Tess

FREE
Spirits

with best wishes
Rich

BY
GRANT SIMPSON

First Published in Great Britain by Vicksburg Press
First Edition
© 2017 Richard Wilmot-Smith
The moral right of the author has been asserted.

This is a work of historical fiction. All characters and events in this publication, other than those of historical record, are fictitious.

A CIP catalogue record for this book is available from the British Library

ISBN 978-1-912299-02-7

Typeset in Sabon by Juliet Arthur
Jacket design by Henry Hyde
All images used in the Public Domain

Printed and bound in Great Britain by Clays Ltd, St Ives

Paper used by Vicksburg Press is from well managed forests and other responsible sources.

Vicksburg Press
3 Essex Court, London EC4Y 9AL
www.vicksburgpress.com

To William Still and Charles W Chesnutt
with thanks

The past is not dead. In fact, it is not even past.
William Faulkner

One

Lucy

I had never thought that I would end up in a Baltimore prison cell, only a short ride from the family plantation. I was a West Point Cadet just past my twenty first birthday, with an "understanding" with Ellen Emerson, the poet's daughter, and had been mentored by Dr. Oliver Wendell Holmes, the best-selling author and Dean of the Harvard Medical School. My future seemed set.

Yet here I was in jail and all that was about to disappear as I awaited the charges to be levelled against me. I was resigned to exposure and almost willing it on as I recalled Lucy and my first memory of her.

I was five and had just arrived at the Baltimore plantation for the first of many summer holidays. I wandered around the plantation's inner grounds, feeling a little lost as I'd never been left alone before. Mother was always anxious as to my whereabouts to the point of suffocation and the liberty felt, at first, welcome; but then it became strange and slightly frightening. The plantation's grounds were large and overwhelming. I first explored the front and the stable yard. Then I lost my fear and ran down to the back.

On the grass between the slave-quarters and the house, Lucy was doing the laundry. I felt she was looking out for me and I ran over to talk to her.

Each of the following summer holidays began in the same way. Mother and Aunt Victoria would go and talk together; my cousins would be out visiting and Lucy would be at the back doing the laundry, ready for me.

Most of the things I told Lucy over the years related to what I had done with my friends in Boston and what had happened at school. Even math wasn't boring to her. I was nine years old when I told her about how I was learning about the states in the Union and I couldn't get over her big smile when I said I was learning to read maps.

The summer days floated by as I worked with the horses watched over by the plantation's groom, Brushes. In the evenings I went into the kitchens and was able to tell Lucy what I what Brushes and I had done together.

My privileged home life in Boston and school life at Phillips Academy were far from hers. But I still wanted to talk to her about them. My parents were interested in my progress. With Father, the judge, it always seemed to me to be of a monitoring nature and I felt that I was being checked on. With Maud, the woman who I called Mother, her interest seemed to be founded upon a great anxiety, which projected itself into me and made me feel protective towards her. From a very early age, I struggled in vain to understand what it was about being with me that made her so nervous, ingratiating and worried.

With Lucy it was different. She was interested in me, but not worried by me. I felt natural with her and didn't need to explain myself or try to please her.

She was Lucy. I was Jack. We could talk.

After that first meeting at the washtub, whenever anything good or exciting happened I thought: "I must tell Lucy." And I did so each summer. I would tell Maud of the same things, but with no felt compulsion to do so but just to make conversation as she asked, in her anxious way, how I was or what I was going.

I was thirteen years old when I had my first dream about Lucy. I was at home in Boston reading a Latin primer for school and trying to memorize the meaning of the word "Amo". The book dropped from my hand. It didn't feel like I was falling asleep, but rather that I had moved to a place above my bed. Then I was in the parlor of the plantation house in Baltimore where I could see that my Uncle Neil, Father's brother, was in his chair asleep. He had drunk his last brandy for the night. My cousins were trying to read and not be annoyed by their father's snoring. This amused me as I had seen it many times during my visits. Uncle Neil was an embarrassment to my cousins on account of his drinking. He was also a source of annoyance to them because over the years he favoured me. He complimented me to my face and in front of them, particularly on my horsemanship which, he told them, was as good as Brushes's. That was real praise since Brushes was a trophy slave of high value because of his magic way with horses. The next thing in the dream was that I found myself in Lucy's bedroom and saw a Bible under her pillow. I had never seen any slave with a book or a paper. They weren't allowed to read and I wondered that maybe someone had put it there to get her into trouble. Then, I woke up.

Nearly all my dreams I forget. But this I remember. Whether it's seeing the Bible under the pillow or Uncle Neil's snores annoying my cousins and remembering their resentment of me as I watched them, I do not know. I wasn't going to tell Maud about it. But my inner voice said: "I must tell Lucy". I counted the days to when Maud and I went to Baltimore and I would see her again.

On the night before we left for Baltimore, I had another dream. I was hovering on the ceiling of Lucy's room and saw her sitting up in bed in her night-dress reading her Bible. It was black with a golden cross on the front cover and had very thin paper, which rustled. As she turned the page, she looked at the ceiling and I felt she could see me. I heard another page turn and then woke up in my bedroom in Boston.

When we arrived in Baltimore, Maud and my Aunt Victoria got talking and my cousins were nowhere to be seen. Lucy was in her usual place at the back of the house. I was hot from the journey and ran to the icehouse and poured two lemonades from the clay jar on the slab by the near door.

As I presented Lucy with the drink, I realized that I might be getting her into trouble. I'd never seen a slave drink lemonade. I didn't know what punishment she might get for having it, but assumed that there might be one and this made me anxious. I felt as worried for Lucy as Maud was about me. Her smile, as she took the lemonade, settled me down. "No," I told myself, "she'll not get into trouble because of this. I'll not let that happen. I'll tell them the drink was my idea and that I made her have it." She was the second adult to whom I felt protective, but even Maud's anxieties did not cause such a strong feeling to erupt inside me as this incident did then.

I couldn't tell Lucy about that protective feeling, so, to cover up, I started to tell her about my friends in Boston in a quick, disorganised and disjointed way. As I did so, I saw a look of understanding pass through her eyes and I knew to stop talking about my friends. We didn't need to say anything.

"Lucy," I said, breaking off my narrative as tears stabbed the back of my eyes.

"Jack," she smiled back at me.

I lowered my voice to a whisper.

"In my dreams I saw that Bible under your pillow and then I saw you reading it. Do you have a Bible under your pillow?"

"I knew it was you," she whispered back as she lowered her head to concentrate on the washtub.

"What?" I said. She put her hand to her mouth to shush me.

"You came to my room a while back and I saw you on the ceiling," she whispered, looking intently at the laundry.

"You mean you could see me?"

"Just as I do now young Jack." She turned from the washtub to face me.

"I won't tell."

"You can tell Brushes. Now let's talk about your school."

I was fifteen when I first spoke to her about Ellen. I was at the plantation for the summer and we were standing by the washtub. I had talked of school and Father taking me to look at West Point.

"You look softer," she said.

"Softer?"

"Like you've kissed someone. Is she nice?"

4

Nobody knew that I had kissed Ellen Emerson. Had anyone else said what Lucy did I would have gone red and blustered because boys my age didn't speak of girls like that.

"She's Ellen Emerson," I said.

"That's a nice name."

"She told me she loves me," I said with a mixture of boastful and bashful. "I'm going to marry her."

"Does she know that?" Lucy smiled as she asked this question, but it was a kind and confiding smile and she seemed almost protective of Ellen as she asked it.

"I've told her that's what I want to do."

"Did she say she wanted to marry you?" Lucy asked.

"No. But she did kiss me after I said I'd marry her. I couldn't kiss another girl now."

"Will she come here?"

"I'd like you to meet her. But she says she doesn't like the South."

I had said to Maud earlier that Ellen didn't like the South and she told me Ellen's father didn't either but went anyway.

Then I started at West Point and the summer visits stopped.

Two

West Point

W est Point was an escape from the tension at home. The academic year was from September to June. From July to September, in the first three years, we went to what they called "encampment", where we drilled in the field. It wasn't until our fourth year that we could go home for vacation. We all counted down to June 1860, when we passed out in front of our families. But in the meantime we looked forward to the summer holiday in our fourth year.

A fifth year had been added by Act of Congress because, they said, the Academy was not sufficiently rigorous and graduates were not well enough equipped by four years of study. We cadets joked that it was because they didn't think our class had learned anything in our first year and needed to start over.

It's a magnificent place, high on a bluff overlooking the Hudson River. I don't know what is more beautiful, the grounds of the Academy or the views from it.

Some parents stayed at the West Point Hotel, which was on Trophy Point overlooking the Plain. A few of my classmates would unofficially see their family there. Aside from letters home, that was all the family contact anyone could have. Mine did not visit. That was a relief to me. Maud's mood swings and general anxiety were hard to cope with. West Point took me away. Father was often distracted with me and sometimes we were embarrassed because we seemed to have nothing to say to each other. We did write letters once a week, but they were an effort as I struggled for something to say to my parents and it was obvious from their letters that they did too.

Ellen visited regularly, staying at the West Point Hotel. She arranged our rendez-vous through code in notes delivered to me by Lester, the cellarman, who carried such messages to cadets for a fee.

During her visits, we made love in her room and our closeness was only broken by the coming dawn and my slipping back to the Academy. My nightly escapes were never noticed.

"Being one of Prof Mahan's scouts, you need to visit me undetected as part of your training," she joked to me after one night together and we were discussing how I was to avoid getting caught out of bounds. As we talked, she showed that her grasp of topography was better than mine as she had worked out a new route back to my quarters avoiding the Plain. I was both impressed at her acumen but embarrassed at my failure to spot what was obvious when it was pointed out.

"Where does your father think you are?" I said covering my embarrassment by pulling her towards me. "Ralph Waldo Emerson, poet and lecturer in matters natural, might not be so lyrical and benign if he knew where his daughter was."

"He knows I'm travelling," she said looking away from me as she did and blushing slightly.

"Where do you travel to?"

He body stiffened and a hunted look flashed across her face, which it did when she didn't want to answer a question of mine. I noticed that look in my second year at the Academy. When I started to tease her about it she said, "I'll tell you if you press me and because I shouldn't tell you, I get scared." That answer baffled me, but when I saw that look I didn't ask her about what she was hiding from me; at the same time I felt a mixture of resentment that she was keeping something from me and pride that I was not insisting she tell me. I didn't press her this time either and she relaxed and said, "Hush, make love to me Jack."

The Academy was headed by the Superintendent. When I arrived in September 1855, he was a remote and awe-inspiring figure in his last year. We "Plebes" didn't have much to do with him.

7

Once during "Off Time", the short period between classes, I was standing on the bluff over the river. I called the look-out place my special spot, and felt I had taken it as my own from my first day there. I was preparing Professor Mahan's next class on "Reconnaissances" and I read from my notes:

Trustworthy guides are invaluable, but most rare in an enemy's country. The best, from the information they acquire by their habits of life, are to be found amongst those classes whose avocations keep them much abroad, going from place to place within a certain sphere constantly; such as common carriers, hunters, smugglers etc.

I put the notes aside and started reciting them from memory, when a heavy hand touched my shoulder. I stiffened.

"It's my spot here too, Cadet."

"I'm sorry, Sir," I said.

I didn't know who it was, though the voice was familiar. I turned round.

"Superintendent," I said and saluted. He saluted back.

"Cadet Ruffin, I see you come here a lot."

"This is where I calm down."

"Cadet, you don't have to remember Professor Mahan's lecture word for word. You just need the essence."

"Thank you Sir," I replied. I wanted to say that when I had learnt it by heart the essence would remain and that Professor Mahan was impressed by memorising. That would have been impertinent and earned a demerit.

I just said, "Sir, I think it's time for me to go back to class."

"It is. It's my time to look over the river here, Cadet. But remember, you need the essence. The most important thing is to think."

I saluted and turned back towards the library where I had left my books, and then go to Professor Mahan's course: *The Science of War.*

"Cadet."

I turned back to face him.

"Give my regards to your father when you write home. He may not remember me. I met him when I was doing engineering work in Baltimore. A fine man, your father."

"I shall, Sir."

I was used to people telling me that Father was a fine man.

There was no sign of recognition in his eyes when our paths crossed during the rest of that first year and it felt to me like our conversation hadn't taken place. I saluted him, but we didn't speak. When he left, I never thought to say goodbye. I was too in awe of him to do so. The words at the top of the bluff were the only ones I spoke to Robert E Lee whilst he was there.

In my second year, Professor Mahan said that Lee had predicted that I would graduate first in the class. As Mahan told me this, he paused and wrinkled his nose and said, "I would not always agree with that man's judgment."

I wondered why he would think that. When that heavy hand hit my shoulder, I was finding it hard to understand mathematics, which was dragging me down to the bottom half of the class. It was only in the latter part of my fourth year that I started to understand the subject and rose up the ranks.

During a summer encampment, I received a letter from Father, which I have kept ever since. I can recite it from memory.

10 Montgomery Place
Boston, Mass
18th August 1857

Dear Jack
I am sorry to have to tell you that Maud's health finally broke down this week. As you know, she has always had a difficult time with her health but, with God's help, she has been able to hold herself together for as long as she has. The strain finally got to be too much for her and she was taken to St Evelyn's Hospital, Cambridge yesterday morning.

She is now resident there and, I am told, will be there for the foreseeable future. I have been asked not to see her for a while. But I shall visit as soon as I am allowed to do so.

As you also know, Dr. Holmes has been a tower of strength through-

out our married life. She has been under his care since before you were born and he was always keen for her to stay outside institutional care. But even he had to agree that St Evelyn's is the best place for her.

When she, at last, conceived a child I hoped that her fragility would end and that she would return to being the strong individual I knew when we married. But it was not to be. The event of your birth and our taking you into our care was not the cure which I and Dr. Holmes hoped it would be.

I know how this will devastate you, as it has me. She loves you very much. If you could keep writing your letters to her at home here in Montgomery Place, I shall make sure that she gets them. I know that they will do her the power of good.

I have written to your Aunt Victoria with the news.

Your ever loving

John Ruffin

After I got the letter, I was summoned by Superintendent Delafield, who had heard the news from Dr. Holmes. He offered compassionate leave but I declined.

Feeling that I had been abrupt in saying no, I walked to my spot over the bluffs and tried to think of what I would say to Maud if I visited her. I couldn't think of anything. I hadn't noticed Father's words in the letter about my being taken into their care but I did try and make sense of Father referring to her in his letter as "Maud", which he had never done before when speaking to me. It felt as if he was writing to a friend and not to his son. That made me feel even more detached from my family.

I looked forward to Ellen's visits to West Point, which now felt like it was my home. Boston and Baltimore were becoming remote. Mother was institutionalised. Father was too busy or too proper to come on an unofficial visit. The Baltimore plantation receded from my mind but my memories of Lucy remained as vivid as ever.

Three

Family

My family was unusual in that Neil and Father were brothers and Victoria and Maud were sisters. Neil met Victoria at Father's wedding to Maud. My cousins were as closely related to me as it was possible to be, but we were distant because I was much younger than them. Neil's favouring of me did not help, but it wasn't just that. There was a difference in temperament and outlook, which meant we were never going to be friends. During the summers they would often be out visiting. They had no interest in working or horses so I never spent much time with them.

My Aunt Victoria was a sane version of her sister. Whilst I didn't have the connection I had with Lucy, I had an easy relationship with her and enjoyed her company. I often asked myself why Mother couldn't be like her. The time when Mother was closest to being like her sister was when we visited in the summer and she and Aunt Victoria were inseparable. Uncle Neil was, like Father, more of an observer of me. He praised me to my face, but it was with a heartiness, which concealed a reserve which I didn't comprehend.

It was a heart attack in the street. Father died before he hit the ground.

I was told that the strain of his work had brought on his early death. Superintendent Delafield summoned me from drill and I had to rush to Boston with a funeral to arrange.

Our house in Boston was big and comfortably held the house-party

11

of Neil, Victoria and my cousins, who had all arrived before me and set up home. I felt over-run. Father, an important man, required a large funeral. Being the only child and with Maud unwell, I had to arrange it. The vice president, the governor, the mayor, two congressmen and a senator were the guests of honor.

I had to write a speech (I wasn't going to allow Neil to embarrass his brother with a drunken address) and appoint someone to make the oration regarding the judge's public life. The house was in chaos and I immediately said I was going to see Dr. Holmes.

I had regarded the Holmes household as if it were my own when they lived next door to us in Montgomery Place. It was a refuge from Maud's depressions and it was there that I met Ellen. The Holmes's recent move to a grander house by the river in Charles Street was inspired by the noise of the new construction in our neighborhood. Dr. Holmes could afford it. His book, *The Autocrat of the Breakfast Table,* having sold ten thousand copies in only three days, was a best-seller.

It was from Dr. Holmes's house that I made the arrangements, returning to Montgomery Place in the evenings to preside over a 'family dinner'. I told Baines, our manservant, that Father's place at the table would be laid but empty. Uncle Neil sat in his place on the first night, causing a hush around the table as he did so and an awkwardness amongst us all as my gesture of respect to Father was ignored. On the second night the chair was left empty. Maybe it was because Aunt Victoria had spoken to him or that Baines left the place unset.

I expected to see Ellen at Dr. Holmes's
    "She's on her travels," Dr. Holmes said when I asked about her.
    "Can she come? The funeral's three days away."
    "Waldo says not."
    "Can't she be wired with the news?"
    "Waldo says not."
    "Where is she?"
    "We don't know."
    "What do you mean you don't know? Surely Mr. Emerson knows

where his daughter is." I said this with a rhetorical flourish I had learned in class. I was frustrated and disappointed beyond measure.

"If she's wanted us to know, she would have," Dr. Holmes said. His voice was mild but his eye was sharp brooking no argument. I decided to change the subject, remembering Ellen's hunted look.

"Where's Mr. Emerson?"

"He'll come from Concord for the funeral, but he has to leave immediately after."

"I'd like him to stay for the Reception," I said.

"He would too, but he says that either of us at the Reception would mean people swarming around us and not talking about your father. So I'll come here after the Service. Neither of us will be at the Reception."

Ellen was away and not there to support me when I needed her most and the two adults I counted on were not going to be beside me at the Reception either.

"Will you do the Oration at the Cathedral?" I asked. "Please at least do that."

"I'd be honoured to do the Oration," he said with a sly smile. "Indeed I've written a few words already. How long have you got before going back to West Point?"

"Two weeks."

"There are some things we need to discuss after the funeral."

"What things?"

"I was his best friend. I…"

"Okay," I said angry with myself for cross-examining the man I respected most in the world. "I'll come over when my family's gone. I hope to be rid of them the day after the funeral. I can't stand any more of them."

"You've scarcely seen them. But I understand. They are an odd lot."

"You think so? It's not just me then."

"No it's not just you. Do you know about your father's will?"

"No. It's a bit soon to talk about that."

"Yes it is. He's left you everything by the way. But the odd thing is that your uncle, no sooner had he arrived in Boston, went to your father's lawyer and demanded to see the will."

13

"What?"

"Quite. Anyway there was no reason for your uncle not to see it so he showed it to him. Your uncle then came round to see me to tell me all about it and asked me if your father was in his right mind."

"In his right mind? He was trying cases."

"Don't get het up. I think there are money worries. You're a rich man now."

"I'll give some to Aunt Victoria as soon as I can get it released after my majority."

"Not long now. Yes. Do that," he said in the quiet voice he used on Wendy, his son, to get obedience. It was as if he had instructed me to do what I had volunteered. I let that pass and asked him to show me his funeral notes.

It was all an act, but I got through it. My detachment meant that I scripted myself as the grieving but rising son of an eminent man. "Thank you so much for coming Mr Vice-President...Yes he was a great man...Irreplaceable...We are all so sad...I am grateful to you Governor...Your words give us all more comfort than I can say...If I could give only half the service he did..."

I stayed dry eyed throughout except for a short hiccup half way through my address in the Cathedral. Even today I can't say whether that was scripted or genuine. I longed for Ellen's support and felt so alone.

I can give you the date, time and place. It was the afternoon of 20th May 1859, the day after Father's funeral. My family had left after Aunt Victoria said, somewhat unconvincingly, that urgent plantation business meant they all had to return as soon as possible. I was in Dr. Holmes's parlor.

He spoke of a mind which had slipped its mooring. It was the mind of Maud Ruffin, the woman I had called 'Mother' all my life. Her baby was stillborn. The days were a long nightmare. Maud refused to believe her child was dead. She dressed him. She talked as if he was alive. She told him how clever he was and how his mother loved him and his family had waited so long for him.

Dr. Holmes, who had attended the birth, had seen this anguished response in other patients.

"It happens when reality is so brutal that madness is a blessing," he said. "People say that insanity is an evil to be cured. In this case it took the place of something worse."

There was a surreal life of apparent normality in the days that followed. Maud and Father were a "family" with a silent baby. If Maud said that the baby needed "feeding", then the corpse was taken away, while she thought her sister's pregnant maid was wet nursing him. She would then ask for her baby back and talk to him again.

They were imprisoned in the house. Maud was mad and the baby was dead. Visitors were told that Maud was not well and they left.

Knowing that reality in the form of a decomposing baby was about to surface. Father told Maud that it had to go to the hospital. He took the body to the undertakers and registered the birth and death. The records show that Thomas James Ruffin was born and died July 15th 1838. His grave is marked only by the name and the date. Father was the single mourner at the funeral. Maud had taken to her bed, anchored by the lie that her baby was in hospital and would return soon.

My birth is also recorded as being on July 15th 1838.

Four

Lucy Ruffin's Slave Narrative

I had been brought to Boston from the plantation in Baltimore as Victoria Ruffin's maid. Victoria was visiting Maud, during her confinement.

Shortly after Maud's baby died, I was stopped in the street by a woman who took my hand. I was afraid that I was about to be kidnapped like my mother was, so I broke free and continued walking.

"I know you are a slave in the Ruffin's house," she said, "I want you to come with me."

I followed her. We walked about a mile. My pregnancy slowed me. I felt a rising panic. I did not know where I was going, nor the way back.

We entered a house which was as big as Judge Ruffin's. I was given a chair in a large sitting room. Across from me was a man in his thirties. He was nearly bald but his dark hair circled his egg shaped head. He wore a black suit, white shirt and a large black bow tie and small round spectacles with no frames.

He introduced himself as William. He asked me about myself. I told him that I was a slave, brought up in New Bern, North Carolina, that I had been sold to the Ruffin plantation in Baltimore and was now in Boston as my mistress's maid while she helped her sister during her pregnancy.

As I talked, he would ask questions. After half an hour, I became agitated, because I was going to be late getting home. I got up to leave.

Then he asked the question, "Do you want to escape?"

The answer was visible on my face, but I had no idea what freedom meant and I did not want to be kidnapped. Most of all, I did not want to leave my new husband, Brushes. If I escaped then, most likely he would be sold away and we would never see each other again.

"I belong to Miss Victoria." I said, shuffling my feet as I had been taught to do when a white man threatened my well-being.

"Eleanor will walk you back to where she collected you," he said. "Retrace your steps carefully and remember this house. Come here whenever you want. I can arrange for you and your child to go to Canada. You need only say the word."

"What about Brushes?"

"Who is Brushes?"

I told him.

"From what you say, he will not be difficult to find." William had a small thin mouth that it grew a huge smile. His eyes, which had been cold and watchful, suddenly beamed. As quickly as the smile came, it left.

"We'll look for him. If you come back in a week or so, we may have found him by then and we can coordinate your escapes. You should both escape at the same time. If you go first, they'll think him an escape risk in wanting to join you and then they'll sell him. Give us maybe two weeks to find him."

A week later Maud had taken to her bed. Dr. Holmes was the only visitor. I cleaned her room in silence. Maud followed my every move. I felt a sharp pain and cramp. It was the first sign of labor. I continued to clean for a few minutes and then went downstairs.

Dr. Holmes arrived. My mistress Victoria, boiled the water and saw that I was comfortable. I remember the pain and the need to stay silent so that Maud, who was upstairs, did not hear what was going on in the basement. The birth took place in my bedroom and the sound of the baby screaming was the first that I knew that he had actually come. The pain was suddenly over.

Dr. Holmes picked up the noisy bundle and left the room. My instinct was to feed him. He was crying for my milk, but I could not shout for his return.

One hour later, Dr. Holmes brought him back to me to nurse. A baby as white as anyone in Boston or Baltimore, with a birthmark on the side of his face just by his eyebrow, just as Master Neil had. It was small but visible and distinctive.

I felt panic as I nursed him. If we went back to Baltimore, then he would look like Master Neil's child. Would I be sold and he would stay? Would he be sold? Could I escape with a baby? Then I remembered William's words to me. I could go to Canada with my baby and Brushes could follow.

It seemed to be only a matter of time before Maud, hearing my baby's cries, would see him. I dreaded the knock on my door. Maud never appeared.

Three days later I was up and working. The baby was in the basement sleeping and I wanted to go for a walk on a "day off". I wanted to tell William of the arrival of the baby and that I wanted to escape quickly. The two weeks he needed to find Brushes had not passed, but I was desperate.

Victoria only looked at my baby once shortly after his birth and she gave him back without saying a word. I looked back at her. We were both crying as if from the same pain. After she met my eye she walked out of the room.

The next day I asked Victoria if I could go out. Having just fed the baby, he would sleep for hours.

"Do you want to take the baby?"

"No Mm. He'll sleep, Miss Victoria. I'm just going for a walk." I could sense that she wanted me to leave with the baby and not come back. I would take him when it was time for the coordinated escape. It was best to let him sleep.

William welcomed me and made some tea before returning to his desk. I was much smaller now and my movements were quicker. I felt relaxed. I was nothing like the shuffling girl who could not answer his question about freedom.

"We've found Brushes," he said. "He'll leave when we say. When can you get here again?"

"Tomorrow," I said. I wanted to leave as soon as possible.

"That's too soon. I need to get a message to him telling him of the day you'll be leaving so he can go then too. A week today will be fine. Can you come here then?"

"Yes."

"Come alone and only with your baby. I'll not be here. You'll meet a man named Joseph. My people know Brushes. He's helped us before. We can arrange that he meets you in Canada."

The prospect of freedom with Brushes and the baby overwhelmed me. I had never felt so happy. As I stood up, I was so excited I punched my fists against my thighs like I remember my mother Sally did when she was excited. I had never done that before and felt embarrassed that I had inherited my mother's mannerism.

My excitement dimmed as I walked back to Montgomery Place. Escaping to Canada and evading the slave catchers would not be easy, whatever William said. Brushes could ride north, but if he was caught he could be killed, mutilated or branded. My excitement became suffused with fear.

On my return, Maud was in her nightgown carrying Jack, who was screaming. Victoria ran to the door to explain, but Maud spoke first.

"Lucy, my baby's back from the hospital and I want you to feed him."

Here eyes were staring with desperation and conviction. She had made herself believe that the baby with the Ruffin birthmark was hers and she needed me to wet nurse him.

"Yes Miss Maud." I said as I took the screaming child.

As I was feeding Jack in my room, the Judge came to see me. He told me that if I gave Jack up to Maud, he would be brought up free and white, as the son of a judge. Jack would visit Baltimore in the summers and I could see him then. He said that I could escape with Jack. He would not stop me, but he could not prevent slave catchers doing so and returning us to Baltimore if we were caught. If that happened, he would not be able to stop his brother selling me or Jack or the both of us. I was unable to tell if that was a threat or simply the way things were. Maybe it was both.

19

Then Dr. Holmes came to me. He said the judge would keep his word that I could see him in the summer holidays and Brushes and I would not be sold away. This was the same as what the judge had said to me. But there was something in his eyes which made me believe he was not threatening me. Then he said to me words I have never forgotten:

"I live next door. I'll watch over him as he grows and make sure he's all right. But when he is grown, I'll tell him about you and how and why you gave him up. He'll know you are his mother and you are the reason he grew up a free man. This is between us. Right now as far as John and Maud are concerned, he will never know. But he will. That I promise."

That night, I dreamed of the slave catchers, the dogs and the whip. I saw Brushes being pulled away from me to be castrated and killed. I saw Jack as a young man in the fields down south, with stripes on his back, picking cotton as I pulled water from a well.

The next morning I took a letter to William saying I had to go back. I could not go inside and face him, so I slipped the letter under the door.

For most of the journey back to Baltimore with Victoria, I looked out of the coach window. I had only talked to the Judge and Dr. Holmes about Maud taking Jack. When my eyes strayed inside the coach, I looked away from Victoria. We did not speak until we were near Baltimore.

"I can ask Master Neil to make you free."

I looked up at her. I did not feel hopeful or even pleased. I knew of people who had been promised their freedom and had never been given it. Also freedom meant separation from Brushes, who was too valuable to them to free. Freedom meant not seeing my son on his visits because they would not free me and then pay me as a maid.

"I want to see my boy," I said. It was all I could think to say, but I knew that as a mother she would understand.

"You don't want to be free?"

"I want to stay, if you'll let me … and see my boy in the holidays like I discussed with the Judge and the Doctor."

"I wanted you to escape."

"I was going to leave, then Maud took my boy."

20

There was a long silence between us. This was the moment when she could have said that I would be sold anyway. My stomach tightened as I worried whether I had said too much. Then my anxiousness left me. My boy would be free whatever they did to me.

"Master Neil didn't do right by you when you came to us," Victoria said.

I looked out of the window and shook my head.

"He didn't do right by me either," Victoria added.

"No, Mm."

My tears stopped me seeing anything and my stomach convulsed. I felt a handkerchief being put into my hand.

"You know not to say anything to anyone about this arrangement."

"Yes Mm."

"I won't say anything to Master Neil either. I'll tell him you lost your baby."

"Yes, Mm."

"I'd have lost my sister without Jack," she said. "I won't let Neil sell you. I owe you that."

I wiped my eyes and saw we were nearly home.

"My sister really thinks that Jack's her child," Victoria said. "We have two things in common, you and I. We both love Jack and hate his father."

The coach stopped. We had arrived at the plantation.

Five

When Dr. Holmes had finished I sat there stunned, not by the truth, which I felt explained so much, but by the telling of it as it seeped into me. I knew the power of silence to make people talk so I waited for him to speak first. As I waited for him to do so, a numbness came over me.

Dr. Holmes was sweating; looking at me; waiting for a reaction with a kind of cornered desperation in his face as he looked in the eye the reckoning he had promised. I tried to move in my chair, but the shock paralyzed me. My memories of Lucy - of the washtub, the Bible and our talks in the kitchens – all of which were never far away, came back as I sat paralysed at what Dr. Holmes said. As the last of the memories came I felt feeling return to my legs as my stomach heaved. Finally Holmes could stand the silence no longer.

"I spoke to Lucy alone. I was prepared to take you away from Maud and give you back to Lucy. If I had insisted upon it, there would have been nothing that could have been done. Lucy didn't want it." His voice moved up an octave and the words, sounding like they were shouted in a hollow cave, came out faster than I've ever heard him speak.

"Why didn't she take me back and escape with me as William Garrison had planned with her?"

"She wanted you to be free. You would always have been an escaped slave even had you escaped the slave catchers."

"Did she feel she had no choice?"

"She felt she made the best choice for you. And there was my promise to her."

"Promise?"

"That when you reached your majority you'd be told of all of this."

"That explains Maud's anxiety." I was already referring to the woman I had always called 'Mother' as Maud.

"No. We didn't tell her. This was between Lucy and me. Maud's stability was precarious enough. She really thinks the baby... you, are hers."

"What did Victoria tell Neil?"

"That Maud gave birth to you and Lucy lost her baby."

"He doesn't know?"

"Victoria had to promise to me that they would never sell Brushes and Lucy. He might have found that odd. He also remarked to me upon the bond between you and Lucy at the funeral. But...no. There's no reason for him to disbelieve."

"Why did Victoria keep her promise?"

"It was the price of her sister's... Maud's, sanity. If I had said what had really happened, Maud would lose 'her' baby and John would have been ruined."

"Would you have disgraced him? You were best friends."

"No"

Then a silence grew between us. I'd asked enough questions. The numbness had gone.

"I must to go back to West Point and finish the term," I said. "But there's just time to go to Baltimore."

"I can go with you."

"You've done enough."

Holmes winced. The edge in my voice was obvious.

"What are you going to do?"

"Bring her and Brushes back here."

"What will you say to people?"

"I don't know. That I bought her. Something like that."

"What makes you think they'll let Brushes go?"

"What do you mean?"

"Your uncle's broke and, aside from the farm, Brushes is his principal single asset. You'll be able to free Lucy because Victoria'll let her go. You'll never free Brushes unless you're prepared to buy him."

"Buy him?"

"You're rich now. Or will be soon."

"I shall, but I'll pay Victoria not Neil. Brushes stayed for her. Lucy stayed for me. It's over now."

"They can stay here while you finish the year at West Point."

"Thanks. I'm not sure they'd get on with Mr. and Mrs. Baines."

"Why not?"

"You've met Baines. So proper he's almost English. Mrs. Baines is so nosy she'd ferret out the truth."

* * *

I packed and set out for Baltimore immediately. With plenty of time to think on the journey, my first thoughts were not of Lucy, but of Ellen Emerson and our 'understanding'.

Our letters and secret nights together had deepened the bond between us such that I couldn't imagine life without her. But it was clear to me that her knowing of my real identity would change everything. I was no longer a white man from the family she knew so well. I didn't know how to say this to her, nor could I pretend to her that I was someone else. She was close to her father, who I was sure, would not want someone like me as a son-in-law. He'd say he wasn't bothered, but he would be. Nobody married the sons of slaves; even an Emerson. Particularly an Emerson. He's pretend to be serene, but Ellen and I would know he wasn't and it would eat away at us.

So my journey was not spent thinking about my life with Lucy as my mother; If I was to stay a scion of a Boston Brahmin family, my origins would have to remain secret. I was trying to imagine life without Ellen and I was not finding it easy. I was almost pleased that she was not there for the funeral with its shattering aftermath and that she was away on one of her mysterious journeys. That meant that I didn't have to face her and, right then, I knew I wasn't ready for that.

The journey went quickly. The plantation was the other side of Baltimore. There was a road which took you round so you didn't have to go through the business district and, too late, I realized that I should have taken it because as I went down Pratt Street, I saw from the posters that a slave auction was to be held the following day. My stomach turned and I rode quickly on, pushing it from my mind. I had seen such posters many times before and they had never registered as being anything more than part of normal life. Now I was disgusted. Lucy's vision of me in a cotton field in the Deep South came into my mind's eye flickering alternately on and off like light does when you ride fast through a forest in sunshine.

As I approached the Plantation, I felt I was crossing into to a different world from the one I had known. I was as different as that new world. Nothing could be the same from that moment when Dr. Holmes had told me who I was.

Somehow it seemed the easy part would be my reunion with Lucy. Acknowledgment of her as my mother was only to be among a limited circle if I was to stay free and remain in the army, passing as white. For over twenty years I was not as I had seemed. The only difference was that now I knew it. Only a few would know. One of those would be Ellen.

It was one thing to deceive your father and go on a mysterious journey to see your lover and fiancé-to-be, which would end with marriage to a respectable soldier. It was quite another thing if that lover was the son of a slave. My pain at the imminent rupture with Ellen tarnished what I felt should have been the pure joy of my anticipated reunion with Lucy.

I told myself to act enthusiastic and happy. As I rode to the front of the main house of the Ruffin Plantation, Victoria was sitting on the porch as if she was waiting for me. No sooner did she see me than she jumped up and waved excitedly. I rode round the house waving my hat and yelled. Then I jumped off.

"So the Cadet has returned for his holidays," she said, a little too brightly. She knew the term had not ended. She was still pretending; probably waiting for me to make the first move.

"Yes indeed," I responded as I tied up my horse.

As I climbed the steps to the front door, I wondered, whether I was too calm.

"Cup of tea for me, please?"

Victoria nodded and went into the house.

It was clear that Lucy was not there. Sometimes she helped out Victoria's neighbors. I felt relieved. I should have been ready and I was not. After about a quarter of an hour, Victoria came out with a tray set for two.

I tried a sally. "Doing your own work now Aunt?"

She laughed in hollow acknowledgment, as if she was trying too hard. Her laugh was brittle. For the first time I could see the resemblance with her sister Maud. I had always thought of Victoria as calm as her sister was nervous, but she was as nervous as her sister when under the same pressure.

"It's good to be here Aunt. Tell me your news," I said. I did not mean to be cruel, but I was enjoying her discomfort as we hid behind fake heartiness.

"No. You tell me yours," she said.

I was happy to do so and recounted my time at West Point, my classes and what I liked about them. Then I told her the story of me standing on the bluff when Superintendent Lee surprised me so. That incident was old but I had not put it in a letter. I had not even told Dr. Holmes.

"I'll take a room in Baltimore." I said.

"You are welcome to stay here you know that."

"I know. I want to buy a valet to look after my kit when I leave West Point next year. If I did, I'd like him to stay with you until next year. If I am in the cavalry I will be posted to Sacket's Harbor soon after I pass out and then I may not have the time to find someone suitable."

I don't know why I said this. But I felt that I couldn't stay the night at the house and I needed sleep after the journey. So an excuse to check into a hotel came into my head. The thought of actually going to the sale disgusted me so it was a pretty poor excuse.

"We could look for you. How much can you afford?"

"I can pay. If I can't find a valet on this trip, I'd be grateful if you did. "

Once the lie started, it went on and I squirmed with shame. I was about to mention Lucy and then I remembered Neil with a mixture of apprehension and hatred.

"Where's Uncle Neil?"

"Baltimore on business."

I felt huge relief. I wasn't ready to face him.

"I thought I'd go into town, do the auction tomorrow and then come back and ride some horses with Brushes." As I said this I couldn't have got a more dramatic reaction had I mentioned Lucy first. Suddenly she was in tears. I had seen Maud cry many times before, but never Victoria. The pretense was gone. We were alone and she wanted to talk.

And Victoria talked.

Six

1858

Neil was short of cash, even though all his children had left home. He needed one thousand dollars to satisfy the bank. His brother, John, had told him he wouldn't leave him anything in his will. That hurt Neil a little. He had thought that if he would inherit some money in the future, it would save him from embarrassment because he could borrow a bit more against the expectation. Given the boom times in agriculture and slave prices, it was unusual for established planters to struggle financially. Alcohol made Neil inattentive, incurring losses.

Neil's father, Grandpa Clive, had never sold a slave, Neil had reflected over the years, why that should be. He prided himself on keeping the slaves he had. Some slave owners bought and sold slaves like stocks and bonds and made the occasional profit. Others used their slaves until they were near exhausted and then sold them when they could still fetch a good price. Neil had never sold and had bought infrequently. The slave children grew up and added to his labor force as their parents grew older and less efficient.

Field hands were for most people the natural place to start if you had to sell. Domestics were too intimate. Artisans, whose labor was sold, made money so selling did not always make economic sense. Selling field hands meant that fewer people would be able to harvest the crops which represented money lying in the fields. Even old and inefficient hands harvested crops and the prices were good that year.

Not counting the field hands, Neil had only two assets he felt he could sell. Brushes and Lucy.

Brushes had value because of his skill with horses. If he sold him he would get a good price, but then he would get no more cash for Brushes' outside work, which had yielded a steady income. That left Lucy and the promise he gave to Victoria not to sell.

Victoria would have to manage without a maid, he thought. He would have to brave her anger. He suspected who I was and had confided them to his best drinking companion once. Those suspicions grew stronger over the years and they had influenced him a little in his favoring of me. He couldn't help having a little pride in having a son who was doing so well. But that made it easier for him to think about selling Lucy. Better to have her away, he thought, rather than the constant reminder and reproach growing stronger as each year went by, which came from who she was.

Careful not to tell Victoria what he was doing but fortified by a few drinks at home, Neil drove into Baltimore to see the trader Colin Stevens, from whom he had bought Lucy years earlier. Before Neil got to Colin's offices, he needed another drink so his first stop was the saloon bar where he was a regular and which was located opposite the trader's offices.

"Whiskey?" asked the barman.

"Hell yes," Neil said.

"Bottle?"

"No, just one. I got business."

"Buying?"

"Maybe."

"Sale's not for a week."

"Yeah, but I want to know what is there," Neil said. "I haven't been to market for a while now."

His eyes were bloodshot. The barman was being kind. What Neil took for conversation was pity. The word had got out from a talkative banker that he was doing badly and would have to sell slaves or land.

Neil had another whiskey. He could see the barman move away slightly as he handed him another shot. The barman wondered whether

Neil noticed. But he needn't have worried. Neil was too pre-occupied to care about either the barman or his own breath.

"Colin's in," the barman said.

"Better go," Neil replied.

Neil didn't move. The barman didn't pour him another whiskey. Neil noticed. The barman usually was free with his offerings.

"Does he want me out of here?" Neil wondered. Then the barman said, "I'll give you one on the house, after you see Colin. Folks usually need one after seeing him."

"Better go." Neil said again and walked out of the saloon with the care of the drunk who wishes to look steady on his feet.

Neil crossed the road and then went up the stairs into Colin Steven's office. It hadn't changed he had come see him to buy Lucy. Colin Stevens stood up and smiled at Neil. His hair, no longer black, was iron grey, though it remained thick. His face was bloodshot. The veins had burst giving his face, what was once pale, a red hue. Neil grabbed the back of the chair in front of Colin's desk and steadied himself. Colin waved at the chair and Neil sat down.

There was, Colin could see, fear and greed in Neil's face. Neil put a foot on Colin's desk then allowed it to fall off which caused him to start a bit in his chair.

"Drink?" Colin asked.

He could see in Neil's face that that the answer he would like to have given was "yes". What Neil remembered of the meeting was that he felt he ought to have been in charge of the conversation and that a breezy dismissal of the offered drink was called for. He was going to get a free drink at the saloon after the meeting.

Neil's face became impassive. Fifteen seconds passed in total silence. Neil felt tension, then desperation and was the first to speak.

"I need to sell someone. I need one thousand dollars now." He emphasized the word 'one' as if it was important that such a sum should be seen as small. But somehow Neil had lost the pretense that he was unconcerned.

"Who are you thinking of selling?"

"Lucy."

"Who's she?"

"The maid I bought from you about twenty years ago."

Colin searched his memory. "I don't rightly recall."

"She came up from North Carolina."

"I remember. Not our usual type of sale. It was south to north as opposed to the other way round. We were one of the few that had a sideline in that type of trade. Illegal, of course, but that law against import for sale wasn't enforced then. I don't do it now. Too risky. How old was the maid then? Fifteen?"

"About that."

"So she's thirty four or thirty five now. Being a maid she won't be strong unless you put her in the fields occasionally and keep her in condition. Did you do that?"

"No."

"She's not worth a thousand. You might get seven hundred. More likely five."

"I need money and can't spare a hand. She's Brushes's wife." As Neil reflected that Lucy would not solve his financial problems, Colin spoke.

"Can you sell both of them?"

"No. I want to keep him." Neil did not need to say that his income was useful.

"If his wife goes South, what'll he do? Some of them niggers get mighty strange when their kin is sold. He's real good with horses. No one's better. Even the Fleming groom Nathan ain't as good. But if he is mad at you because you've sold his wife, he won't be worth anything."

Neil sobered up. His eyes seemed less bloodshot. The decision was easy to make. He couldn't afford Brushes to lose his value and neither could he afford to lose a field hand.

"How much can I get for Brushes?"

"Ten thousand, easy. Probably more. Maybe up to fifteen. Folks round here know how good he is and they'll get a return from letting him out."

"Fifteen thousand?" Neil was staggered. With that sum, he thought, all his problems would go away. He'd never have to sell land nor a field hand or anything ever again.

"Possibly as much as that," Colin said. "There's not been anyone like him on the block that I remember."

Neil had adjusted to the need to explain the loss of Lucy to Victoria. They were in a financial hole. This would get them out of it. Never mind the past and its promises, he thought.

Colin repeated his advice. "I can get more if I advertise a bit, or see some people."

"No posters," Neil said. He was thinking of the shame of Brushes' picture going up locally. Everyone knew Brushes. It seemed all right to sell him but not to advertise with posters showing Brushes' face announcing the time and place of sale.

"Word of mouth," Colin said. He winked at Neil. Neil was relieved people would learn of the sale that way. Posters would announce failure.

"I'll get them now," Colin said.

"Why?"

"Makes it easier. Also I can show them to selected clients for a possible private sale."

Colin didn't want Neil to change his mind. Neil sensed that, but he also felt that he didn't want anything to change his mind either. This way out of financial trouble felt almost too good to be true. He didn't want it not to happen. He felt, it'd be worth putting up with Victoria's anger, if it saved the family fortunes.

"Private sale?" Neil asked, as re-assurance.

"Yes, sometimes you get more for a nigger on a private sale than you get on the block. Some folks don't like bidding openly and like to feel that they're getting a bargain from inside information."

"Ok," Neil heard himself say as he rose from his chair. But the enormity of what he was doing was starting to dawn on him and he felt he should back down. Yes it was too good to be true. Colin sensed Neil's changing mood.

"Say, why don't you get yourself a drink while Porter gets them." It was not a question. Neil patted his pockets. He had not paid for his whiskey in the saloon. He had forgotten the free drink. He felt a small surge of alarm. He had no cash. Sensing this, Colin put his hand into his pocket and took out a stack of dollar bills and handed a wad over to Neil.

"Advance on the sale."

Neil took the money. He was committed.

After Neil left, Colin called for Porter. Porter had worked for Colin for over twenty five years.

"That was Neil," Colin said not managing to conceal a smile of triumph. "We're to sell Brushes and Neil Ruffin's nigger maid."

"Brushes?" shouted Jim, Porter's new assistant.

"Yes, Brushes," Colin ignored Jim's exuberance. "We can get a good price for him. I want you two to go bring them both here. Neil can't change his mind when we have them. I've given him a payment on account."

Colin took down two pairs of leg irons. They were made to fit any adult. For the smaller children you needed special irons, but for the ordinary adult the buckle-like mechanism enabled them to make the leg iron fit either a thick or thin ankle. Brushes was wiry. Lucy was not fat but her legs were a bit stouter. It didn't matter. Any would fit. Porter came out of his office with the leg irons and a whip. He didn't carry a gun. A whip was all he needed.

Porter looked at Jim. "Better get going," he said and they left Colin's offices and went downstairs to their wagon. Like most slave trader's wagons, Colin's had a flat bed behind the driver and upright poles through which leg irons could fit, so that slaves were secured to the wagon. Some wagons had a fence-like structure around the circumference. Colin's wagon did not.

Although Neil had not sold slaves before, Colin's wagon was one of the best known amongst his field hands because either it had been used to transport them to the Ruffin plantation or to transport their friends in neighboring plantations to and from the markets where they were bought and sold. Slaves in the county knew that if his wagon came to where they were living, at the very least one of them was to be sold.

The wagon came up the main approach of the Baltimore plantation house. Slaves and overseers alike stopped work and ran to the track leading to the front of the house to see who would be taken. Lucy came out onto the porch and started to open her mouth as it drew up. It was as if she was about to ask a passing stranger what he wanted.

Before she could say anything, Colin Steven's assistant, Porter, called out.

"Go get your clothes."

Lucy stood still. Victoria came to the front door and looked out, paralysed. Porter shouted out again.

"Girl, get your clothes."

Lucy could see that Porter was addressing her. She ran her hands down the side of her dress and felt the outside of what appeared to be a pocket.

"Have it your way," Porter said. He jumped to the ground with a pair of leg irons in one hand and a hunting crop in another. Lucy turned to walk inside. As she did so, she was pulled to the floor by the hooked handle of the whip.

"Too late nigger girl," Porter said, as he attached the irons to Lucy's legs. She lifted her head up, trying to push herself to stand up and began to shout "No. No. No." Then she called out "Miss Victoria," over and over again.

Victoria came onto the porch. Her lips moved as if she was about to speak and at the same time she was trying to swallow something too large to fit in her mouth. Her strength was failing her. By the time she could summon the strength to speak, Lucy was already chained to one of the poles on the back of the wagon. Her face was covered with what appeared to be dirt and bruises. She turned to Victoria, looking at once quizzical and betrayed. Her screaming had stopped. Her cries gave way to her body jerking out of control.

Finally Victoria found her voice.

"What is the meaning of this?" she shouted. Her breathing had become deep and regular. Her voice sounded reedy, as if there was no conviction in it. Any tone of command in her voice was faltering.

"Where's Brushes?" Porter shouted at her.

"He's working at the racetrack. You unchain her now."

Porter shook the reins and the wagon's horses found an instant canter.

Seven

Victoria had spoken for an hour. My breathing had become quick and shallow and my hands numb. My body was getting out of control. Professor Mahan taught us that some soldiers were like this when the battle got noisy and the muskets hot and, once they did that, they were ready to run away from the battle and needed an instant command to breathe properly, which calmed them down.

I then did as I was taught to order soldiers. I exhaled all the breath from my lungs, waited ten seconds and then started to breathe in slowly, held my breath and exhaled, repeating the process again and again until I got the feeling back in my hands.

"We've lost them both," Victoria said after she described to me the wagon leaving. "Brushes never returned from the racetrack. I don't know where they are or whether the were sold together. I've been to town to ask several times. Nobody knows, or if they do they won't say."

"When's Neil coming back?" I asked. I had my breath and wits back. "He might know where they are."

"He doesn't. He'll be back in another half hour or so I guess."

"Have you visited Mother, sorry Maud?"

A smile flickered across Victoria's face.

"No," she said.

When the family was staying in Montgomery Place before the funeral, I had written to St Evelyn's to ask when there could be visitors and had been given an evasive reply which I showed to Victoria and Neil at the time.

"You can go visit her." I said chancing that they would let her eventually. Then I saw no point in further evasion so I said, "Tell her that I know everything and I still love her."

At that point Victoria broke down again; but this time it was uncontrollable. Part of me wanted to comfort her and say all would be well. But we neither of us knew that and the words would be meaningless. A small part of me, probably a larger part than I would admit, even to myself now as I tell my story, felt that this was well deserved pain for her and she should take it to the last full measure. It took a while for her to regain her composure. I had asked myself if I could trust her. I knew that I could, when she cried at her sister being loved by the 'son' she stole. I was surprised at how coolly I felt about her and how calculating I had become. I absolved myself by thinking that this was how it was to be for the rest of my life. I was never going to trust anyone again, aside from Lucy and Brushes. As for Ellen I didn't know. I thought I had loved her, but, right then, that love was receding like a ship over the horizon. When Victoria recovered her composure, she nodded to me as if she was asking for me to speak.

"Could you consider moving to Boston and looking after her? " I asked.

"Of course."

"I must find Lucy and Brushes. I don't know how I'm going to do that. She needs you. You could bring her here, of course."

It wasn't true when I said I didn't know how I was going to find them. I was going to see Colin Stevens and ask him where they were. If he wasn't prepared to tell my lady-like aunt, he would tell me. I'd do to him what it took to find out, I told myself.

"No, I won't bring my sister here," Victoria said quickly. "I'll look after her in her own home. Your home, if you don't mind. There is nothing keeping me here."

My cousins had left home. I knew better than to ask about Neil. Her affection for him, tenuous at best given his many drunken binges, must have departed with Colin's wagon and Lucy's cries.

"I'll write to Mr. and Mrs. Baines that you are coming. They'll look after you. I kept them on to look after Maud if she recovered."

"You know," Victoria said, "I think he guessed the truth quite early. He's told me many times that he's proud of you, and in a way that shows me he feels the truth even if he hasn't been told it. I'll follow your letter to Mr. and Mrs. Baines."

"I'll wire them," I said.

"Then I'll leave tomorrow. I'll wait at Montgomery Place until St Evelyn's say I can visit."

"I'll wire Mrs. Holmes too. She'll be pleased to see you." Then I had a thought. "Don't tell Neil you're leaving him."

"Of course I wouldn't," she said. Her words were hurried and soft as she waved frantically at the parlor's door. "I'll say I'm looking after my sister. I can't leave, he has all my money."

I heard Neil's footsteps on the porch. They were steady. It must have been a good day. I stood up.

I had wondered on the journey down how I would react to him when I first saw him. My mother's rapist; my aunt's jailor; the casual breaker of promises and families. Rage welled and then a cooler head enveloped me like a cold white mist of freezing fog.

"Hello Uncle Neil," I said as he entered the parlor. I didn't just try to sound affable. I was affable. A look of fear was haunting his face as if he knew we had been talking of him and as if he had dreaded this moment for the previous twenty years. My friendly greeting of a beloved uncle, intoned in the same manner it had been for many years, eradicated the anxiety in an instant.

"Why Jack," he said. His voice was as hearty as ever with only the slightest of catches in it and his eyes showed the delight of the felon hearing a 'Not Guilty' verdict after a long wait. "Come to look after my horses?"

"No sir," I said, as if that question was the most important I'd heard that day. "I need to buy a valet for after I pass out of West Point. I was asking Aunt Victoria if you could look after him for a while after I've got him."

The contrast that he had sold out of desperation and I was talking of buying from choice hung in the room like tobacco smoke.

"Why not wait?" he said.

"The market's rising. Now's the time to buy. It'll be much more expensive next year. Anyone with any sense knows not to sell with the market having so far to go up. Besides I'll not have time after I pass out."

"Of course we'll look after him," he said. "We'll be allowed to work him?"

"Not as a field hand. As a groom maybe but I'd prefer it if you kept him as an inside man."

Neil nodded sagely as if I had explained a clever stock buy. "Are you staying the night?"

"No sir, I don't mean to be rude but I need to get back to Baltimore. I've an appointment with a trader."

"Well, you'd better go like the wind, like you usually do. Y'all come back when you can stay." He was breezy as he said this; relieved that there would be no fight about the sale of Lucy and Brushes and oblivious to the fact that I was looking for a servant in Baltimore when I should very soon be in class at West Point.

"I shall, sir." I said. "Good night Aunt Victoria. Good night, sir."

"Oh, I have a wire for you," Neil said. "I was walking past the telegraph office and Bill ran out to give it to me."

I took the envelope without a word, put it in my pocket and left; dispirited and unable to think of anything than attacking Colin Stevens, which would take me no further if they had been sold on by a pin hooking trader. I couldn't do this on my own, I thought. But I didn't know where to turn. Dr. Holmes knew nothing about the South. I thought of Ellen and wondered if she would help me at least think of what to do. The exhaustion from the journey swept over me.

I was a mile out from the plantation when I opened the wire.

COME BACK STOP URGENT STOP HOLMES

Eight

I'd like to think that it was trust which made up my mind to go back. Actually it was partly the budding soldier in me. I'd received an order and I could obey it. I was tired and had no idea what else to do. So I rode immediately to Boston, stopping only to change horses.

By the time I'd got to Charles Street, I was deranged with fatigue. I'd never been so many days without sleep having ridden from Boston to Baltimore and back again with only stops for tea with my aunt and to change horses. After crossing the Massachusetts border I was starting to see things. Weird faces and crashing waves mostly. Light was flashing in my eyes and there was a constant ringing sound in my ears as I rode on and on relieved that I had a destination, which let me push aside depair.

I tied my horse up outside Holmes's house and he opened the front door as if he was waiting for me to appear. I stumbled across the threshold, fell and picked myself up.

"Christ Jack," he said. "When did you last sleep."

"I'm falling down Doctor. Falling down. I'm here. But I'm falling down."

"Let's get you to bed."

"What's the news? Please what's the news. Then I can sleep."

"You're in no condition to take it. Use Wendell's room and sleep."

For the next twelve hours I was between slumber and delirium.

Occasionally I saw Mrs. Holmes wipe my brow and Dr. Holmes look on. Finally I slept the deepest of sleeps.

I was woken by Dr. Holmes, who shook me hard.

"There's a tray of breakfast over there," he said pointing to the bay window overlooking the river. His voice was urgent making no concession to my condition just like when I was ill as a child.

"Come down as soon as you can. There's someone you need to see now and he can't stay long."

I jumped out of bed and saw that I was still in the clothes I'd been in on the ride from Baltimore.

"You're a wreck, but you can change at your house. Meet me downstairs."

No more than ten minutes later I'd eaten the bread, drunk the tea and splashed my face with water from the night-stand. Holmes was waiting by the front door.

"Are you fit for a small walk?"

"Yes, sir," I said. "Can you tell me why you got me back here. Lucy's gone."

"That's why I sent the wire. You need to promise me that what I'm about to show, you'll not say a word to anyone, even Ellen."

"Even Ellen?"

"Yes, it's that important."

I was going to tell the whole truth about me to Ellen when she got back from her travels. That my secret was to be replaced by another made something die in me. But, compelled by Holmes's urgency, I nodded assent.

"You have to meet someone in my old house. He's waiting and we don't have much time."

We walked full speed. Holmes had his eyes fixed firmly on the road ahead. His face was grim, his manner urgent. There were so many builder's wagons to dodge, it would have been difficult to have asked him anything as we raced through to Montgomery Place. It took fifteen minutes of brisk walking. Holmes almost made me run. He stared as if he wasn't looking at anything. If he was not possessed by what he was to show me, he was at least consumed by it to the exclusion of all else. I tried to talk with him once, but he walked on with his head forward ignoring me.

The front door was unlocked, as if the builders were in. There were sounds coming from the kitchen.

"Cook sometimes works here until the new people move in," Holmes said as we walked towards the cooking smells.

"New people?" I asked.

"The sale goes through in a few weeks. Until then I have some things here. Cook…"

Dr. Holmes broke off. I saw a man of medium height and a non-descript face you could easily forget. His even features were of a sort which Holmes called goodlihead, but he was totally forgettable.

"Cook," said Dr. Holmes. "Can you introduce our friend here."

Cook opened her mouth and was about to speak when the man put out his hand.

"Tracker," he said.

"Jack."

"I know. Follow me."

The first hiding place was in the cellar. Behind a rack of wine, which had cobwebs all over it, stood a fake brick wall and behind it, in a space through a small vertical gap, were two beds.

The second was an attic leading off from the spare bedroom I'd often slept in when things at home got too much. Even though much of my childhood was spent in that house, I didn't know that there was an attic above that bedroom and no-one would ever know it was there except for a screw recessed into the ceiling. Tracker went out to the hallway and picked up a large stick with a screwdriver on the end. He stuck the end of the stick into the screw. About a minute later it dropped onto the floor and a hinged ceiling flap opened.

"Pick it up," he said, pointing to the screw. He went back into the hallway and got out a set of library stairs. This time he he shut the door behind him with the familiar clunk I had heard so often when Mrs. Holmes left me after putting me to bed. He placed the steps underneath the hole in the ceiling and gestured for me to climb up. It was pitch black. He handed me a candle and then I could see that, hidden inside Dr. Holmes' house, was another home in which a family could live undetected. There was a sitting room and a bedroom area, with furniture.

My head was spinning and I nearly dropped the candle. I climbed down the ladder.

"You'd better go see Dr. Holmes," he said.

"Are you...escaped?"

"You need to talk to Dr. Holmes."

"Where will he be?"

"Where he keeps the whiskey. I have to go. I'm glad to see you. We'll meet later I hope."

"You're going?"

"Yes. Like I said, glad to meet you. I have one question. If we help you free your Lucy, will you stay in the army and help us?"

"Who's 'we'?"

"Dr. Holmes will explain. I need to go. If we help you free your Lucy, will you stay in the army and help us?" His tone was unruffled but relentless.

"And Brushes?"

"I meant both of them," he said. No irritation appeared in his voice but his even tone made me think it should have.

"You know about Brushes?"

"Of course."

"Who are you?"

"Dr. Holmes'll explain. I must go. Can you screw the ceiling back up?"

"Of course. If you can find them, I'll do anything."

He handed me the screw.

"Finding them's normally the easy part," he said. "We've got our best spy down there now looking. We help you. You help us."

"I understand," I said; though even then I realized that I didn't really.

I screwed the flap back up and when I turned to give him the stick back he had left. The door, which had always shut with that familiar noise, had silently closed behind him so that even my acute ears did not hear. Panicked, I dropped the stick and ran downstairs and into the street. He had gone.

I went to the old study. Holmes was at the whiskey cabinet which was behind a small round turning bookshelf. He grinned at me.

"Good, aren't they?"

I nodded.

"How often did you use them?"

"Once a month, sometimes twice. It all depends. They can use the whole house now. When they come, Cook leaves food for them. If anyone catches an escapee in here, you could imagine how shocked I would be at the use to which my empty house has been put."

"How did you feed them when you lived here?"

I knew the answer. There was always too much food. I saw so much go to waste.

"Oh. You know, leftovers."

"Who knows about this?"

"Aside from Amelia?"

"Yes, aside from Mrs. Holmes."

"Cook of course. Of the children just Mellie and Wendy. Not Ned, he's too young."

'Mellie' was the name we all used for Amelia Holmes, Mrs. Holmes's namesake and 'Wendy' for Dr. Holmes's namesake, Oliver Wendell Holmes junior.

"It's good practice for us to conceal them from Ned. Cook fed them the 'leftovers'. She always cooked too much so no one noticed any extra food being bought. It's all accounted for by my eccentricity."

"Who's Tracker?"

"Ah, he is a fine figure of a man is he not?"

"Yes," I said, not sure what Dr. Holmes was aiming at.

"Describe him."

"What?"

"You've just seen him. Now describe him."

I couldn't. The term "nondescript" was apt. Dr. Holmes relished my discomfiture and continued.

43

"He's my station master. He directs the people here and then sends them on to the next station. He comes and goes. I never see him come.

We were sat on stools in the old study. He poured each of us a small early morning whiskey and told me about how he got involved.

A man knocked on his door in a state of panic and asked if he could come in. Mrs. Holmes was away with the children. The man was bedraggled. Holmes beckoned him inside and asked him his business.

He was an escaped slave who had, through many different stopping places, managed to find his way to Boston where he got work in the harbor, cleaning offices and carting goods on the wharf. He joined the community of free blacks and tasted freedom and security. He made the mistake of confiding his position to a young freedman who helped him with his daily tasks. Wanting his position, the freedman gave him away to the slave catchers. The escapee heard them come to the front door of the boarding house in which he was staying. He climbed onto the roof of the house and managed to get away, catching a glimpse of his potential captors as he ran across the roofs of Boston.

For the next two weeks he stopped at four different houses of work mates. On a move to a fifth house, he was recognized in the street by one of the slave catchers who had knocked on the door of his boarding house two weeks before. He ran until he found himself in Montgomery Place, where, exhausted, he stopped and pounded on the door he was about to drop in front of. He did not know who lived there, it was the only chance he had of escaping his pursuers.

Dr. Holmes hid him in the attic, which then consisted of storage space and nothing more. No sooner was he safely stowed than the slave catchers came on a house to house search. Dr. Holmes assured them that he was not hiding anyone.

He was taking a risk. Congress had just passed the Fugitive Slave Act, which required all slaves to be returned to their owners regardless of where they were caught. Slaves in Massachusetts had to be returned to their owners on pain of the imprisonment of anyone who harbored them.

The slave catchers who had knocked on Dr. Holmes's door demanded to search the house. It was, they said, "to eliminate the house from the search". Dr. Holmes was due to teach at the medical school.

"I have to leave in ten minutes. Will your search be over by then?"

"It will take as long as it takes, sir. You don't want to be the hider of a runaway, do you, sir?"

"Doctor."

"Doctor who?"

"Oliver Wendell Holmes."

They made a quick exit saying that they meant no harm, but that people were hiding fugitive slaves and to do so was theft, if he understood their meaning.

He did understand their meaning and as a gesture of magnanimity assured them that they would not appear in his column in *Atlantic Monthly*. Not only that, to prove his bona fides, he said he would not even ask their names.

He rescued the slave from the attic and ensconced him in his study. He wrote a note for Mrs. Holmes and asked him to hand it to her if she strayed into the study. Otherwise the escapee was not to communicate with anyone. Mrs. Holmes did not discover him until dinner time, when he joined them for roast beef and Yorkshire pudding, rustled up for them by Cook who was told to prepare dinner for five people that night and to make it grand.

There were six. Dr and Mrs. Holmes, John who was Dr. Holmes' brother, Wendy and Amelia, his son and daughter, and the runaway. Little Ned was out with a friend. As their guest told his story, Wendy was enthralled and kept asking questions until Holmes senior was driven to say, "Wendy, be quiet. Let the man eat."

He stayed at Dr. Holmes' for three weeks. Cook liked the large appetite of the household and the lodger was discreet, either hiding in the roof, or the spare bedroom or occasionally in Dr. Holmes' study. At the end of the medical school term, the family and the lodger took Dr. Holmes' private carriage to the Emerson's house in Concord, New Hampshire. I remembered this because it was one of the very few trips to Concord to which I was not invited by the Holmeses when I was in

Boston. I was a little put out because it meant I would not see Ellen.

Dr. Holmes had no other idea as to what he could do. Neither did he know where the slave could go once he had outstayed his welcome with Mr. Emerson.

Mr. Emerson was amused to hear about the Holmes' attic and showed off his own hiding place, which he had made some five years earlier. He suggested that Holmes have some work done to his house by some Quakers, so that his guests could rest and hide in more comfort.

That was the start of Dr. Holmes' introduction to the Underground Railroad. Visitors began to arrive at his house. Some came singly. Others came in families, mother, father, children and sometimes even grandparents. They stayed as long as three weeks, though sometimes only a day. He would sometimes take them to the Emersons' house in Concord and from there they went to Canada.

Occasionally he would get a letter thanking him for his kind hospitality. One ran to several pages in which the writer, as in Christmas family newsletters, gave an account of how well everyone was doing, adding at the end how much their freedom owed to him.

Dr. Holmes did not keep a record until he received a letter from an escapee he did not recall and could not picture in his mind. He then kept a journal so he would know whether such a letter was a forgery designed to catch him out or whether it was genuine. He knew the risks of written records, therefore he wrote it up in his own cipher.

Soon after he started, Holmes was visited by Tracker. The first visit was brief and involved Tracker saying, "Thank you for all your help," and disappearing again as if he had never knocked on his door.

The Underground Railroad kept its integrity because nobody knew who else was involved aside from their immediate dispatchers or dispatchees of the "parcels" as they were called. There were others in Dr. Holmes's immediate neighborhood, but he did not know who they were until Tracker made his second visit.

Nearby there were five safe houses. Then one of them was discovered by slave catchers. The householder, who was supervisor of the local station masters, avoided prison and got away with a large fine. Suffering social disgrace and his cover blown, he moved to New York City.

Tracker was sent by someone, who Dr. Holmes only knew as Grace, to ask him if he could be the new supervisor in his district. Dr. Holmes and Tracker were the only people to know the identity of all the safe houses in Beacon Hill. His work involved nothing except that each of the owners of the safe houses could come to him if their "packages" were too large to be taken in by one household. Dr. Holmes would organize the individual's or family's dispersal around the neighborhood followed by their re-convening for onward transmission up north.

Tracker was an "Area Manager", who visited Dr. Holmes' house to see if everything was all right and whether there were any more households who might be interested in helping. If Dr. Holmes thought that someone might provide another safe house then Tracker arranged for a freedman to ask for shelter. The freedman always had his papers with him so that he could say that it was all a misunderstanding if the householder tried to turn the fugitive in to the slave catchers. Six more safe houses were found that way, replacing four whose owners "retired" on account of local suspicion.

"That's all I can say really. I haven't met Grace. All I know is that she runs the whole thing. She's a Boston Girl whose sister was kidnapped. Tracker talks about her occasionally."

"I had no idea," I said.

"I was worried you'd spot the attic. If you look carefully you can see the door's outline in the ceiling. But it's very well concealed."

"I didn't see it."

"Well, that's a mercy. Tracker's men are going to fill that attic up soon. How're you feeling?"

"Tired still. My leave runs out tomorrow. I promised him I'd help him from the army if he found them."

"He's got spies everywhere."

"How did you know to send the wire and that Lucy'd been sold?"

"You'll find out soon enough. What you say I take you back to the Academy and let the spies do their work."

Nine

I was a day late back, but Holmes's celebrity ensured that no questions were asked by Superintendent Delafield when I was presented to him by Dr. Holmes. It was interesting to watch Delafield react to a famous man.

"You look awful Cadet," he said finally after he had finished fawning on Dr. Holmes.

"I'm tired, Superintendent, that's all."

"It's a big thing losing a parent, Cadet. I'm so glad you have the Doctor here to help you. You'd better go now."

"Yes, sir."

I fell back into the routine of West Point life for those final four weeks. It was a relief that all I had to do was some soldiering and that the Railroad's spies were looking for Lucy. I became sustained by the knowledge that my instructors were teaching me things they never would, had they known the truth about me. My fellow cadets would have found it horrifying if they knew. This gave me a distance from them, which they attributed to grief.

I found this double life exciting but I was fearful at the same time since all I had been taught about spies was that they were cowardly despicable turncoats deserving only of contempt and being shot.

Lester didn't signal a visit from Ellen, but he did bring me one letter from her shortly after my return.

"Is she there?" I asked.

"No sir," Lester said.

"How did you get this then?"

"I can't say I'm sure," Lester said using a voice of dumb insolence I'd heard so often from uncooperative staff.

Knowing better than to alienate him, I ripped open the envelope. The letter was full of local Concord gossip and fears about the health of her father, whose memory, she thought, was not as it was. She ended by asking that I go straight to Concord at the end of term rather than back to Boston and that she'd be waiting for me there.

In those last weeks of term I threw myself into my work and left off escaping to the local Inn with my classmates, studying instead. Mathematics was starting to make sense. Superintendent Lee's prediction that I would be first in my class did not come true, but Lee was more right than Professor Mahan. I was number three.

When the vacation finally came, I felt excitement and dread at the same time. Without the overwhelming yearning for news of Lucy, I wouldn't have had the courage to face Ellen in Concord and tell her a truth, which would tear us apart.

When I got there, I was greeted by Mr. Emerson, who ushered me into his study. Dr. Holmes was sitting in a wing backed chair reading *Richard II*. He remained engrossed in the play when Emerson and I sat down.

"How was term?" Emerson asked.

"Okay, I guess."

"That's all?"

"I've done okay. But that's not why I'm here."

"We're all under cover," Dr. Holmes said as he put his Shakespeare aside.

"Even my own Ellen," Mr. Emerson said.

He saw my confusion and continued. "Ellen found my hiding places when she was twelve. I had to tell her everything or she wouldn't speak to me any more. She's very discreet."

"She never told me," I said.

"Exactly."

"Is there any news?" I asked.

49

"None that we've been told," Emerson said. "But that doesn't mean anything. If they've found her they'll not tell us and finding them's only the start. Tracker's sending someone here with an update. Because first you need an education."

"An education?"

"Yes. You can't just go to Baltimore and pick them up. It's not that simple."

"I've got money."

"That's unlikely to be enough. Her new owners may not sell and you can't go round Baltimore asking where she is. If you do, you'll be the first suspect when she goes missing," Emerson said and then turned to Holmes.

"Wendell, someone must educate this boy before he goes south. Meantime Jack, go see Ellen. She's in the gazebo"

Ellen had dark hair, almost black, parted in the middle. Down to where it covered her ears it was straight, but it then changed into ringlets. She had blue eyes, a full nose and a straight mouth, which, in repose, curved upwards in a kind smile. When we were small I teased her because her left eye seemed higher in her head than her right and she teased me back about my birthmark.

I walked with her as I told her my story, taking care to look ahead and away from her making space between us so that she would not have to move away from me.

She did not recoil. She took my arm. She then released it, turned and looked at me.

"You were worried I wouldn't accept you." she said.

I blushed. My relief at her taking my arm gave way to embarrassment.

"I know you better than you think, Jack Ruffin. My father and Dr. Holmes often spoke of you amongst themselves. It's amazing what a curious daughter can pick up if she pays attention."

Dr. Holmes's many trips to Concord involved discussions about me. What Holmes had done troubled him and he needed to talk to Emerson from time to time. Emerson alternately scolded him and gave him the comfort of confession.

About three years previously they spoke with the study door ajar. Ellen, who wanted to see her father about their latest "packages" received from the Railroad, overheard enough of their conversation discussing me to know everything.

"So you knew before I did?"

A pang of jealousy stabbed me.

"Yes."

There was silence between us.

"I wanted to tell you that I knew in my last letter to you at West Point. But this wasn't something for me to say in a letter. Jack, I couldn't tell you what I had overheard. I had to bear it myself."

As she said this, the dagger of jealousy evaporated. Her thoughts were the same as mine.

"I knew long before you destroyed my virtue."

"You never shared it."

"I wasn't supposed to know and couldn't tell you. I guessed you knew when you stopped writing me. I came to West Point and stayed at the Hotel for a week, trying to pluck up courage to send you a note to say I was there. I watched you drill on the Plain from my hotel window. I didn't think you'd want to see me and I gave Lester a letter and left. I couldn't have borne it if he came back with nothing."

"Of course I'd have wanted to see you."

"I didn't know that, just as you didn't know. I should've asked you to come, but I was frightened."

I kissed her hard.

When we broke apart she spoke first, in what I had often teased her as being her 'brisk voice'.

"I have to leave for the South tomorrow," she said. "I have a job to do. If you see me, you mustn't recognize me."

"You're changing the subject." I said.

"Yes."

"Why?"

Her eyes recessed and she got that hunted look she had when she felt cornered. That warning sign I knew well, so I backed off and changed the subject.

"How could I not recognize you?"

"Because I shall be playing the part of Marylyn Griffin and you'll not have met me before."

I stood still, my mouth open wide. She turned to one side curtsied, smiled and said, "I am Marylyn Griffin," in a deep Western North Carolina accent. She then reverted to her New England voice.

"Don't ask me any questions because I would answer them truthfully to you and I should not tell the truth to anyone who doesn't work for the Railroad." At that she put her index finger to her lips. Then she changed back to her North Carolina accent.

"I'm Marylyn Griffin and I'm right pleased to meet you."

"Jack Ruffin, the pleasure is all mine."

Whilst she was flirtatious in this exchange, I was solemn as if a gentleman on first greeting.

"Ok Jack, one more time," she said. I kissed her again with urgency and relief. Eventually we broke apart.

"However surprised you are, if you see me, that is what we say. And there must be no sign that we know each another."

I wanted to ask her about Miss. Griffin. I had arrived with what I thought was my own secret. She had one and I was intrigued. With the girl I loved since I was five years old, there was mystery. I felt a strange mixture of jealousy, relief and acceptance.

"Make love to me tonight," she said and ran towards the house.

We didn't make love. She put on her night-dress, turned away from my side of the bed and fell asleep immediately. When I awoke the next morning she was gone.

At breakfast I met a Mr. Brown, who was an old friend of Mr. Emerson's. He was a wild looking man with long flowing white hair and an equally long white beard. Mr. Emerson said he had a reputation as an anti-slavery speaker, but I'd never heard of him. Emerson introduced him to me as being part of the Underground Railroad.

"The Kansas Branch," he said, appearing to require none of the secrecy that the others had shown. "But I know a bit about Maryland and Virginia and I'm here to teach you about them before sending you off for basic training."

"Basic training?" I said.

"Yes. An army term I believe young man. You should know as you're in the army. Don't they teach you anything?"

"Not about basic training"

Brown ignored my joke.

"Never forget this is a war," he said. "One side of the country is fighting another and you need to know both of them. Shall we start with your side first? No. Let's start with the Patrol. They're your enemy. If what you hear doesn't make you want to kill them, then there's no hope for you young man."

As he said this his eyes flashed with the madness of a fanatic; with the type of insanity I'd seen in people Father avoided when we were in South Boston and they were handing out leaflets with instructions as to how to save your soul.

"I see you think I'm mad."

"No, sir," I lied.

"Mad I may be. Nevertheless listen. First the Patrol. Then the Railroad. First your foe. Then your friend."

Ten

The Patrol

Tim and Jake Smith were brothers. As their story was told to me, they were in their early twenties. It was hard to tell them apart, even as adults.

The game they liked to play when children was "Patty Rollers", taught to them by their father when they were small. It was the children's game hide and seek, but the child who had to hide was a make-believe escaped slave and those who had to seek were the Patrol, whose job it was to search for and apprehend escaped slaves and take them back "home".

It was played by children everywhere in the South, the slave and free children on plantations and the children of the poorer whites such as Tim and Jake. After the Civil War, the game reverted to being called "hide and seek" in the South.

Tim and Jake were the only children of Dick and Patty Smith, small farmers who eked out a living about fifteen miles to the south west of Baltimore. They lived an isolated life on the farm. Dick hit Patty and she did not want to show off her bruises, so they kept to themselves. Dick would go to Baltimore alone to purchase provisions. My Aunt Victoria would occasionally comment that it was strange that Patty was never seen in town, but nobody intruded upon the Smith farm to find out why. When I was traveling with Brushes in the summers, he always gave the Smith place a wide berth.

It was a hard living because the farm consisted of about twenty acres of difficult land to till. The crops they grew were wheat, corn, rye and sweet potatoes which Dick sold in the markets in Baltimore. It was hardly enough to live on and, with two growing children to feed, Dick found himself a sideline.

Like on any other day in that time of year, he started to load up the sacks of wheat, which were piled up in the far corner of the barn.

The sacks had formed a wall and their removal reduced its height sack by sack and it was not long before he saw that someone was cowering behind it. A man of about five feet eight in height, light brown skin but nondescript features, he looked around nineteen years of age. Runaways were not an everyday occurrence and it took Dick about five full seconds to work out that an escaped slave was hiding behind his sacks of wheat. Dick himself did not keep slaves. This was not out of principle, but economic reality. His farm was too small. Dick would occasionally hire a field hand. Sometimes it was impossible to hire someone at a reasonable price and he had to manage without. Ideally Dick needed another hand at planting and harvest time. During those months hiring a slave was at luxury prices, which Dick increasingly could not afford.

The sight of this teenager did not cause him to change his expression. He carried on loading his wagon.

Dick reflected that the harvest was almost all in and he could have used some help a bit earlier. Although he felt less pressed then, there were still things to do. As he loaded the last sack onto the wagon, Dick turned around and, without looking directly at him, said: "Do you want something to eat?"

There was no response. He raised his voice and said, "Boy, do you want something to eat?"

The runaway looked at Dick standing beside the wagon. He reckoned there was a space between him and the barn wall through which he could jump if he was quick. That would be about as far as he could get because Dick could have caught him on horseback. He had no weapon and was not confident he could disable Dick.

"I am hungry, Sir," he said.

Not many people called Dick "Sir". If he rented a slave he was called "Master". While "Master" satisfied Dick, he found the appellation "Sir" arresting and appropriate. Come to think of it, none of the free blacks in Baltimore called him "Sir". "Mister Smith" seemed be their address of choice, not that he had much to do with them anyway.

Dick occasionally heard the words "poor white trash" behind his back. He wondered if they applied to him but invariably he dismissed the thought and carried on about his business.

"Come with me," he said and, without looking at the escapee, walked to his house and round to the back door. The teenager followed. Defeated.

"Wait here."

Dick went inside. His boys, now also in their early teens, were still asleep. He took a plate and filled it with some bread and sweet potatoes and brought it out

"What's your name?"

"Tom, sir"

"Eat, Tom."

Tom ate the food and Dick went inside, got a cup of water.

"Thirsty?"

"Yes, sir."

"Here."

"Thank you, sir."

"Can you work?"

"Oh, I work, sir."

"I'll just get the wagon out of the barn and I shall give you some work to do."

While Tom ate, Dick hitched his horse to the wagon and drove it out of the barn and onto the cart track, which would take him to Baltimore.

"Can you plow?"

"Yes, Sir."

"I want you to plow up a field for me. Can you do that?"

"You show me where, Sir."

Dick got down from his wagon and unhitched the horse.

Half an hour later Tom was plowing the field from where the wheat crop had come. Dick, an amateur blacksmith, watched him as he mended his tools. As Tom plowed, he thought of unhitching the horse and making a break for it. The plow-horse was strong but slow and he feared he would never make it either on foot or with that horse. He told me later that this was one of the biggest mistakes of his life. It taught him that caution is sometimes folly.

Tom proved an efficient plowman. Dick was relieved that part of the backbreaking work was being done by someone else and pleased he did not have to pay for the labor.

"Do you want to go to Baltimore?" he asked after the plowing

"Yes, sir, that's where I am heading."

Dick had made a gap in the sacks so Tom could climb aboard the wagon into which, with a squeeze, he would fit. Dick reckoned that he could drive Tom into Baltimore and let him go. In the back of his mind, he wondered about rewards, but there was no guarantee that Tom would bring him one and he dismissed the idea. Besides he was grateful for the plowing.

"Come here," he said and then showed Tom the place in the wagon for him.

"You lie in there. I'll cover you up with these sacks and I'll take you in and let you out when it's safe. I'm going there anyway to sell this last bit of harvest."

Dick was not used to being kind to "niggers". But Tom had been so quiet and willing that it was hard not to think of him as another human in trouble. Stuck away on his hardscrabble farm, with just his wife and two small boys most of the time, Dick was not used to unsolicited company.

Dick thought he saw Tom hesitate, but then dismissed the idea from his mind. "Yes, Sir. Thank you, Sir," Tom said as he jumped onto the wagon.

Tom had spent his plowing time working out the odds of a successful escape from this farm and a continuation of his journey. If he stayed at the farm he would be caught by the Patrol. If he left in full view of Dick in the daytime, then Dick could alert the Patrol. If Dick took him to Baltimore, then at least he had a chance that he could find aid from amongst the freedmen before continuing his journey. He had been to Baltimore only once, when he had been sold to his current owner eight years earlier, arriving in chains and a neck brace with his mother and brother on the back of a wagon. It was not Colin Stevens's wagon but that of another trader, Pat Buchanan.

Tom planned to jump out of the wagon and make his escape when he got into town. He could then get lost in the crowds. He lay down and allowed Dick to arrange the sacks over him.

Eleven

Dick had figured that there was enough air for Tom to breathe because, although the space in which Tom hid was small, he had made two cracks along the length of the sacks through which air could filter.

As the wagon approached Pratt Street, Tom heard the noises of commerce. The journey was jarring as the wagon went over every possible bump in the road. He could no longer take the heat and bumping, let alone lack of air. He pushed hard on the sacks. They were unyielding. He could get no firm purchase and his perspiring hands slid on the sacking. In the heat of the tiny hole in which he hid, his upward push became progressively weaker as each effort seemed greater and became more desperate. Overwhelmed, he passed out.

On Pratt Street there were a series of shop fronts and small billboards on which advertisements were placed. As a commercial district there was much to advertise. Harvest sales, slave sales, leather and dry goods and other merchandise and services.

One of the up and coming items of business were runaway slave rewards. The posters were mostly amateurish and not truly descriptive of the owner's property. However with Tom this was not the case. His owner, Gerald Butler, Esquire, liked horses and hunting. His plantation was looked after by his overseer and he paid little attention to the day-to-day management of the farming business. He was of medium build, thin with salt and pepper hair parted in the middle. One of his hobbies was drawing portraits.

On the day that Tom went missing, Butler drew him from memory and found that what he had created a very good likeness. Tom's portrait appeared on billboards on which posters of runaways were placed.

The wagon was trundling down Pratt Street when Dick hit its side and shouted: "Boy, this is Baltimore. I'll stop down a side street in a minute."

There was no response.

On the corner of the next street, he saw the poster. It had Tom's picture on it, in a staggeringly accurate likeness, and above it in large type

"$200 REWARD FOR SAFE RETURN". Below the picture was a short narrative and description:

Tom Butler. Medium height. Good legs. No markings. Missing, possibly lost or escaped. Trustworthy nigger groom and gamekeeper. Harmless to approach. Any Baltimore dealer authorized to give reward money, no questions asked.

Instead of turning off Pratt Street, Dick stopped the wagon and peered at the poster, oblivious to the traffic jam he created. He understood the significance of two hundred dollars. This was more than he would receive from his crop sales that year. In an instant he could double his income and all he had to do was turn in the "nigger" to a dealer.

Dick tapped the side of his wagon and shouted, "We have to go a bit further boy. Just you lay low a bit longer." There was no reply and Dick scratched his head as he tried to decide to which dealer he should give his business.

The regular merchant to whom he sold his products did not include slave trading as a central part of his business. He was a feed and seed merchant who advanced money to farmers but occasionally handled slaves as a sideline, usually in conjunction with a large slave dealer like Colin Stevens with one-off deals, rather than a partnership or franchise.

The merchant's slave dealings were seen by him as a favor to his usual clients, but some were lucrative, depending on the size of the reward or commission. To be in the business more than occasionally you needed a storefront, a jail, ironmongery and men to control the slaves on their way to and at the market. Leon Bott could not afford these overhead costs. The main barriers to starting slave trading were connections and capital. Leon had some connections with small "cracker" farmers like Dick, but he had no capital, no slave jail and no men in his employ who could act as the muscle. In this business you needed full time people you could trust. Colin Stevens had them. The Campbell business did. Leon Bott did not.

If Dick went to Colin or the Campbells', he would be giving the brokerage reward to someone with whom he did not usually deal. A brokerage reward was the reward given to the slave trader to whom a runaway is turned in. You could turn in runaways to the authorities, and, under the Fugitive Slave Act, that was a recognized means of restoring property to his or her lawful owner. Many people did not like dealing with the Sherriff, as it put them into contact with an authority they found intimidating. Allowing for this, posters, such as this one with Tom's face on it, had on them the alternative of turning the slave in to a dealer, who would pay the reward and restore the slave to their owner for a fee.

The thought in Dick's mind was that if he turned Tom into Leon, then Leon would get the brokerage fee and as a result might give him better prices for his crops. Leon did not always pay the best prices. He did advance money on account of a crop before it was in the barn and for that reason he was able to get a large proportion of his business from people like Dick.

Having toyed with the idea of turning Tom in to one of the bigger traders and expanding the circle of people with whom he did business in Baltimore, Dick settled on Leon. He continued on Pratt Street and turned up Penn Street to Leon's premises, and parked his wagon outside.

It had a large shop front, lightly off the beaten track in the sense that the larger and more prosperous businesses were directly on Pratt Street and further towards the port. It was nevertheless close enough to be considered part of the main business district. Leon was behind the counter.

"I was expecting you a bit earlier."

"Well I got me a runaway and am here to turn him in to y'all."

"Which one?"

To the left of the counter on the wall was a set of slave runaway posters. They were largely out of date and scrappy. There was no poster depicting Tom.

"Damn."

"Not there?"

"No"

"Some new ones came in yesterday. I just haven't got round to picking them up. Let's see what you got."

There was a side door behind the counter, which enabled Leon to go outside and into the store at the front. He had no flap to pull up, since he preferred the strength and stability of the continual counter. Leon picked up a pair of leg irons and went to Dick's wagon. Dick was already taking away the sacks that covered Tom. He pulled the sacks off, exposing the feet first.

"Tom, we're here," Dick said. Tom did not move. "Nigger must be sleeping," he said to Leon.

"Did you leave any room for him to breathe?" Leon asked. He stopped himself asking Dick why he covered the runaway with sacks of grain.

"I guess." Dick dislodged the sacks with greater urgency. He felt a rising panic. The reward was not "Alive or Dead". He could lose the reward and would be perceived by Leon Bott as an incompetent. He had caught a slave and could not turn him in alive. Leon could not be trusted to keep silent. Dick became so agitated he dropped a sack spilling the contents onto the road.

"Careful with your cargo," Leon admonished as Dick stared at the broken sack before checking whether his prize was still breathing. Leon was already on the wagon and put his ear to Tom's heart.

"Well, I guess he's okay. Let's get your sacks in while we wait for him to wake up." Leon attached the leg irons to Tom.

Between the two of them they managed the task of getting the sacks into Leon Bott's barn in just under half an hour. In the meantime Tom lay prone and manacled on the floor of the wagon. The sun's heat had begun to dissipate and he was no longer breathing foul or stale air. Even so, by the time Dick and Leon had finished unloading and storing the crop Tom was still unconscious. Leon went to the back of the store and returned with a wooden bucket and handed it to Dick.

"You'd better fill this up and then wake him up with this. The nigger must have fainted in the heat."

There was no hint of reproach in Leon's voice. It was simply practical and matter of fact and Dick was relieved. He was ready for a sharp word from Leon because he had not left enough air for Tom. Although Leon did think that Dick was a bit of a fool, he wanted the commission this runaway would give him and Dick's continued business. Relieved that Tom was alive and that Leon was not blaming him for Tom's state, Dick took the bucket and walked the hundred yards to the water trough leading his horse there so that he and his horse could drink the water.

Dick was not ready for comment from passers by. The moment of unloading had been essentially undisturbed as the two of them got on with the task. No one commented that two white men were manhandling sacks whilst a black man appeared to be asleep in their midst. But the sight of Dick leading his horse pulling a cart, with a shackled and unconscious Tom in it, could not pass unnoticed among those doing business on that day.

"Hey Dick," said one as he walked in the other direction, "your nigger's supposed to lead you."

There were two other pieces of unsolicited advice given to the embarrassed Dick as he went to and from the trough and watered his horse. Dick was too chastened to say anything. At one point he felt like justifying himself, but he knew there was no point. Besides, he was up for a reward and these people who were making fun of him were not.

On his return Dick put the pail of water down and went into the store to discuss business with Leon, who had by then found Tom's poster. They agreed that Dick would receive fifty dollars for the grain. Leon gave Dick a receipt for Tom. The receipt was written on the of back Tom's reward poster which Leon had found amongst the pile in the front of the store.

"Well, I guess I needn't stick this one up," Leon said as he turned the poster over to write out the receipt.

Dick had never turned in a runaway before, and did not know the procedure and his legal rights. He was to receive a receipt for the slave, who was taken in exchange. On the receipt was written the promise to pay the two hundred dollar reward if the slave was accepted by the owner as his.

"How much do you want in cash and how much in credit?" Leon asked. Normally the question was answered by the degree to which Dick was in debt to Leon, because the amount owed on the advances Leon gave his crops was so large that Dick usually came away with no cash. The two hundred dollars wiped the slate clean. By Dick's calculation, Leon would owe him one hundred and eighty dollars when his debt to Leon and the amount due for this load of crop was taken into account.

"Fifty fifty," Dick said. He had, on the trip back from the water trough, worked out the amount of goods he was likely to want from Leon in the following six months and ninety dollars should cover it and that would leave him ninety dollars cash and all debts paid.

Dick had never made so much money at one time. His trading life with Leon was a cycle of debt, which receded as each crop was brought in for sale but which increased after he almost reached balance or even, briefly, credit. Every year Dick's debt to Leon, at the peak of his indebtedness, increased slightly and Dick worried when he asked for more credit that Leon would say no and that Leon might ask for payment of what was owed. This anxiety reached its peak when his whole crop of beans failed through a blight because he made the mistake of planting beans on the same land for three years in a row. Dick knew of crop rotation, but he had planted the same crop twice with success because the price was good and so he felt that it did no harm the third year. He was to discover that doing so nearly wiped him out.

That time Leon told him not to worry but that he would have to increase the rate of interest. Dick was so grateful that he thanked Leon and assured him that the crop the next year would clear his debt. Both knew it would not, but the fiction made Dick feel better.

"I'd better wake him up," Dick said to himself and went out to the wagon.

Tom had awakened shortly after Dick started to lead the wagon back from the trough. His mouth felt dry and he remembered the claustrophobia and heat of the journey's start from Dick's small holding and the impression of being entombed as the sacks were put around him. Then it came back to him. The tearful goodbyes, the flight in the night, the North Star, his sight of Dick's barn and the decision to rest the day behind the sacks, his discovery by Dick, the offer to go to Baltimore and freedom and his blackout.

As he moved his feet to get up, he felt the leg irons and then the splash as a bucket of cold water hit him.

Twelve

The Railroad

Tom did not have to worry about the paperwork and the money which had to change hands when he was returned. All he had to concern himself with was that he had been caught in the stupidest way he could think. He reflected on not discussing his plan with "The Birdwatcher".

A former army sharpshooter and now a man of leisure, The Birdwatcher had a red face which never tanned, dark curly receding hair and medium build. From Lynchburg, Virginia, he traveled round Virginia and Maryland looking at birds and writing descriptions of them in a book.

What drew people to him were his shooting and his field glasses.

With a Sharps' rifle, he could demonstrate hitting a target from half a mile away or more.

The field glasses were exotic apparatus from Europe. A frame with two telescopes mounted onto it, the glasses magnified thirty times. People would ask if he would allow them to peer through this strange device. He was always ready to hand it over, have them train the glasses on a faraway target and then tell them a story as he hit it with a single shot. I remember once looking through them myself when I was about eleven years old and out with Brushes. I never saw his shooting, though I did see the rifle.

By his second year on circuit, The Birdwatcher had become an institution and he received invitations to the best houses. By his third year, he'd made a comprehensive map of the principal plantations on his circuit, the topography of the land, the location of the main houses, where the overseers lived and the slave quarters.

Had Tom discussed his plan with The Birdwatcher, he might have received more help identifying safe houses on the route north. He later discovered that his route to freedom was unnecessarily roundabout and prolonged as he took many diversions trying to avoid the Patrol. His lack of a safe house got him into trouble and stranded him at Dick Smith's place.

Before the failed escape, Butler had asked Tom to show The Bird-watcher round. As they walked, He asked Tom about the plantation, the buildings, where the slaves, the overseer and his family lived and where all the white people who worked for Gerald Butler resided.

Thin almost to the point of emaciation, Tom cut an odd but not unfamiliar figure to The Birdwatcher who took an immediate liking to his guide. He was careful of his mission and did not divulge it to anyone, not even the slaves. He was making a full map for the woman he knew as Grace.

To have told Tom that he was drawing up a definitive map for one of the branches of the Underground Railroad would have been folly. Grace wanted good topography, the locations of safe houses and where the members of the Patrol lived and their normal riding patterns.

People like The Birdwatcher did not give anyone any information about their true purpose and mission in life unless the Railroad needed them to know.

Their walk around the plantation took two days. The Birdwatcher would stop and say he had to sketch. He drew pictures of the terrain and paced out lengths of fields, identified the crops grown and searched for ditches and watercourses. He was able to fool his guides as to his true purpose because he had many explanations as to why he was doing a particular thing.

Searching for ditches was explained as looking for possible habitat.

Pacing out the size of a field was searching for perspective.

Finding the slave quarters was either looking for the help or discovering where the route of that most people took to work the land so that disturbance of the birds could be predicted.

Finding the overseer's home was similarly explained.

Discovering the Patrol was a hit and miss business and he did not ask on the plantations. He looked in the towns and villages for them. He made no secret of his drawing of the topography, but he hid the dimensions, which he placed in code in a separate notebook that referred to the sketch he was making.

Occasionally he would stop and draw a bird. The most common birds he sketched quickly and most of his time was spent mapping. Each topographical sketch had a large letter N on one edge which signified due north from the middle of the sketch.

Something about the professional way in which he went about his business told Tom that he was not as he seemed. The Birdwatcher presented himself as a friendly and absent minded type to Gerald Butler. When not telling stories in society, his manner was fussy, his tone deferential and he seemed an enthusiastic amateur, except for the shooting. Some talked of him having been a sharpshooter. Most ignored the incongruity.

In Tom's company there was no amateur air, his eye was sharp, his tone almost pre-emptory and his manner clinical and professional. He was, in his previous life in the army, used to command and he had no difficulties in ordering Tom about. He was a man who knew what he wanted and acted as if he knew how to get others to give it to him. However there was something in his manner which Tom had never seen or felt before. He asked him to do things with authority and in a way which assumed obedience. There was no menace to his command and no threat in his voice.

The conversation which made them friends was a short one. The second morning of their work had been spent tramping fields. Tom paced and The Birdwatcher counted his steps as he sketched. Tom returned to where The Birdwatcher was sketching and assumed his usual deferential manner of speaking with white men. It consisted of a non-threatening child-like servility. Tom, however, had not always spoken to him in that fashion. On the first day The Birdwatcher had asked questions about the distance of the plantation to the river and what course it took. Tom answered swiftly and professionally.

On the second morning Tom kept rolling his eyes obsequiously in a manner to exude a lack of threat. The Birdwatcher was used to slaves acting in that way and he normally suppressed his irritation. But from Tom's crisp answers of the day before he knew that was not how he really was. Something in him snapped.

"Oh for Christ's sake stop it."

"Stop what, Master?"

"Stop it. If you roll your eyes like that again I'll scream, I swear."

"Tell me what you are doing then," Tom said, as he sat down beside him.

"Sketching."

"Sketching what?"

"Birds."

"Show me."

The Birdwatcher got out his sketches.

"Those are the same ones we looked at yesterday before you started."

The Birdwatcher looked flustered. He had mislaid yesterday's sketches. They were, he thought, probably back in his room and he had only done one bird sketch that morning. He felt his aura of command leaving him, but he had only himself to blame.

"I'm sketching the way to freedom," he said.

The words just came out. Grace would kill him, he thought, as he put himself and his mission at risk by divulging it to a complete stranger.

"We'd better get on then," Tom said.

Tom asked no more questions that morning as they continued with their mapping. The Birdwatcher gave Tom a map showing the route to Baltimore omitting the location of safe houses and the information about the Patrol. He was not yet willing to divulge that information to the boy he knew as Tom. Even so, they had made such a connection that Tom was able to tell his story to The Birdwatcher.

***

69

Tom was bought at his mother's knee. She was a field hand who "married" his father after she was pregnant with him. Shortly thereafter his father was sold south and neither wife nor son knew where he went.

He remembered his sale to the Butler plantation vividly and he spared no detail in the telling. Their master took them to Baltimore in order to exchange them for a strong man. Tom's mother was not the best field hand since she was so slight in build and she fainted in the heat. She was whipped by the overseer, who reasoned that if all the field hands stopped working when the sun got hot, the harvest would not be brought to market. However the inert body and bleeding back of Tom's mother persuaded the overseer that her fainting was genuine.

She was a willing but not overly productive field hand and was, at the time of her sale to Gerald Butler, about twenty six years old and pregnant with Tom's half brother by her master's eldest son. She was never to know whether her sale had anything to do with her condition, except that being six months pregnant at harvest time was not the best advertisement for her willingness and productivity. Tom demonstrated no curiosity about who had sired his future half brother, although he, along with everyone else in the Quarters, knew the truth.

Tom was a wiry child taller than the average for his age and his master must have been in two minds as to whether to keep him. He would, in a relatively short time, turn into a useful field hand himself and at little cost to his master. To the relief of both Tom and his mother, they were sold together.

They stood together on the block of one of Pat Buchanan's sales in Baltimore, his mother stripped to the waist, with prospective purchasers sizing them up and feeling them for muscle tone. The scars on his mother's back had to be explained in the sales particulars because they were a sign of intractability. If she were horseflesh the term would be whether she was "genuine". The question for a prospective purchaser was whether she was willing. Here there was a dilemma. The sales particulars, if inaccurate, could result in the seller facing a lawsuit and, if completely accurate, could reduce the purchase price. To have sold her "as seen" or "at buyer's risk" would also have dramatically affected the price. Instead the particulars said: "Slightly scarred when whipped after fainting in the hottest sun". People understood the hottest sun and the seller was protected even though she fainted at least twice a year.

Although Butler bought Tom's mother as a general laborer, he really bought her because there was something about the look of her son, which appealed to him. He reckoned that the boy would be a better prospect for the work he had in mind for him if his mother and brother came too. He had the normal theories about the education of black people, that it was dangerous and made them unhappy and was not to be encouraged. Nevertheless he wanted to see if he could have the young boy educated to be a game-keeper. Someone who would look after the hunting drives and make sure that the birds were undisturbed until the season got under way.

Tom became an apprentice at the age of ten and by the time he was eighteen years old his knowledge of the locality, its flora and fauna was unsurpassed. He had been the natural person to show the Birdwatcher around the plantation.

Thirteen

G erald Butler did not connect the walks with The Birdwatcher and Tom's interest in freedom. After The Birdwatcher left, Tom made his escape and found his way into Dick's barn and thence to Leon Bott's store and to the slave jail where he waited for Gerald Butler to come and collect him.

Tom over-heard his master using his best English gentleman's accent as he negotiated his collection. Butler paid his reward money and commission and was given a receipt to sign, which he handed over to the jailor once the key in the lock was turned. Gerald had adopted an ironic banter with the jailor. When he looked into the cell, his manner changed.

"I am surprised at you, Tom," he said.

Tom did not reply.

"I thought that you, of all people, should know better."

Tom hung his head, but said nothing. Gerald turned to the jailer and motioned to Tom's leg irons. The jailer stood still. Annoyed, Gerald told him to take them off.

"You've paid enough for him, you can have them as part of the deal," the jailer said.

Gerald sighed. "No, take them off."

Within half a minute the irons had slipped off Tom's ankles. Gerald turned down the passageway and walked, ramrod straight, towards the jail entrance and out to the waiting buggy. Tom followed behind him and Gerald did not look to see if he was there. His whole manner assumed that Tom would follow, as he did.

Gerald climbed up onto his cart and sat down. He waited for Tom to come alongside the cart and he nodded towards the reins. Tom jumped up and took them and Gerald pointed in the direction that would take them home.

There was silence between them as they took the road out of Baltimore. It was Gerald who broke it.

"So, you want to be free?"

"Oh no sir, I just got lost. I don't want to be free. I belong to you Mr. Butler, sir."

"You got so lost that you hid in a cracker's barn."

"Tom needed to sleep."

"Tom did, did he? You expect me to believe that?"

Tom said nothing. Caught between self-preservation with no dignity and punishment with it, Tom would say no more on the subject.

"You got quite a distance."

"Yes, sir."

"On your own."

"Yes, sir."

"I'm impressed."

Tom wanted to say, "Thank you sir." He felt that it would not be safe to say more than "Yes, sir." Neither could he share the fact that his actual distance covered was considerably greater than it seemed, with all the diversions he had taken.

The loss of Tom had been a blow to Gerald Butler's ego. He had been proud of the way in which he treated his slaves and he felt that he had a happy community under him. A mark was not laid on any of them. His lifestyle was substantially trouble free. He could not understand why people mistreated their "people" as he called them. It made no more sense to him to mistreat a slave than it did to vandalize his farm machinery. If a slave did not behave then he or she could be sold. Whipping slaves was, to Gerald, a sign of uncouth cruelty.

Harvard educated, Gerald Butler was proud to be a farmer, a scholar and a gentleman. His friends and neighbors were not always sure of when he was serious and often felt they were being patronized. Their feeling was not misplaced. Gerald's acreage and lineage ensured that nobody took him to task for it. For Gerald, people were not to be taken too seriously and he found it hard to be earnest when life had so many diversions for a gentleman.

His slaves knew that they were treated well in comparison to others and they did not tempt fate and sale by not doing what was expected of them. Gerald could not understand how people did not see that this was how things should be. Tom was his first escapee. His disappearance was a surprise, a source of gnawing doubt and tarnished his self-confidence.

Butler reflected that the large two hundred dollar reward had got Tom back. He had gone a long way from "home" and might not have been caught. Another attempt at escape was inevitable. If, as Butler planned to do, he moved closer to Baltimore and the racetrack, then Tom's escape would be even easier and he would not get him back. Butler knew he'd either have to sell Tom or give him a reason to stay.

The next part of the conversation between Tom and Gerald Butler seemed to Gerald, almost as if he was not a party to it. The noise coming out of his mouth sounded to him as if someone else was talking through him. Yet the words came out and were his.

"Tom."

"Yes, Master."

"You want to be free."

"Oh no Master. I made a mistake."

"No you didn't. Look, if you work for me for five more years, I'll set you free."

Tom was stunned. That would mean that he would be twenty three or twenty four when he was free.

"Master?"

"There is one condition. That you tell no one else until the day you go. That includes your mother. Tell anyone and the deal's off."

"Yes, sir."

Tom's instant agreement was accompanied by a stab of disappointment. He could tell no one of the biggest news of his life.

His return was a low-key affair. That he had been missing was known. However his mother stayed silent about the escape, no hue and cry had been made on the estate and it was assumed by the other slaves that he was on one of his master's errands. When Tom turned up with Gerald, nobody said anything.

Fourteen

Tom now had a third life plan almost as soon as he had lost his first two. His first was to become as good and useful a gamekeeper and horseman as he could be. His second, after meeting the Birdwatcher, was to free himself. That was shattered in Dick's barn and on the stifling trip from Dick's small farm to Baltimore. This was different. He could be free after five years. He had to be prepared when freedom came and he would spend the next five years getting ready.

He determined to keep himself an expert in topography and geography. He would know every track, every road and every route to his freedom in the county. He would learn the maps, which the Birdwatcher brought, so that every field, hill and house was known to him. He would be the best gamekeeper and horseman possible so that, when his freedom came, he would be employable and appear employed.

Most of all, he had determined that he would never be defenseless again. Every day for the rest of his life he would recall the moment when he woke to find the shackles on his ankles.

Over the next five years Butler felt the new happiness and willingness in his gamekeeper. He'd made a sensible bargain, he reflected. He got good work out of someone he never could have kept.

Five years later, Tom went to the back of the mansion and knocked. The housekeeper answered.

"Why hello Tom."

"Can I see Master, Ma'am."

"He's in his study Tom. Go right in."

Butler was proud of the friendliness which he encouraged in his slaves and it was normal for Tom to be sent into his study to report.

"Good morning Tom."

"Master."

"Yes, Tom."

"It's been five years."

Butler had made no plans for Tom's replacement. Part of him hoped that by not doing so and not saying anything he would not need to because it was all a dream. But the time had come.

"What are you going to do?" Butler said. As he asked this question, he understood that one option was to renege on the deal, keep Tom a slave and sell. His self-regard as a man of his word ruled that out.

"I don't know Master. I thought I'd go north and find work."

"There's good work to be had down south, Tom."

"I know Master"

"I could pay you and you could stay here."

"Thank you Master. I would like to go North and see what's there."

"Wait a moment."

He took a pen and wrote:

I hereby free Tom Butler who shall from this day forth be fully and absolutely free. Signed Gerald Butler.

"You need this," he said and handed over the manu-emission paper to Tom.

"Thank you, sir."

"You are the best gamekeeper and horseman I ever had."

"You need a new one, sir."

"I was hoping to persuade you to stay on, so I've not looked for one."

"I'm sure you can find someone else. I can stay until you do"

"I'm sure I can find someone. No. Go now. We can manage. When had you planned to leave?"

"Tonight."

"Does your mother know?"

"No sir, you asked me not to tell her."

"It's up to you what you say to her."

"Thank you, sir. Can I visit them, sir? After I'm gone, I mean"

Tom could see that his gave Gerald a dilemma. It was not healthy for a freedman to keep returning. It might give others ideas. Tom was an exception. The five-year offer would not be repeated and he had not lost hope that Tom would return to work for him.

"Once a year, Tom, unless you come and live with us. I'll pay you if you do."

Tom was relieved.

"Thank you, sir. I'll come back and visit in a year."

"Good boy. There's always a place for you here, Tom."

"You've treated me well, Master."

"That's very kind of you Tom. Right kind to say so. I believe I have. When I'm at the racetrack, which I hope to be soon, y'all come and see how the horses are doing."

"I shall, sir."

With that Tom left Gerald Butler's study and went to the quarters to find his mother. She had watched her talented son grow with pride and not a little wistfulness. Freedom was not to be for her or her youngest. But then Tom had skills, which she did not have. He would thrive in freedom, she thought.

She was not sure about herself. Some of the slaves on the Butler Plantation had spoken of the North Star to freedom and Canada. That had been just talk and without meaning for her. Although she wanted to be free to go where she wanted and to work for whomever she wanted, she feared starvation. She hid the stripes on her back from others and that included any potential lovers and therefore men who she could contemplate escaping with and making a new life.

Her previous master had repeated to his slaves many times that if he did not take care of them, they would all starve. There was enough truth in that for her to be glad for Tom's freedom but not anxious for her own. Besides she had the little one to take care of.

That afternoon, she was allowed to leave the fields early to say goodbye to Tom, who would be leaving that evening. Tom sat with her and his little brother.

All Tom and his mother could think to do was to sit and face one another as the tears came. What there was to say had been said. Tom could not turn down freedom and stay because his mother and brother were slaves. Tom told her that he had work to do, though that he did not say what that work was. Something in his eyes stopped her from asking. That was his private world, she knew, and he would tell her when he wanted to. She knew it wasn't game-keeping.

"Does that mean I can look after the Master's hunting?" his brother asked.

"You'll have to ask him," Tom said. "Go play, I need to talk to Mama."

His brother was getting restless and did not need persuading.

"Don't go without saying goodbye," Tom said as his brother ran off.

"I've been lucky to keep you so long," his mother said as she thought about their sale and how easy it would have been to have been separated then. Tom remembered too. Then he did not want to be separated from his mother. Now he knew he had to be.

"I'll be back in a year Mama," he said. "The Master may have bought his new place by then, but I'll know and I'll come."

"You keep your freedom papers safe," she said thinking of how easy a kidnapping and return to slavery would be.

"I'll keep it all safe Mama."

"At least you're free," she said. "That's all I could hope for."

"I'll be back," he said. "When I do, I'll come and get you both."

"I can't run like you," she said.

"You won't have to run, just climb into my special wagon when no one's looking."

They had spoken of special wagons. The type that had a hidden compartment which could conceal two adults. Tom had described them and how the compartment was concealed and could be uncovered.

"On the day I come, which will be one year to the day, you all don't go to the fields. I'll stop the special wagon next to the Quarters. While we all look for you in the fields, you climb in with him and wait."

One year seemed an eternity. The special wagon felt like a work of fiction. The chances of him actually being able to return seemed too remote to believe possible. It felt like their last meeting.

Fifteen

Sundown was at 9pm when he left the Quarters. His objective was to hike the twenty miles he needed to reach his first station. Armed with his manu-emission papers he was intent on reaching Philadelphia.

Every summer after his failed escape he and The Birdwatcher walked around the estate "to look at the birds". The maps The Birdwatcher had shown him on those walks meant he knew every step of the way. He had got to know of Grace, the woman whom he had agreed to work for should he arrive safely in Philadelphia. His challenge was to find her. He was given no address by The Birdwatcher and only knew he was to go to Philadelphia via Baltimore.

It was fifty miles to Baltimore and another hundred to Philadelphia. His sole contact was the first stop on the road. To him it was "Town A", a small hamlet. He was not given the name and address of the house. Its location was made known to him by its place on the map drawn by The Birdwatcher in front of him. It was shown to him for a minute and then withdrawn and destroyed. Should anyone ask him where he was going he could not answer, though he knew the destination from the map in his mind as if it were planted in his memory and X marked the spot.

Twenty miles by night over countryside, walking along the roads, listening for the approach of strangers and ducking into shelter, is hard. But it is comparatively easy if you are a fit young male on your own. His objective was to make the distance with time to spare whilst finding places to hide along the way. Trees, ditches, barns, bridges all served a purpose and his eyes were keen as he sought places that would keep him safe from the roving Patrol.

The exercise that he set himself was to see that no one saw him. Were he found alone there at night, his freedom papers, signed by Gerald Butler, would be no protection against an armed, aggressive and suspicious night Patrol. His prodigious memory of the maps, his alertness and his ability to make himself almost invisible had to be put to the test at some point. The day, since the ignominious time the boy Tom was sprung from the slave jail by his master and for which he had waited so long, had come. He was now a new and free man.

The first thing he had to do was test the Birdwatcher's route. With his new freedom he needed a new name, a *nom de guerre*. He was no longer Tom Butler, his master's slave. He had to have a name by which he was known as a free man.

He had not given the name much thought. As he strode along the dirt road towards his first destination and tracked in his mind exactly where he was, the name came into his head as the obvious one that reflected the life he was about to begin. His intention was to reach 'Town A' without being stopped by a white man or even being seen by one. On this first night he met no one. He heard no dogs, no horses or wagons. It was eerie and strange.

As The Birdwatcher explained, night was the safest time to find a safe house in the middle of a town. The darkness gave him a better chance of not being seen. The noise of his shoes on the dirt road seemed to him to be thunderous as he walked down the main street of 'Town A' before turning left down the side street where the general store, the first stop on his designated journey, was. His footfall was inaudible to most. It would be a while before he was able to move completely noiselessly.

Large letters *Sam Streatfeild: General Merchant* hung over the main window. To the side of the front door was a smaller sign, *Hawkers, tradesmen and niggers use the side entrance.*

Sam Streatfeild was forty years of age, with an open face, which concealed a quick intelligence. To all appearances he was a tough businessman and custodian of the order of things in the town, which boasted a "Chamber of Commerce" of which he was the chairman. He slept in the store on the nights when he had no guests. From his bed he heard three quick knocks on the side door.

"I need shelter," whispered the stranger at the door.

"You are welcome to shelter here."

"I have come twenty miles."

"I have a bed for you to rest yourself."

"God bless you, sir."

The code having been exchanged, Streatfeild let in the stranger and shut the door behind him. The stranger put out his hand. Streatfeild took it.

"Sam Streatfeild."

"Tracker," replied the stranger.

Sixteen

The door shut behind Tracker. He saw the bed in exactly the place where The Birdwatcher had told him it would be. Above it was a window with the latch open. If anyone came and saw a runaway, Sam would say that the man climbed in the window.

The Birdwatcher had described Tracker to him, but had not given his name. Sam saw a man of medium build, a young unlined face, nondescript features, alert eyes and a graceful coordination of his movements. He had listened for half the night for his arrival. There was, however, no warning of the three sharp raps on the door. This was a new experience for Sam who always heard the footfall down the side street.

Usually when he opened to door, runaways looked at him anxiously, unsure whether to trust him and knowing that at that moment they were putting their life in his hands. Sometimes they were young men, sometimes young women and occasionally a family of mother and father and children, even babies. Sam had space for six, including babies and toddlers in his back warehouse.

His contact was The Birdwatcher, who had found him six years before and ever since he was the first station in The Birdwatcher's Branch 5 of the Underground Railroad. Branch 5 was not a name disclosed to Sam. All he knew was that someone would be knocking on the door at a specific time or on a specific night and he was to take the runaways and others who accompanied them and forward them to the next stop.

This one was different because he was to be met by Grace. Someone whom Sam had never met but of whom he had heard spoken of with awe. There was a high price on her head. She had frustrated the best efforts of the Patrol, Sheriffs and all the forces of law and order for years. Her legend matched Harriet Tubman's.

The price on her head had started at one hundred dollars when she was a young female escapee from a Virginia plantation. As a field hand, Grace was at her peak of productivity and therefore value. Field hands could reap about one ton of cotton, or its equivalent in grain or other crop. Her value, had she not escaped, would have started to decline slowly over the years of her thirties and then would have dropped more quickly as she approached forty and her annual tonnage decreased.

So far there was nothing remarkable about her, nor the reward for her capture. She had left behind a "husband" and two children aged five and eight, none of whom could say where she had gone.

That was because they did not know.

They were as baffled as her master. She had never traveled to town since she was bought. Nor had she ever left the plantation since she had arrived there as a young girl, telling tales of having been kidnapped near the wharves in Boston while looking for her sister. She was quickly told that she should not say such things and immediately she did not. An unremarkable field hand, she was only noted for her alert eyes and loud laugh.

Perhaps she had met with an accident on the plantation, they thought. That seemed most likely and for a day all one hundred slaves combed the land looking for her.

Her family was genuinely baffled and the wailing of her children and the bemusement of her "husband" convinced their master that she had not become a runaway. Single women rarely escaped without a companion.

It took three days before she was reported and her master arranged for reward posters being put up around Richmond and Baltimore. By the time a portrait of her had been posted she had reached the North. When she had crossed to Canada the posters were ready to come down and the mystery of her departure ceased to be of interest. Hers was an unremarkable escape of a forgettable female field hand and was soon forgotten.

Horton Field was an experienced patrolman. The leadership of his Patrol was unquestioned. When I met him he was a man in his sixties. When he was in his late twenties he was already standing counsel to the best slave traders. When he started out the best was *Franklin & Armfield*, which was a big concern with offices and agents throughout Virginia and Maryland. They had the respectable end of the market and the owners were paid up members of society.

The profitability of that firm of traders and its traditions came from the simple formula of buying cheap in the upper south and selling high in the lower south. Over the years others caught on - people like Campbell, Buchanan, Moody, Kephart and Stevens. The biggest was Kephart whose firm *Kephart & Harbin* had offices in New Orleans as well as places like Baltimore and Frederick.

By the time I met Horton Field in 1859, *Franklin & Armfield* had dissolved, the traders were greater in number and smaller in size and Field had rivals for the lawyering trade. When Grace first came to prominence, he was the only "go to" man with considerable resources behind him. Now life was less easy and he made his living with legal work and the occasional deal as an agent buying slaves for owners who didn't want to be identified as being in the market and for local owners who didn't want their new slave's old owners and slaves to know where their slave had been sold to. Many people felt that it unsettled slaves in both the old home and the new one if it was known where the slave had been sold to. If the slave was being sold to the Deep South, this did not matter. But with domestic slaves - maids and manservants – it did.

If Horton Field was the buyer as agent, nobody would know who the new purchaser was. His discretion was unquestioned. Most owners reckoned that the slave's new whereabouts would be found out eventually, but 'eventually' was the operative word. Also in the more reclusive of households, the word about the whereabouts of the newly sold slave would take years.

Exactly one year after Grace's escape, her 'husband' and two children disappeared. The young Horton Field who, kept a register of escapees, with the time and place of their going and the identity of those that remained, took notice.

Most escapees did so singly and those left behind stayed until sale or death. In Horton Field's view this loss of the family was unprecedented. Nevertheless to everyone else there still appeared to be nothing remarkable about her and the loss of her family. Grace's use of anniversaries as a signature or message was not understood then.

Exactly one year after the loss of her immediate family, her "father-in-law", who had been separated by sale to a plantation fifty miles to the south, was missing. Nobody would have understood the coincidence except Horton Field, who thought the previous year that something odd was happening. He was now sure. His register of dates enabled him to see the connection, which others overlooked.

The use of anniversaries was not a loud message because it had not, by then, gone outside the boundaries of one family.

The next year it did. On the anniversary of the escape of her father in law, another slave on that plantation disappeared and people started to talk. Fleeting glances of the woman who came to be known as Grace were seen, or thought to have been spotted, all over the area. The trouble was that there were many likenesses as people guessed what she must have looked like. She appeared on the posters variously as a field hand, an old woman and even, embarrassingly, as an almost white woman.

Horton Field held a meeting of his combined Patrol covering Maryland and Virginia. They passed a resolution to ask that the price on her head be increased to one thousand dollars, paid for by all the slave owners. With such a wide area and the addition of money from the top slave traders which Field represented, the levy was not too much for each individual to contribute. This was someone who had to be caught.

As Grace was spotted and almost captured, her reputation became the stuff of legend. By the time she was due to meet Tracker at Sam's store, the reward had risen to ten thousand dollars, a price way beyond that of a good field hand, indeed you could buy ten for that price. The posters for her reward were confusing because they pictured her in whatever disguise in which she was last seen, or the clothes she was thought to have been wearing. Her status meant the disappearance of any slave led to individuals going to either the newspapers or the Patrol declaring that they had caught sight of her but had just missed catching her.

Because she had many disguises, her height was the only constant in her description, which was five feet four inches. This meant that, after an escape was announced, all black women of between five foot two and five foot six became objects of suspicion and were subject to arrest. The trouble was that Grace was usually seen in broad daylight in towns and villages. Those who thought that they saw her only realized that they may have done so long after she disappeared from their sight. On many occasions it was indeed her. On others, it was some other "legitimate" person, such as a slave belonging to a stranger who was passing through the area.

People served as decoys. Their 'owners' were nearby and were ready to bail them out once they had got to the slave prison where the reward for Grace was to be paid. The 'owner' picked up the person who was their "slave" expressing gratitude that they had found their lost servant. Once again the captive was not Grace. The period, between the decoy being caught and it being established that it was not her, diverted the attention of the Patrol, facilitating Grace's escape.

That the reward money far exceeded her true value on the market as a field hand did not matter. Slave-owners of Virginia and Maryland felt as if they were under attack and were being made to look fools. Grace had to be caught.

After Streatfeild left his store to go home for the night, Tracker started to look around. The back was a huge warehouse filled with all kinds of products including hay and straw bales. In the front part, near the main shop area, there were piles of saddles, belts and boots along with barrels and boxes and even coffins. The shop was described as a feed store, which, of course, it was. But it was more than that. Virtually everything which a farmer wanted to buy was there.

Sam was not an undertaker, but his piles of coffins were noticeable.

They were of all sizes. One pile, a stack of five, almost reached up to Tracker's shoulder. As Tracker looked at it, he heard a voice from behind him.

"Get in."

He was used to sudden noises outdoors, where few things caused him to start. He was so in tune with nature and aware of the effect of humans on land, and his ear was so acute, that normally he could hear someone approach one hundred yards away. Tracker flinched because he had heard and felt nothing. He turned around. About twenty feet behind him was a short dark woman, five feet four inches tall wearing a black mourning dress and a black scarf on her head. Her eyes twinkled white and her teeth were a bright yellow.

"Who are you?"

"Get in."

"Get in what?"

"That coffin you are looking at."

"Why?"

"Because I am asking you to."

He looked at the size of this woman and remembered that he had not heard her approach. It was the person The Birdwatcher had told him about.

She raised her left eyebrow. Tracker started to laugh. Grace put her finger to her mouth. "You'll wake the dead. Now get in"

Tracked picked up the coffin and put it on the floor, took off the lid and slid in. He was just too big to lie absolutely straight and he raised his knees slightly.

"You don't fit," she said. "I guess you chose the small one. They better make bigger coffins now." She pointed to the six-foot long coffins.

Tracker got out, stood up and put out his hand.

"Tracker," he said.

"I know." She shook his hand. Tracker looked at her. To Patrick, the Birdwatcher, he was "Tom" and he must have been "Tom" to her.

"Patrick told me enough about you for me to know that you wouldn't keep your name once you left. Tracker's a good name."

"Patrick told me enough about you for me to know that you might think that."

"Patrick's a good man. Now let me see if I fit in there." With that a short, slim woman wearing a large black dress got into the coffin which Tracker had just vacated.

"Pass me the bundle and put the lid on." Tracker had not seen a bundle of anything and he was just about to ask what she meant when he saw a pile of what appeared to be men's clothes on the stack of coffins next to the one she had climbed into. Tracker did not know where they had come from and had not seen them before she had got into the coffin. He handed her the bundle and covered her.

"Now you go and sleep on the bed and I shall sleep here. We have an hour before Sam returns."

In order to be able to look at him when she said this, she had slipped the coffin lid sideways. She now slid it back. Tracker moved towards his bed. The coffin lid opened again.

"Put the other coffins on top of me."

"Why?"

"There's a price on my head."

"You had better have some room to breathe," he said and left the lid slightly open, then he put four coffins on top of that.

As he lay down, Tracker heard footsteps. It was still early in the morning, too early for business people to be walking up and down the street. There were two men, Tracker reckoned, who walked past the store and about one hundred yards down the side street away from the main road. One of Tracker's gifts was to be able to assess the size and height of men by their footfall. One man sounded to him to be about the same size as Streatfeild, the other sounded about two inches taller and of heavier build. Tracker heard mumbling in the distance, but no words. The people were speaking quietly to one another. They then walked back towards Streatfeild's shop.

Tracker recognized Streatfeild's voice. They were now underneath the window over Tracker's bed.

"You sure?" Tracker heard Streatfeild say.

"It has to be the trail has gone cold here," said the other voice.

"I've got a free nigger sleeping in the back," Streatfeild said, rather more loudly than when he last spoke.

"A free nigger?"

"Yup, "said Streatfeild. "I call 'em that because they work for free."

Horton Field laughed. It was an old trick to get labor from a freedman and then send him on his way unpaid. Streatfeild laughed with him. The door opened. Tracker pretended to be asleep.

"Nigger, wake up," Streatfeild said as he led Field to the place where Tracker lay.

Tracker did not stir. Streatfeild stood over him.

"Nigger. Wake up," he shouted this time and hit Tracker on the face hard with his right hand as Field looked on.

"Yes sir," Tracker said, smarting from the blow as stood up whilst doing his best imitation of someone awakened from a deep sleep.

"You let anyone in?" Streatfeild asked.

"No, sir, I've just slept here like you told me to"

"She could have got in while he was asleep," Streatfeild said to Field.

"Could she have a key?" Field asked.

"She gets in everywhere, she doesn't need a key," Streatfeild said.

Horton Field turned his attention to Tracker.

"Papers."

Tracker took from his trouser pocket his newly written manumission papers.

"Well, well. So you want to help out Mr. Streatfeild then."

"Yes, sir," Tracker replied. Streatfeild was now standing behind Horton Field.

"You move quick, boy," Horton said.

"Thank you, sir."

"We'd better look around," Streatfeild declared.

"Its like a needle in a haystack here," Horton Field commented. "I'll get the boys. Mind if I take your nigger with me?"

"Go right ahead."

Horton was wary of Sam Streatfeild. Too many escapees had come from these parts. Streatfeild was a leader of the local Patrol. But his

Patrol never seemed to catch any escapees. On a hunch he had gone down to search for runaways and look over Streatfeild's Patrol. While there, Field heard from one of Sam's patrolmen that the slave with the ten thousand dollar reward on her head had been spotted. The latest poster read "Ethel also goes by the name of Bertha". In fact she went by neither name. Those names belonged to two other escaped slaves.

Horton Field had, by now, convinced himself that she was hiding in Streatfeild's store. Her legend was making a mockery of everyone, he thought, and was a rebuke to his Patrol, which, it was being said, could not even find a small and nondescript field hand.

The reward was ridiculous, Field thought. Ten thousand dollars was an absurd price for a slave. But she would nevertheless be a huge prize. He needed to get a message to the other men who were checking the adjoining side street. If he went himself to get them, she might walk past everyone again and he would look really stupid. He had to use Tracker.

"Boy,"

"Yes sir,"

"Do you understand me, Boy?" Field always spoke more slowly when he was instructing a black person to do something.

"Yes, sir," Tracker said.

Tracker knew it would not take long to find her if there was a thorough search. Horton Field himself was dressed in a suit and had no gun, Tracker had no doubt that Field had armed help.

"Go down this street here and make a left and you will see two young men walking up the street next to this one. They are called Mr. Jake and Mr. Tim Smith. You tell them that Mr. Horton Field sent you."

"Yes, sir," Tracker said and started toward the main street.

"I ain't finished." Horton said.

Tracker stopped and turned.

"Yes, sir."

"You tell them I am at Mr. Streatfeild's store"

"Yes, sir,"

Tracker went to where two young men in their late teens were peering into windows.

"Sir," said Tracker to Jake Smith. "Mr. Horton Field told me to come and get you. He is at Mr. Streatfeild's."

About five yards behind Tracker was an old man of about five feet four in height with grey hair and a shabby hand-me-down suit, shambling and leaning on a stick. Tracker had not heard Grace in the store. That he could explain by not being attuned to listen inside a shop. But this old man was on the street. He had not heard him at all. If he could not know about this man following him, how could he ever trust his instincts?

The two looked away from the windows and towards Tracker.

"Say it again," Tim Smith said. The request was made in what was, to Tracker, a familiar overbearing manner. He immediately felt fear replace the alarm over his failing instincts. This young man would not hesitate to hurt or even kill him. They were armed and Tracker was not confident he could disarm them both.

By now the old man was passing him and shambling towards the two men. Tracker's mouth went dry. He asked himself how he could recount the message without provoking them into violence.

"Mr. Horton Field asked me find you, sir, and to say that he wanted to see you at Mr. Streatfield,'s store." As he said this he looked down and shuffled his feet.

Tracker's fear vanished as they ran towards the store. The old man carried on, walking away from him as if nothing had happened. Tracker rushed back. With two armed men and Horton Field against him, he did not fancy his chances of stopping them from capturing Grace even if Streatfeild was ready to attack at the same time as he did. Considering Streatfeild's physique, Tracker doubted he would get much help from him. He would have the element of surprise.

The door was open and he saw Horton Field, Jake and Tim Smith and Sam Streatfeild. As he entered, he looked for a weapon, but saw none to hand.

"Okay," Field said. "We look and we look good. She's here some-where and we only have to find out where she is hiding."

"Well, if you fellows don't mind I shall go home and have the breakfast you stopped me from having." Streatfeild turned to Tracker,

"Come on, Boy," motioning that he follow him.

Tracker did not know what to do. Grace was hiding in a coffin and Streatfeild was proposing to leave these people to turn the store and warehouse upside down and find her. He felt powerless. He could not make any suggestion to Streatfeild. It would only attract more suspicion. He started to form a plan in his mind, which involved him returning to the store almost as soon as he left it.

Streatfeild led Tracker through the warehouse. As they passed the coffin into which Grace had climbed, Tracker saw that the lid was on. But the side of it lay flat on the ground. The coffin was empty.

Seventeen

treatfeild's house was five minutes walk and he pointed the way. "It is down there a piece. Fancy breakfast?" Streatfeild's voice seemed to Tracker an octave higher than normal. His casual manner was a front.

Grace was at Streatfeild's kitchen table. She had on the old man's clothes but the stick which she had used to such effect stood in a corner.

Their nerves were taut. No one was hungry. Streatfield served coffee. Grace broke the silence.

"The Railroad's station masters have tried to stop me traveling before," she said. "I always said to them: 'No, I must continue. At least until I find my sister.'"

Grace let her words sink in.

"You'll be my eyes and ears from now on, I'm going to take you to Baltimore and Philadelphia. You'll meet some people and I'll tell them you're taking over managing the road and I'll direct things from Philadelphia. You can manage the safe houses for your Mama and the little one."

Tracker was momentarily disturbed that she assumed that he had been hired into the Railroad without even being asked and saying yes to the offer. Then he remembered his talks with The Birdwatcher. He had, over the years, accepted the role. He just did not know it until then.

During the five summers after his abortive escape, Tracker met The Birdwatcher who taught him about maps and topography. In the second year Patrick told him about Grace and how she had to stop traveling at some point and someone had to take her place tracking all the points of the underground railroad as far as Philadelphia, helping with escapees and communicating whether there were problem stations which needed closing down and where they could find new stations to take their place. Grace also wanted him to go to Boston and meet with safe houses on the route from Philadelphia. During all this time Tracker did not mention his family to Patrick. Yet it was clear then, that she knew all about it.

Grace's branches of the Underground Railroad had taken years to build. Each station had to be within between ten to twenty miles of the next stop, so that it could be reached in a single night's travel. The length of the distance between stops depended on topography. Twenty miles required the escapee or "package" to move quickly. Each station had to have alternatives, or sidings, through which escapees could pass if their main station was closed off. That required constant vigilance. It also needed morale boosting. Grace understood the need for the station-masters to know how their cargo, or "packages", had fared. Whether they had made it, and if they had what sort of life they were leading.

Every year for ten years she had traveled her routes stopping off at each station telling each station master how the previous year's packages had managed. The visits were more than morale boosters. They were also the means whereby she was able to keep in touch with problems along each stretch of line, to open new stations and "rest" others which may have come under suspicion.

She explained that for the past five years she had narrower and narrower escapes and that Patrick had discovered that the price on her head was about to rise to fifteen thousand dollars. The local slave owners wanted an end to her, whether the sightings were real or imagined. The increased price with the greater ensuing vigilance meant that her luck felt finite and depleted. Tracker's freedom came not a moment too soon.

Eighteen

One year to the day after he had been freed, Tracker arrived in a special wagon at the new Butler plantation and riding stables and parked it by the Quarters. Butler had moved to be near Baltimore having bought the new horse and hunting farm, which he had wanted to purchase for seven years while he waited for the owner to die. He had taken Tracker there a couple of times as he explained his plans for an equestrian centre.

Tracker's cover in his new found freedom made him occasionally act as a carter and he had used the wagon frequently. Butler was surprised to hear that he had come in a wagon. Tracker explained to Butler that could sleep in it on long journeys. He was commended for his enterprise in making good use of a trip to see his family. He told Butler that he had been hired by a Doctor Jones of Boston, who wanted to purchase his mother and half brother to keep his family together.

He gave Butler a letter from Dr. Jones, which asked if the mother and son could be bought for six hundred dollars. Tracker explained that their price would be set off against his wages. The work "Tom" did for the good doctor was similar to that which "Tom" performed at the Butler plantation although "Tom" worked for other people as well. The doctor had an estate just outside Boston, the letter explained, and he rode to hounds in addition to having land for hunting.

Butler asked Tracker to take a letter to Dr. Jones, asking him whether he would like to do some hunting in Maryland and yes of course he would sell the mother and son. It was a Monday morning. Having written a letter to Dr. Jones, Butler gestured to Tracker that the interview was over. Butler was relieved to have made the agreement. If "Tom" was not to work for him, he decided on further reflection that he would not have him visiting his family, even if it was only once a year. He felt it would be too unsettling for the other slaves.

Tracker left and wandered around the area of the plantation where he was told his mother normally worked. He called the names of his mother and half brother. He asked the overseer where they were. The overseer thought that they must be in the fields, though he did not know which one. Eventually he enlisted the support of the overseer to look with him. Tracker and the overseer went round the fields, barns and outbuildings, calling and looking. Giving up the search, the overseer himself became alarmed. Tracker returned to the main house and knocked on the front door with the overseer by his side. Butler answered the door himself.

Tracker blurted out, with some anguish, "They ain't there Mr. Butler."

"Well, they're probably working in the fields already. It is a bit late in the morning."

"I can't find them," the overseer said.

Butler was annoyed at the failure, of his servant and his former slave, to find a field hand and a child. "Did you both look in the far fields?"

"No, sir," the overseer said. It was true, they had not done so. Tracker did not know that Butler had bought the extra acreage and the overseer did not think anyone was working there.

"Well then," Butler said. "There is work to be done there, you know."

Relieved to have overlooked a place where they might be found, the overseer relaxed.

"Look, you've taken too much time on this." Butler said. "Why don't you come back tomorrow morning and we'll make sure that they are here to see you,"

Then Butler had another idea. "Even better, you come back on

Sunday, then you can have the whole day with them. Enough time's been spent on them this morning."

Sunday was six days away. Given the acceptance by Butler of the offer by Dr. Jones to buy his family, Tracker asked if he could he return in two weeks with the purchase price from Dr. Jones and he could take his family away then? Relieved, Butler agreed. In the wagon with the false bottom lay his mother and half brother. It left for Baltimore with Tracker carrying with him the good wishes of their former Master.

When Tracker took his special cart backto the Butler Plantation, the hue and cry about the loss of Tom's mother and half brother was almost over. Horton Field's Patrol of Dick and his sons Jake and Tim had done their best, searching every creek and ditch, all to no avail. Posters had gone up in Baltimore but there were no sightings. Tracker knocked on the back door and asked to speak to Master Gerald, who was in his study.

"Master," he said quietly as he put his head around the door. "Do you know where my mother is? I've come back to see her today, just like you asked and they say that she's not here." Tracker did not, at first, notice that Horton Field was also in Butler's study.

"I just don't know what to say to you," Butler replied.

"Master Gerald, what's happened?" The quaver and distress in his voice was palpable.

"She's gone."

"Gone?"

"Yes."

"Master Gerald, I don't understand. I've come to pay for them on behalf of Dr. Jones."

"It looks like they left or were taken just before you came last week. Mr. Field here says you took them away in your cart."

Tracker stood dumbfounded. Field got out of his chair.

The distress that he showed at the disappearance of his mother was persistent and convincing to Butler. "Tom's" acting was particularly good since he recognized Field from the day, one year ago, when he had met Grace at Sam Streatfeild's store.

99

Butler disliked Field but knew that "Tom" was "a resourceful boy", therefore he allowed Field into his study and the Patrol onto his farm. As the distraught "Tom" recovered himself, he said, "Master Gerald, sir, I have a letter for you from Dr. Jones."

The letter was from an address on Beacon Hill in Boston thanking Mr. Butler for his kind invitation to come south to go hunting, but he was getting rather old now and would not find it easy to leave his home. The bearer of the letter had a Bill of Exchange drawn for seven hundred dollars to pay for the freedom of his mother and her child.

"You're a good boy," Gerald said at last. He showed the letter and Bill of Exchange to Field, who, at last, spoke.

"Am I right in thinking that you came here exactly one year after you got your freedom?"

"I don't know, Sir. I guess."

"I've got my boys looking at your cart."

"My cart's ok, sir, thank you sir." Tracker felt a slight panic. The anniversary was Grace's trademark. Tracker had used it so his mother would be able to remember and count the days precisely. Whilst Tracker understood the practical use of the trademark, he now felt only fear.

Field knew of the use of false bottom carts. There was now a flicker of recognition in Field's eyes.

"Aren't you the boy I met at Streatfeild's store?"

"Yes, sir," he said to Field. Turning to Butler he said "Can I take a reply to Dr. Jones?"

"Yes, Tom."

Fortunately for Tracker and Dr. Holmes, Gerald Butler did not venture to Boston and Beacon Hill to seek out Dr. Jones. The reply explaining that Butler no longer possessed the property to pass to Dr. Jones was the only communication which Butler sent north. As he wrote out the reply, Tracker stood in front of the desk and Field waited in his chair. The wait seemed interminable. Tracker sweated. He tried to control his fear of Field but it came at him in waves as Butler wrote his letter and Field looked at him with a steady gaze.

There was a knock on the door.

"That will be Mr. Field's men, Tom." Butler said. "I guess they've looked at your cart. Open the door for them will you."

Dick Smith ignored Tracker.

"Mr. Field, there's nowhere to hide in that cart."

"Well, I guess you folks will be on your way," Butler said. "I never doubted you Tom."

As Tracker left, amazed at the failure of Dick, his betrayer, to recognize him, his relief at Grace's insistence on the precaution of duplicate and similar carts was matched by the certainty that the training and instruction which she had given him on bluff and precaution had been, and would be, essential for his survival.

Nineteen

Mr. Brown's stories took nearly the whole day to tell. The house was empty. The Emersons had gone to Boston to visit Harvard before Mr. Emerson went on another lecture tour. Leaving me behind with the mad story-teller had alarmed me at first. But his tale telling was easy.

"Have you met Grace?" I asked over tea.

"No. I've met Tracker though; and the redoubtable Mr. Horton Field. He's a dangerous man and the one you'll have to be most scared of. That is if you want to stay alive."

"How do you know. Lucy and Brushes could be anywhere."

"Law of averages. Most sales are local. It's strange that no one knows where Lucy is; but my guess is that she's looking after some old people."

"Why's that?" I asked.

"Figures. She's not been seen about and neither have her new owners. When you get a new maid, you boast a little. It's natural. Nobody's boasted."

"Doesn't that mean she's been sold out of the area?"

"Maybe, but, as I say, most sales are local and Colin Stevens's clientele is mainly local. Besides there's no point in paying Baltimore prices for an Alabama maid. Anyway you have to start somewhere and Field's bailiwick is the first place to start."

"I'm out of my depth." I said.

"I said you'll need some basic training. You'll get that first and let the Railroad have a look at you. Haven't you learned anything at West Point?"

"Your talk of topography felt a bit like a revision course from Professor Weir's class."

"That's a start. You mustn't be afraid to kill or die, you know."

"I am afraid."

"Good," Brown said, "Now I have your orders."

The train journey to Philadelphia was quick. My "medical" appointment was at two o' clock the following day and I stayed overnight in at The Girard House where I had been with Father on breaks from Maud's breakdowns. I remembered the breakfasts we had there and they were just as good as when Father and I stayed.

The address Brown gave me was a house a mile away just off Broad Street. I knocked on the door and it was answered by a white maid in full uniform. I was to ask for Dr. Cass. I was invited in and told that he was seeing patients but if I would like to wait he might fit me into his schedule. I started to protest that I had an appointment. But by the time I summoned up the wit to speak, the room was empty. It was an ordinary doctor's waiting room.

I picked up a weekly paper and started to leaf through it. It was five minutes past two. I had an appointment with Dr. Cass at two. I obviously had to wait but I started to wonder whether I was in the wrong place. The maid had not even asked my name.

At fifteen minutes past two, another patient entered the waiting room. He was tall and wore a large Quakers hat. He thanked the maid and said that if the doctor could fit him in, then he would be most obliged.

"You have no appointment?" I said, trying to make conversation but also keen that no one was going to jump the queue.

"No. I'm Luther Hodges." He put his hand out.

"Jack Ruffin" I said.

"Pleased to meet you, young man. You had a two o'clock from Dr. Holmes?"

"For Dr. Cass."

"A referral from Dr. Holmes?"

"Yes."

"You must go to 41 Walnut Street at three o'clock. It's a short walk, so you should get there on time if you hurry. Say that you were sent from Dr. Cass."

"But..." was all I could think of to say before he pointed to the door and settled himself down with a weekly magazine as if to wait for the doctor.

I had a handbook of Philadelphia and saw the house was a short but brisk walk away. I knocked on the door and this time a manservant opened it. "I have been sent from Dr. Cass."

"A referral from Dr. Holmes?"

"Yes sir."

"Step this way please."

I walked down a long corridor to a library where there were no medical books. In the middle was a round table and standing by it was a woman who could have been any age between forty or sixty. She was about five feet four inches high with short unkempt black hair and wore a homespun black dress.

She gestured to me to sit down.

"Tell me your story son," she said as she sat down.

She closed her eyes as she said this. I was brisk and probably a little confused. The woman at the desk just sat there. Occasionally I thought I saw a nod and sometimes a smile, but I was not sure. If I had to swear as to what she was doing I would have said she was asleep.

"Don't worry, son," she said. "Tubman falls asleep sometimes. I just like to look like it." She broke out into a loud and shrill laugh. This had to be Grace.

"When you see Dr. Holmes, will you tell him from me that I appreciate all he does."

"I will. He wants to meet you."

"So he may one day. But there's no need for it now. You know the penalty for helping folks get free?"

"Yes, Ma'am."

She smiled. "I like it when you ma'am me. You are a young boy."

I shrugged.

"And from West Point?"

"Yes Ma'am."

"Can you read a map?"

"Yes Ma'am."

"Can you hide yourself on the land?"

"Yes, Ma'am"

General Taylor had cut his army off from its sources of supply in the Mexican War. At West Point we were taught his campaign in class and also we were shown how to live off the land and all the ways to hide ourselves if we were separated from our supplies.

"Because that's what you will have to do. Now, let me see if I have got this right. You want to get your Mammy. You don't know where she is. You want to take her somewhere where she'll be free and you don't know how you're going to do it. Am I right?"

"Yes Ma'am."

"Do you think you're ready?"

"No, Ma'am."

"There are patrols and slave catchers, sheriffs and marshals in a country where all us niggers are being kept in one big prison. Do you know that if they found out you were a nigger, you could be bought and sold yourself?"

"I'm at West Point, Ma'am."

"Yes you are and none of that counts for anything if they know you are the son of a slave. That makes you a slave and someone's property. Unless you have your freedom papers and you don't have them. Where are you staying?"

I told her. She looked impressed and relieved at the same time.

"Well, we've had enough time with your doctor's appointment. I want you to go back to your hotel. Do what you like today, but stay in the hotel tomorrow. You don't need to know any more than that, son."

Twenty

I was not to leave the hotel, but, I assumed that I could leave my room. At about seven thirty, I went downstairs for breakfast. I had some oatmeal and coffee. Dinner had been rich and I was not in the mood for the huge breakfast of the day before. I struck up a desultory conversation with a paper salesman by the name of Wilson Calhoun. He sold paper to printers and publishers along the eastern seaboard. Gift paper, greeting cards, newspaper and book paper. Philadelphia was the publishing capital of the United States. New York did not overtake it until after the War so there was a great deal of scope for him in Philadelphia.

This hotel was grand for a salesman. Something like the Jones Hotel was more his line I thought. I had never heard of paper salesmen and what they did and, having communicated that lack of knowledge, I could see that I was about to hear all about it at length. I left him quickly.

On my return to my room a maid in hotel uniform was sweeping under the bed. I did not give her a second glance and said, "There's no need. I'm staying here tonight."

The maid got up and stood in front of me.

"How do you know, young man?"

It was Grace, dressed as a maid. I had to look at her twice to see that it was the same person I had met the day before.

"I just thought I'd check your room."

106

I saw that my things had been gone through. I had not hung my suits and now they were all arranged neatly in the wardrobe.

She picked up a piece of paper from the table. It had the name and address of Dr. Cass that I had left in one of my pockets.

"Did anyone see you write this down?"

"No, Ma'am. I did it myself when I got to my hotel so I wouldn't forget."

"Lesson number one. You don't write things down after they are committed to memory."

"But I was only going for a doctor's appointment."

"Yes you were, but you don't write. Besides niggers aren't supposed to read and write." With that she started to let out a gale of laughter and then stopped herself.

"If Dr. Cass needed to deny that you were coming to him, would he be believed if his name and address were in your pocket? Now I think I have finished up here. You go to the Bates Coffee Shop, near where the new hotel is being built. Be there at ten o' clock and someone will meet you. If you are followed, you have one cup of coffee and come back to your room. Otherwise you have a second cup of coffee. Now, son, isn't it a nice day?"

I looked out of the window.

"I guess it is."

She was gone. How she left I will never know. She was standing by the door, but a good two steps from it. I did not even hear the door close.

At nine thirty I left the hotel. The warning about being followed caused me to look around as I was about to leave the hotel. Wilson Calhoun was in the lobby.

"Well, we meet again," he said.

"Are you selling much paper today?" I asked. At breakfast we had not discussed his day. We had only gone a short way, I would guess, into all the uses of paper.

"Just a bit. Where are you going?"

"Just to walk around, maybe have a coffee somewhere."

"I'll walk with you, do you mind?"

"No, sir." I flushed at the lie.

His endless chatter was annoying but I could not cast him off without being rude or arousing suspicion. We walked down Chestnut Street. There was a coffee shop just before a huge building site near 9th Street.

"Here's a good place to stop for coffee," I said.

His inane babble came to an abrupt end.

"Well young man." Everyone was calling me "young man" or "son" now and it was starting to grate. "I guess I'll leave you here. We are not far from my first appointment."

The coffee house had few spare places. In talking to Wilson Calhoun I could not see whether I was being followed. He was so insistent in talking and looking at me as he did that it would have looked suspicious to check if anyone was behind me.

I ordered a coffee and wondered what I should do. If I was being followed, I would not know it. If I was not, then I was wasting my time and the time of Grace who had arranged my contact. As I realized this, I felt foolish and useless. How I would explain why I did not look properly for someone following me, I did not know.

"A second cup of coffee, sir?" the waiter asked. He was a tall and stocky man in his early forties, probably a freedman, I thought. I almost felt a reproach from him when I declined. I thought that he must have known that I did not check for people following me. Why did he say "a second cup of coffee" as opposed to "more coffee"? Did he work for Grace? To make up for my shame, I left a large tip and walked back to the hotel. A whole day wasted. All because I could not shake off this absurd man who was telling me all about different types of stationery.

I walked past the receptionist.

"Back already?" he said.

If I was trying not to be conspicuous, I was failing. I could not check out of the hotel because nobody could contact me if I disappeared.

Upon opening my bedroom door, I saw, sitting in a chair by the window, my companion the paper salesman, Wilson Calhoun.

"So," he said. "who was following you?"

"What?"

"Who was following you?"

"This is my room."

"Look, son, you had to go to the café and order one cup of coffee and only order the second if you were not being followed. Now. Who was following you?"

"You,"

"Precisely. I couldn't see anyone else."

"How did you get in? How did you know what room I was in?"

"Both answers you will have to guess for yourself. I daresay that she will tell you that you passed your first test. You were followed and you did not order that second cup of coffee. Mind, if you had it would have made no difference, there was nobody there to meet you."

"What? I went to meet someone who was going to send me to another place."

"So you thought. You know the risks. You've got money, right?"

"Yes, sir."

"Right, you go out and buy yourself a small briefcase. In it you will put a week's supply of clean clothes and a toothbrush and you check in to the Ethel Hotel and pay for a week's rent. It's a small lodging house and very friendly. Room Eight has a fire escape. Ask for that one." He paused then asked:

"Why are you in this fair city?"

"To see a doctor."

"Well, now you have been to the doctor, you need another reason to be here. Can I suggest that you say you stayed in Philadelphia to see a bit of the world before you go back to the army. There are lots of things to see. You must be enthralled by it."

I was not, of course, though I should have been as this was the place where the government first met.

"You will keep this room as well and stay here every night. After you check into the Ethel, you shall only go there in a case of emergency. Make sure you are not followed to the Ethel and be back here in two hours."

I walked out of the hotel, leaving my new friend there and bought myself two clean shirts, a cheap suit, a briefcase and shaving gear.

I was being followed, I was sure of it. But I could see nobody. The feeling never left me as I walked into the different shops to buy what I had been told to purchase. The feeling became more and more insistent as I went about my business. It took me forty minutes to make my purchases. I had to check into the Ethel and return to my room in one hour and twenty minutes. I did not have very long if I was to shake off the person following me. However whenever I looked around, I saw no one.

There was a back door behind the counter in the clothes shop where I got my shirts. I walked back to the shop, reintroduced myself to the owner, bought another shirt and asked to leave through the back door.

The shopkeeper had made a sale and told me to go ahead. I looked back into the street before walking through the shop. I thought I saw a dark shadow but could not be sure. At West Point I had been sent to the countryside to learn how to avoid being spotted near enemy lines. I was top of that class.

The street at the back of the shop was narrow and a horse and cart had stopped there. The direction of the Ethel Hotel was to my right. I was glad to have memorized the street plan. Since I had learned to memorize maps and topography in the countryside, city maps came easy to me. There was more intensity but less variety of topography. I turned left and took the next right turn. It was a long way round but if I went down three streets I would reach the main road which would take me to the Ethel. I picked up my pace and looked behind me. There was no one there. But still I had the uneasy feeling.

I had gone about half a mile along the main road when a man came out of a side street in front of me. I nearly tripped over him. I apologized and he continued on his way. He resembled the waiter in the café. He was smaller but the face was just as ordinary and unmemorable. There was now a long stretch of road in front of me and behind me. We were away from the hustle of the center of the city and I could see that nobody was following me.

I put my case down and as I did so the uneasy feeling left me. If I had got a ride into town I could have got to the Ethel and checked in and just about make my appointment. No ride came. I was going to

110

miss my appointment. The only comfort was that I did not lead anyone into a trap. "Who knew of my visit here and why were they following me?" I was asking myself.

On the long walk back I occasionally looked around, but the street was empty behind me and I felt secure that no one was following me.

Twenty-one

I checked in to the Ethel but was now an hour late. Returning to the Giraud, I collected my key and went to my room. The man who had almost collided with me was sitting in the chair Calhoun had sat in earlier. He looked familiar, but I could not place him.

"Well, you make a good man to follow, I give you that," he said.

"Tracker," I said.

"Nice to see you army boys know when you're followed."

"I couldn't. I only felt it. How did you get in here?"

"Normal way."

"What's going on?"

"Testing you. Nobody can spot me when I tail them. You're the first. Good move through that shop."

"I couldn't see you."

"You weren't supposed to."

"You made me late."

"Yup."

"How did you find me after I ducked through the shop."

"Easy. I knew where you wanted to go so I guessed where you would try to lose me. The rest was easy. Sorry about running into you like that. We had to get acquainted again and I needed to get back here."

"I'm not sure I did pass. I didn't see you."

"I said you weren't supposed to. Feeling is good. Sometimes it is all you have."

"What do I do now?"

"I'm pretty sure you weren't followed. Wilson was sure of that this morning and aside from me there was no one following you just now. Who else knows you're here?"

"Apart from Mr. Brown? No one."

"Where will you tell people you have been?"

"Here I guess."

"Why?"

"To see the famous places in the old capital, Independence Hall, Liberty Bell and all."

"Have you learnt some lessons today?"

"I don't know who is friend or foe. I feel I am followed everywhere. I ought to pay more attention to cover stories and I should trust nobody."

"Good start. Just remember that if you get caught you go to jail. If I get caught then I'm roasted on their fire. You understand?"

I was both angry with and awed by him.

"Go for a walk. You'll receive instructions."

I took my sketch book to draw Independence Hall. As I was leaving the hotel, I saw Wilson Calhoun heading out of the door.

I got up and walked out turning in the opposite direction to which the Calhoun was heading.

"Hey young man."

I heard the shout from behind me. I turned.

"Wait."

Wilson Calhoun ran up carrying his briefcase. "Good to see you again. I'm looking for some law offices around here and I should know where they are. They are on Broad Street. I've been given a map but I'm not sure that's right."

He was panting slightly. The run had made him out of breath.

"I thought I knew this fair city but clearly not."

I took his map and was able to find and point to the street he was looking for immediately.

"Hope to see you again, thank you," he said and ran off.

"You left me your map," I called after him.

He was well on his way and seemed not to hear me. I looked at his map. On it was a large "X" against a spot on Vine Street, near the port, which was in the other direction. I walked towards Vine Street forgetting for the moment about Independence Hall. The street was narrow. The café at 8 Vine Street seemed to be the place marked on the map. I was not followed, so I sat down and ordered a coffee.

The "X" could have marked several properties. I looked all over the map until I saw the panel with the price printed on it. It was a ten cent map and the price was circled with a pencil. I had just noticed this when I heard a voice.

"Do you mind if I join you?"

A cadaverous man of about thirty years of age, wearing a large Quakers hat and carrying a Bible, stood over me.

"Of course not." I said. Most of the other tables were taken but one or two were free.

"What are you doing here?" he asked.

"Sketching the history."

"It is a great city. The fount of freedom, don't you think?"

"Yes, I suppose so."

"Do you have God in your heart young man?"

I had clearly made an error. I started to get up to leave. He grabbed my forearm.

"Don't you have time to listen to the word of the Lord?"

His voice was loud and if I got up we would be making a scene. His grip on my forearm relaxed but his hand slipped quickly and unobtrusively towards my wrist as he put a piece of paper into my palm.

"You are in the hands of the Lord. Now let me read you His words."

The waiter came up to me and said, "Is he bothering you, sir?"

"No, it's all right," I said, resigned to listening to what Moses did thousands of years ago. When I left the café I looked at the piece of paper the preacher had slipped into my hand. It was blank.

I knocked on the door of 10 Vine Street and a small middle aged and smiling Quaker woman welcomed me in.

"Come in young man," she said. Her face was lit with a welcoming smile.

The front door opened into a living room. Grace was seated in the corner.

"Bolt the door."

I did

"Sit down."

I sat.

"I want you to pick up a family and take them to a safe house and leave them there. Someone else will forward them on. We're going to send you to Virginia. There are three sisters on the Lane Plantation near Lynchburg and they need to get from there to one of three houses. Any one of them will do. It has to be done on a Saturday night."

She explained the rescue mission in detail. Then she said, "I also want you to get to know the Patrol down there and I want them to like you and trust you."

"Why?"

"I need to know about them and so, I think, will you. They're vicious and would kill you as soon as look at you. The youngest one is the most dangerous and slices folks up into ribbons. They travel all over as a kind of roving patrol. Horton Field controls them from Baltimore. Just find out what you can. Who they are, what they do, where they've been and where they plan to go."

"I'll ride with them a week. Why a Saturday for the rescue?" I asked.

"Because they don't work Sundays and won't be missed."

"Am I doing this on my own?"

"In a manner of speaking."

"What does that mean?"

"This is to see how good you are. Someone's going to look over your shoulder. When you come back here, you tell me who it was and where you saw him, if you saw him."

She read my mind.

"No it might not be Tracker following you," she said. "Your hotels are okay?"

"I think so."

"Check out of all of them when you get back and get yourself into Streeter's Boarding House and leave your things there. You were given a piece of paper a while back. What did you do with it?"

I pulled it out of my pocket.

"It's blank," I said.

"Was it folded when you got it?"

"No."

"Ah."

"Does that mean anything? A blank unfolded strip of paper?"

"It was message for me. Folded means 'yes'. Unfolded means 'no'. You were the courier. If you were caught, no one would have suspected anything."

Grace gave me a map of Lynchburg and its immediate environs. I memorized it; the woods, the tracks, the houses and slave quarters big and small. The distance between the Lane Plantation and the first of the three safe houses was about five miles across open country. The next safe house was a mile further on but with some woods in-between and the last one was a mile beyond that in the centre of Lynchburg.

I needed a cover story.

She had read my mind again. "Take a Bible. Use it."

"What about my name? Do I take a new one?"

"If you're undercover, best to have as few lies as possible. Keep your name army boy."

Without a further word she got up and picked up a Bible from a small rickety bookshelf in the corner of the room. It was well used.

"Make sure you bring it back. You have work to do. Remember I need to know all you can about that Patrol and I want them to like you."

"Why do they have to like me?"

"So they don't suspect you when you meet them next."

Twenty-two

I bought a horse for thirty dollars. He was a flaming chestnut called Pierce, named after the former President. He bucked a bit when I mounted him but settled quickly.

I packed the Bible in a bag behind the saddle and rode out of Philadelphia to Lynchburg. The ride was easy and Pierce was worth more than thirty dollars. He was an eight-year-old gelding, built small and muscled like a sprinter, mature and with the nervous energy I liked. But he had the sour mood of someone who had'nt been treated well. That attracted me to him because it gave me something to work with. After about half a day's journey I discovered that he liked to sprint for short distances of no more than about five hundred yards and then slow to a trot to catch his breath.

So I gave him a gallop followed by a trot and then a walk. He liked galloping and was an excellent sprinter but could not sustain the sprint because he quickly got out of breath. That had frustrated him because he could not give what his riders had expected of him. Once he realized that he had to gallop only a few hundred yards at a time and I pulled him before he got out of breath, he started to enjoy the journey. He was able to run, but always had to be within himself and therefore not feel that he was a failure or unable to do as he was asked.

He also liked jumping, but hadn't been trained properly. Every hour or so I schooled him over makeshift materials that I turned into jumps and fences. This regimen sweetened him. It took me four days

117

to get to Lynchburg. I could have made it much quicker, but Pierce would not have stood a steady and even pace. He got bored easily and responded well to my changes of regime. I liked Pierce and wanted to get to know him.

I practiced two of my tricks with him. One was getting him to rear up on a low whistle. That was something I got horses to do with Brushes. When Pierce first heard the whistle and reared up, he was alarmed at the reflex action because it meant running the risk of throwing me off. He felt happier when he saw I would stay on. The other trick was to make him run away from me after I had dismounted. That involved a lower whistle as I expelled my breath and concentrated to will him to run from me. He was less reluctant to do this because that was what I wanted him to do and it did not involve the risk of throwing me off. He still thought it was odd that I would want him to tease me by running away.

By the time I got to Lynchburg, Pierce and I were getting on very well and he had stopped being such a sourpuss. He still sulked in the morning. He did not like the saddle being put on. Like many people he was not a morning person. I had hopes that he would be a good night person.

I checked in to the Middleton Inn in the center of town.

As I rode around in the moonlight, I met the Patrol. Everyone knew they were looking out for runaways and so their principal purpose was deterrence.

There were three of them, all riding together. "Hey, how you doing?" the oldest one said. They looked like the brothers, which they were. Jess, Wade and James Stimson aged twenty two, twenty and nineteen.

"I can't sleep." I said. "Mind if I join you?"

"No problem," Jess said. "It gets kind of boring."

"Thanks, maybe you can give me a tour."

"Be our guest," Jess replied.

They were impressed that I was at West Point and surprised that I knew Baltimore, because I sounded like a Yankee. They'd been to Baltimore recently "on business". Each brother carried a rifle, which was sheathed in a holster off the saddle along the near side of their horse. James, the youngest, carried a knife in his belt.

Conversation was not encouraged because voices carry at night. We did two circles across the countryside, through woods mostly, and at three thirty in the morning it was time to go home.

"Mind if I join you tomorrow?" I asked.

"Sure thing," Jess said. We parted, and I went to catch up on my sleep.

On the following night, they were not hard to find. The moonlight was good and the sky was clear. I felt I was being followed. So, it seemed, did the three brothers.

"Did you hear anything?" Jess asked me as we entered a clearing in the woods. I heard a twig snap the second before he asked me. Mindful that Tracker was probably in the area and annoyed at him putting himself at risk, I stopped Pierce and cocked my ear.

"I thought I heard a stick snap," I said, hoping that Tracker would not curse me for giving credence to Jess's suggestion. But I had to gain their trust.

"Let's ride in four corners," Jess said.

It was explained to me that involved the four of us starting from the same place and riding outwards at ninety degrees from one another. We rode out towards a "corner" and then rode back. This allowed us to search the territory as best we could within the square of the corners.

I rode in the direction of my corner, which by good or bad luck was also roughly in the direction in which I heard the twig snap. I saw a bunch of rags lying on the ground. I willed Piece to see the rags. He stepped over them expertly while I kept my eyes ahead of me looking at the horizon. I could see the rags move out of the corner of my eye. An escapee. I rode on past him and then back again to the centre. There were woods nearby and all he needed to do was get to them for cover. There he was exposed.

As I rode back, towards the center I took a slightly different route to avoid him and also search different ground. After we met in the middle, we carried on an unplanned patrol. There was no method to their searching. That was good in the sense that it was unpredictable, but it was random and therefore, I thought, incompetent, because not all the available territory was being covered.

"Nope, must have been a fox," Jess said. We rode on.

"Do you catch any?" I asked.

"Sometimes," Jess said. "The niggers have to know that we're out, that's the main thing."

"Most of your slaves are happy?" I ventured.

"Yes," Jess said. "But these Yankees put ideas into their heads sometimes. No offence Jack."

Suddenly Jess's horse shied. There was no reason for him to do so. We were in a field riding along the edge about three hundred yards from the wood and near where the man in rags lay hiding. Jess was not a bad horseman and kept in his saddle but in controlling the horse he turned backwards.

"Yes, whoa," he said trying to keep command of his horse. But he had seen something.

"A nigger's over there," Jess said as he pointed towards the woods. "He was looking out of the woods watching us go."

It would not have taken us very long to ride back and catch whoever was there.

"Are you sure?" I asked.

"Yes sir. Let's go get him."

I let out a low whistle to make our horses rear and dump us by the same means that I had practiced with Pierce. Jess hung on the longest, but he was taken by surprise and did not stand a chance. The others came off immediately. I had to make Pierce rear with my reins as he was not keen to do so while I was in the saddle. I slid off. I whistled again and all the horses, including Pierce, ran away from us and towards Lynchburg in the opposite direction to where the runaway was spotted by Jess.

I got up and dusted myself down.

"Do you have snakes here?" I asked.

"There's snakes everywhere."

No one was hurt.

"We'll find him quicker if we get the horses," I said.

The horses were now standing one hundred yards away from us. We walked towards them and as we got to within ten yards they ran off again and stopped one hundred yards from where we were. I was able to do this just by concentrating and did not need to whistle.

I wanted to get the men further and further away from the runaway without them giving up the hope of catching their horses and chasing the runaway themselves on foot. Just as we got close to the horses, they would run off and then halt. The last time this happened we reached the road. By then the runaway had enough time to make his retreat.

Jess got to the horses first. His horse liked him and so was happy to be caught. He thought it was a good game and enjoyed seeing his rider chase after him.

"Something's spooked them," Jess said.

"Snakes," I said. "Let's go find the nigger."

"He'll have gotten away," Jess said.

"Maybe, but you've gotta try." From the map I'd memorized there were slave quarters about a hundred yards from the other side of the woods. The runaway had plenty of time to get there. It was time for me to initiate a fruitless search.

Pierce and I led the three of them to edge of the woods.

"Ok," I said. "Let's go in a line fifty yards apart through these woods. If he's here we'll see him." The Patrol followed my order without complaint. The woods were dense and not easy for horses to get through.

About half way through the woods Jess shouted.

"This is too hard."

"We keep going," I said. "Do you want to tell your Boss you gave up? Get off and lead your horse."

We got through to the other side of the wood and the slave quarters were exactly as the map had shown them. The runaway was safe.

"That was a waste of time," James said.

"Never a waste," I said. "They have to know you don't give up."

We started to go home at four o' clock in the morning with the Patrol trio frustrated.

I had their trust.

Twenty-three

I slept until noon, exhausted. Not so much because the day seemed interminable but because of the tension of discovering the runaway and then making sure he escaped the prying eyes of the Patrol. It was Saturday, which was the day for rescue of the three sisters on the Lane plantation.

By the afternoon all the slaves in the six surrounding plantations were accounted for. This was a relief because a continued search for an escapee would have delayed my mission until that search was complete. All being well, I could take them on that day.

That night I greeted my fellow patrollers like old friends. A few remarks were made about snakes and I said how I hated them and how pleased I was not to see any when I normally rode out. We had ridden for about an hour and a half when the ensuing silence was broken by Jess.

"I don't think anybody's going to try it tonight. Not after yesterday."

I was in a dilemma. I didn't want to return to my lodgings because it would be obvious if I went out again and I didn't want the Patrol to stay out much longer as that would decrease the amount of darkness available to rescue the three children. I told them that I would ride some more on the "main road" (which was little more than a narrow lane) and said goodbye. I was relieved when they rode home towards Lynchburg.

I tied Pierce to a fence post at the bottom of the track leading to the Lane plantation and walked up on the grass, past the main house, to the slave quarters at the back. I knocked on the door once and it opened immediately. Three girls, who must have been aged between twelve and fourteen, were standing dressed in their Sunday best carrying a small sack. Seeing that I was white, they hesitated. I beckoned to them and the eldest took the plunge and the others followed shutting the door behind them. They were barefoot and so their feet made no noise as they walked on the short pathway to the grass.

They were not expecting a horse. Neither was Pierce expecting them. He appeared hesitant when he saw them and started to shy away. That alarmed the children a little but they responded immediately when I put my finger to my lips in a motion to be quiet. I then re-assured Pierce that he need not be frightened of them. I did this by picking up each child and patting Pierce on the neck as I did so. As I put each one down, he greeted each girl as a friend by nuzzling her outstretched hand. Pierce had not had happy experiences with children.

After we got clear of the plantation, we stopped and I told them to practice falling into the ditch. I felt foolish bringing Pierce with me because it meant that I could not go into the ditch with them if we were spotted. Lesson learned. They managed well and one of them nearly giggled with delight in jumping into the ditch in her Sunday best.

The sun was starting to rise as we reached Lynchburg. I wanted to go to the safe house furthest away, if only to show Tracker that I could do it. I knew I could not. People would soon begin to stir. It would have only taken one person to look out of their window for them to see a white man, a horse and three very dark young girls for my apprenticeship to come to a quick end.

I was as sure that no one had spotted me, so I knocked quickly on the window of the first safe house, which was a small cottage next to a blacksmith's forge. The door opened and I pushed the girls inside and pulled the door shut.

Had I been any slower I would have compromised the safe house, its owner and the girls I was trying to rescue. Ten yards away, unsighted by being down a side street, walked a middle aged white man I had not seen before.

"Good morning."

"Good morning," I replied. As I returned the greeting, the man continued on his way. I was relieved and at the same time curious. I wondered what would happen to those three girls. Had their parents gone before them? Had they too received help or was their escape a means whereby their parents could run across country unencumbered? When would they meet their parents? The Railroad was not going to give me answers to these questions. I did not need to have them.

I had to wait an hour before the blacksmith himself arose. His house was located on the other side of the forge, which was wedged between the safe house and the blacksmith's house. I asked him to look at Pierce's shoes with apologies for the early hour and promised to be back at noon. If I was to be an eccentric, I may as well play the role, I thought, as I returned to my lodgings with the Bible in my hand for an early breakfast.

I did not wake until one o'clock in the afternoon. I had overslept, I ran to the blacksmith to claim Pierce.

"Nothing wrong with his shoes," he said.

Relieved that no questions were asked, I paid him two dollars for his time for checking the shoes and, shaking my head, I rode back to my lodgings, booking in for another week.

There was no hue and cry on the first day. In the afternoon of the second day, Jess stopped by the Inn.

"Want to ride out?" he asked.

"Sure."

"Three nigger girls gone missing from the Lane's place."

"How old?".

"About ten up,"

"They can't have gone far."

"Let's get going," he said. I saddled Pierce and we spent the afternoon combing our bailiwick. We searched every ditch, copse and field and no young girl was found by me or anyone else.

I enjoyed the searching during the rest of the week, particularly organizing our group to be especially thorough, knowing the girls had long gone. As before, they responded to my authority.

"I've got to go soon," I said on the fourth night's patrol.

"They've gone by now, we've just got to carry on so Mr. Field's happy. If they've gone north the other patrols will get them."

"I've got three more days to look," I said.

"No point in making them think we give up," Jess said with a laugh, as he imitated my "yankee" accent.

Jess told me about the escapees' parents. Their father had disappeared the previous year. Shortly after that their mother had been sold south. No one wanted to buy the children at a price the Lane family thought sensible, so the Lanes kept them. That was a common commercial decision in that part of Virginia. There was no real trade to the north of Lynchburg or to Maryland. Although domestic slave prices were high in Baltimore, the best prices for field hands were in the Cotton Belt. Plantation owners preferred more mature slaves; patient owners waited for maturity and a better price and the Lanes were patient.

Twenty-four

When the seven days were up, I rode back to Philadelphia. Pierce had found the trip down to Lynchburg and the night time patrolling tiring. He never protested, but I felt that a slower pace was in order. I used the system of "Halts" all the way back. Halts were informal stops for horses and their riders at intervals of between ten and fifteen miles apart. Each Halt consisted of a small fenced off paddock area where the horses could be turned out as well as a number of posts for the horses to be tethered if you preferred. Usually there was a small barn-like structure, which was no more than a roofed area for the riders to sleep. You had to cater to yourself and sleep on the ground where you could.

I didn't particularly like these temporary resting places because they did not have straw or hay unless an occasional hawker came by. Halts were good free places and you could often buy hay and oats for the horses locally. Whilst I preferred to travel longer distances and pay for decent overnight accommodation, Pierce liked them and I was in no hurry.

In Philadelphia, I went out sketching and on my second day back encountered another Quaker who led me to a small house.

Grace was inside as well as someone else I did not recognize and who did not introduce himself. He looked like The Birdwatcher, but much older than the man from Tracker's story. Come to think of it, he would be older. I knew better than to ask who he was and gave both of them a lengthy de-brief.

"Horses can be good," said Grace after I had explained how foolish I felt walking with Pierce when I collected the three girls.

"Don't worry, son. It all worked. How did you manage with the rag man?"

I felt alarmed since I had not got to describing that incident. I tried to continue the debrief without surprise that she knew about him and Grace nodded with approval as I told her the story of the man in rags and my ordering the Patrol through the woods on the fruitless search.

"Good of you to do that, but he had a horse tied up in the woods. They wouldn't have caught him and had those boys done so they would not have stood a chance."

"Who was it?"

"One of ours. I heard they like you."

"Who?"

"The Patrol. They told Field all about you. They think you a little big for your boots, the way you ordered them around and all."

"How do you know?"

"Do you need to know?"

"No."

"Then I won't tell you."

I explained about the close call at the blacksmiths and Grace laughed. "I've had a few and that's why I don't do it any more. But you've got to watch the light, Son. Watch the light."

"So Tracker wasn't there?"

"No."

"Someone was watching me about the time when we got to that runaway," I said.

"It was one of our people. I told the safe houses you'd be coming."

I wondered how many more expeditions like this I would have to go on before I could free Lucy.

"Well," Grace said, reading my thoughts. "We'd best find your Mammy."

"Has your spy found her?"

"That's not for me to know."

"So what can I do?"

"You go to Baltimore. Avoid Horton Field but go to the slave market and pretend you're buying."

"Why must I avoid Horton Field?"

Grace told me.

* * *

On a warm July evening Horton Field settled into his chair and looked across at his friend. Both by now in their late thirties, Horton Field and Neil Ruffin were comfortable with each other. It was to Field, and Field alone, that Neil had confessed his indiscretion with the new maid he had bought for Victoria. It was to Field that he confessed his wife's distance from him after that indiscretion. He had her money and lacked her affection, he had said.

"What's bothering you, Neil?"

"Is it that obvious?"

"We've known each other since we were kids."

"Horton, I don't even know that something's wrong. It's just that something might have happened and I don't know what it is. Or I think I know what it is."

"You feel a little crazy?"

"Some."

"You suspect something?"

"Yes."

"Something crazy?"

"Yes."

"Better spit it out."

"You must keep it to yourself."

"Why wouldn't I? Why do you even have to say such a thing?"

"Because you have responsibilities."

"Look, what you tell me goes no further. It never has. You know that. I didn't even say anything to anyone about that maid you put in child."

"It's about that which bothers me."

"Tell me Neil, or you'll just get more and more miserable. Victoria isn't talking to you still, is it that?"

"She's talking to me, but she's so...polite. We don't talk like we did."

"Talking at all is something."

"I'm thinking that my nephew Jack is the maid's dead child."

"You've said this before. It's ludicrous."

"I have evidence now and don't know what to do with it."

"Another drink?"

"Yes please."

Field tried to look casual as he went to the bar and as he did so he congratulated himself for not, right then, asking what the evidence was. He judged that Neil was three drinks away from falling over. There was enough time to get the evidence from him.

"Two more please."

"Will he need a room?" the barman asked.

"In half an hour."

The barman poured the drinks and gestured to his wife, who was washing the glasses, to prepare a room for Neil.

Field returned to the table.

"The thing is Victoria and Lucy, the maid, came back from Boston with no baby."

"We know. Lucy lost it."

"That's what Victoria said."

"You trust her?"

"What if the truth was worse?"

"You don't know it is."

"I always felt funny about that boy, as if he was my son and not John's. Do you know the first person he goes to see each time he comes down for the summer?"

"You're going to say Lucy aren't you?"

Neil nodded.

"Who does he see after that?" Field asked.

"He goes to Brushes and they work with the horses."

"You're not saying he's Brushes' child. Look Neil, this is crazy."

"I thought so. I felt I was crazy even thinking it. Watching the kid go to the maid, who Victoria will not let me sell, even though I slept with her and everyone knows I did."

"You're imagining it."

"Listen to me. I've just got back from Boston where I visited my brother on farm business. He was judging in court and I had an hour to kill. It's a bit of a walk to the Charles River from his chambers and I didn't trust myself not to get lost. Boston's got no focus. I can't make it out. Not like Baltimore. I walked from his chambers towards Montgomery Place. I know that route. Then I passed a church that I'd seen many times. It seemed a good place to kill time. I wandered around the graveyard, looking at the headstones seeing who died first, husband or wife. It's something I did with Victoria when we were talking. We'd see who died first, the husband or the wife. Husbands die in their forties and fifties and the wives go into their eighties. We'd laughed about that a lot. How the women lived forever..."

"You've said this before Neil. Is there a point?"

"Yes. This wasn't John's church. I'd been looking at the monuments for a good while and was ready to go back to see John, when I saw the gravestone of Thomas James Ruffin, with his date of death 15th July 1858."

"So?"

"That's Jack's birthday. When she got back from Boston after Jack was born, Victoria said the name of the maid's child they buried was Thomas James. The same name as on the gravestone."

"You found where the maid's child was buried, then."

"It's not a darky's cemetery."

"It's the North. They'll bury them all together, sometimes. And you said it wasn't your brother's normal church. Of course the child would be buried somewhere else."

"Not that Church. I met the Pastor," said Neil.

"Maybe the child looked white. You are and the maid are pale."

"I introduced myself to the Pastor. He'd said that John had come to bury a twin, something about the grave being in a different place to where Maud went so she wouldn't be upset by looking at it when she went to her church."

"They had twins then?" said Field.

130

"So John told me when I confronted him."

"Twins often die."

"Victoria never said anything about a twin when she came back from Boston. John never mentioned a twin before then."

"No?" said Field, stunned.

Field tried to remain calm. Neil was lucid even though his speech was slurred. Field revised his calculation. Neil could take only one more drink before falling over in his chair. Neil drained his glass.

"One more? My turn."

"No, I'm okay. Get one for yourself."

The two friends knew the ritual. When Horton Field was done and felt that Neil was on the edge, Neil would get himself one more drink from the bar and when he sunk that one, he would walk upstairs to the room, which Horton Field had arranged for him.

Neil returned to the table and continued the conversation as if he had never left to go to the bar.

"Victoria never said anything about a twin. But she did say that the maid lost her child and it was buried in a darky's grave in Boston."

"This is all circumstantial."

"It wasn't a darky's graveyard. They didn't say anything about a twin until I found that grave. The gravestone has the same name as the maid's dead baby. John said she must have named her child after the dead twin. But they'd have said something about that when they returned from Boston. They didn't. John was covering something up. I could feel it."

"You found a gravestone. That's hardly a cover-up."

"It's a cemetery John would never have expected me to go into. It was for white people and, on his story, was for a nephew of mine he'd never told me about."

"How did he look to you when he said all this."

"I know when my brother's lying. He may not tell lies now, but he lied a lot as a kid. There was no twin. I'd have heard if there had been."

"What do you want to do?"

"I don't know."

"Do you want to ruin your brother?"

"No."

"Then do nothing."

"Nothing?"

"What can you do that doesn't cause a scandal? My lips are sealed. I promise you that."

Neil followed Field to the bar.

"We have a room for you, sir," the barman said to Neil.

"Thank you. I think I'll take it. Thanks Horton."

"Good to see you Neil. Best not talk about this again."

Field walked to his office at first wishing that he had not heard Neil's tale and that he had promised not to say anything. He thought that his duties to the community, as leader of the Patrol and standing attorney to the best quality slave traders, had been compromised by his friendship.

Then he was relieved. That this son of the famous judge, who was taking the academic prizes at Phillips Academy, was the son of a slave, was too horrific to contemplate. It was impossible for slaves to have those abilities. Best, he thought, to forget the conversation and dismiss it as the speculation of a drunken man. Its implications were beyond understanding and would have shaken his community to the core. The lawyer in him said that proof would have been impossible, that people would not accept Neil's speculation and Field's voicing it, as truth, would have spelled his own ruin.

* * *

When Grace stopped speaking we sat in silence for a while.

"How do you know this?" I asked. "It's like you've got into Field's head. How do you know?"

"Do you need to know?" she said.

I shook my head.

"What it tells us," Grace said, "is that you have to watch your step in Baltimore if you want to go there still. Tracker can do this on his own if he has to."

"I'm going." I said.

Twenty-five

I took Pierce to Baltimore, arrived in the early evening and checked into Tiffin's Hotel near the markets on Pratt Street. I had to wait for contact from the Railroad and had no idea who would contact me or how. All I was told was to walk round Baltimore as conspicuously as was respectable and I would be found.

The next morning I gave myself a shave and put on a clean set of clothes. Along with the aid of the coffee and breakfast, I took a walk around the business district and slave market. I'd been there many times, but now I saw its casual workaday ugliness as I had never before.

Occasionally someone raised their hat to me. I was not sure whether that was politeness or because they recognized me. It felt that I was part of a club and this was an acknowledgment of my membership. I saw that there was an auction the following day and the posters were up all over advertising it. They were part of the commercial life of the town, the advertisements and the sales themselves and were ubiquitous.

Sales particulars were obtainable from all the traders on and around Pratt Street. This was a sale in which all the traders participated. On some days sales were specific to the particular trader. On others, as this one, the sale involved everyone. Each trader had a slot and they shared the same auctioneer who could put any amount of excitement into his voice.

It was now about ten in the morning and the Street was buzzing. People were entering and leaving the trader's offices, some clearly from out of town.

I went into the nearest trader's office. It belonged to Pat Buchanan, a large loud voiced man of about forty with dark hair and a stove pipe hat, which he wore indoors.

"What can I do for you, young man?" he asked as I walked into his office which was a basic storefront.

"I was wondering if you could show me your sales particulars."

He pointed to the counter.

"Mine are on pages thirty two to forty five and you can see them down at the jail, just point to the ones you want to see and they'll take you to them. What are you after?" There was a flicker of recognition in his eyes as I had met him before when I was working with Brushes.

"Hey, aren't you Jack Ruffin?"

"Yes sir. I'm just down from West Point visiting."

"And buying. Hey, it's good to see you again. West Point. Well I guess you'll be after a manservant to clean your kit and all?"

"I'm not sure," I said trying to seem interested but not bound to buy. "I may clean my own kit but I want to see what's available."

"Well Jack, I have no manservants myself. All I've got are field hands and maids and you wouldn't be interested in them." He paused and tried an adult joke. "Except the maids of course." He winked at me. I laughed as best I could.

"If only the army would let me sir," I said, while looking down at the catalogue.

"Pity I can't help you. But it's a good sale. I think Brian Campbell may have some."

"Thank you, sir." I said and picked up the catalogue. Going to Campbell's to see what manservants he had would fill time while I waited for contact from the Railroad. Campbell's office was on Pratt Street next to the big jail opposite the Repository by the Circus.

The jail was a two storey building with barred windows, it overlooked a paved yard of about forty feet by eighty feet with benches, a hydrant, wash tubs and clothes lines. The slaves spent the daylight hours there and were locked in the cells at night. The public could look at prospective purchases through a tall stockade gate. Clients could enter from the offices.

It seemed to me to be classier office premises than the others. In front of me was a woman in her twenties with dark hair pulled back in a bun. She had a welcoming open face and milk white skin which rarely saw the sun.

"Hello, I am so pleased to meet you," she said in a thick North Carolina accent, "I'm Marylyn Griffin."

I was stunned.

"Jack Ruffin," I said. "The pleasure's all mine."

Ellen was occupying the front office, while Brian Campbell went out doing what he did best, looking for business. Campbell's junior partner Moody was in the back office. I had seen him around Baltimore when I was growing up.

By now he was forty years old, having worked in the family business before a disagreement with his elder brother caused him to leave *Moody and Downs* and join Brian Campbell as his deputy. Nominally he was Brian's partner, but Moody did not have the entrepreneurial spirit which Brian possessed. Moody was a desk trader who looked after things for Brian in the back office. He left it to Brian to find the business and preferred organizing and scheduling in the background and to have as little to do with clients as possible.

I was nervous and it must have showed. Ellen, however, was completely in control.

"Why I'm sure I've heard a lot about you, you must be Neil's son?" she said, with her eyes twinkling slightly. I knew her well though and could see their sadness.

"Nephew," I said and flushed a deep red.

"Oh I'm sorry I thought..."

I started to feel uncomfortable but I recovered.

"No Ma'am that's Morris. I am Judge Ruffin's son from Boston."

"A Yankee. Well, you can't help that I suppose. You sure don't sound like one." She was smiling as she said it. Somehow her Southern accent got deeper.

"Not all Yankees are bad Ma'am." I returned the smile. Moody came forward and asked for a file, which Ellen gave him then turned to me.

"Can I help you?" Ellen said. "It's a busy day for Brian with the sale and all. He's got a big list. He always has a big list. Did you know he is the biggest and most popular trader in these parts?"

"I thought he might be," I said.

"Yes, he runs a very professional operation, unlike some others I could tell you about. But I'd better not. Brian'll not forgive me. 'We're all in this together' he tells me."

"I'm after a manservant," I said.

"What kind?" Ellen asked.

"Er... the ordinary kind. For when I'm in the army."

"Well, we only have two. They don't come up that often you know. I'm sure that they'll work fine for you. Where are you being posted? If you don't mind my asking."

"I've not passed out yet. But when I do I'll be at Sackets Harbor."

"New York?"

"Yes Ma'am."

"You need a loyal one then."

"What do you mean?"

"You don't want to pay all that money and find them going off to Canada, now do you? What am I saying? I am trying to make a sale and here I am telling you why they could leave."

"They wouldn't want to go to Canada, would they?" I asked. I gave an air of genuine puzzlement.

"What happens up North is that Yankees..." she paused, "sorry, I didn't mean you, put ideas into their heads about being free and all and so they go to Canada where the catchers can't get them."

Ellen glowed. She was steeped in her role. I was about to be sick with a combination of fright and disgust.

"Yes," she continued. "They may not have so many in Boston. Thing is Jack, I shouldn't say this, but you may have to think of doing your own kit. They're all here right down South. They like it here and there are no Yankees to give them foolish ideas. But up North, when you are doing what you young soldiers do, then who knows what is poured into their silly little heads?"

As she was saying this she put her hand on my arm and occasionally turned her head but mainly looked straight into my eyes.

"Well, y'all go look at those boys and come back and tell me what you think of them." She had her back to Moody. Whilst her voice was flirtatious, he face was sad, serious and urgent.

"Well, Miss Marylyn, I'm real pleased to meet you Ma'am. Thank you. Suppose I see these two manservants and then talk to you about whether I bid for them."

"I'd be happy to advise you, young man. On a confidential basis." She paused and picked up a catalogue.

"Now let me see. Yes, here they are. Shall I tell you what to look out for, or would you like to see for yourself first."

"If I don't know what to look for I may not get very far."

"Yes, but some folks want to see for themselves first. No pre judging and then talk it over with a friend. That way they look at the problems in the cold light of day, as opposed to getting carried away and trying to make a private sale on the spot by themselves without our help. Here I am stopping you again. Now what's got into me? You go and see and come back here and we can talk about them. I'm sure I'll have information as to how you can get them."

Ellen wanted me to return and seemed to be telling me in code not to act alone. I dared to think that the words "information as to how you can get them" was her way of telling me that she knew where Lucy and Brushes were.

Moody was chained to his desk. She needed time to write a note to me, probably in cipher. I had to leave to give her time to do it and that meant appraising the valets.

While her deep knowledge of buying and selling slaves shocked me, I was astonished at her bravery in taking a role in the heart of the slave trade where she could so easily be exposed as the daughter of a man whose anti-slavery views were well known throughout the country.

I was overwhelmed. Here I was posing as someone else, because I had to. Ellen was doing the same thing from choice. Now she scared me. The woman I loved had a secret life without my knowing or guessing. Her travels were now explained, but in a way which was disorienting. I wanted to marry her and be her protector as an officer in the army; yet she was courting a greater danger than I had ever faced. She hated slavery with a greater passion than her father, yet she was embedded in a trader's office as the Railroad's best spy. I needed fresh air as nausea came at me in waves like smoke blown from a bonfire.

Twenty-six

At least thirty slaves were in the jail's courtyard. Some were children with their mothers. In the corner was a tub with a young woman of about twenty washing clothes.

The two manservants were lots 56 and 57. One "Wilfrid" and the other "Sloan". Neither had a last name, which was normal in particulars, so as to allow the slave to take the name of the new master. I could see from the particulars that Wilfrid was about sixty years old and Sloan was forty.

I called out Wilfrid's name and from behind the washing bucket, a small coffee colored man stood up, grey hair surrounded his ears. Otherwise he was bald. He wore a suit of good cut and a tie. He did not wear leg irons. I noticed this because I could see that some did and some did not. The women, by and large did not and the men mostly did. He walked over to me.

"Yes Master."

"Jack."

"Yes Master Jack."

"No, just Jack."

"Yes, sir."

"Where do you come from?"

"The Bradshaw household, sir."

"How long have you been a manservant, Wilfred?"

"For as long as I remember, sir. I only came over here as a small boy, sir."

"Over here?"

"From where I came from. In a ship, sir."

"And how long have you been in the Bradshaw household?"

"Twenty years, sir."

"Do you know why you are being sold?"

"No, sir. Mr. Bradshaw told me it was time to let me go, sir. I can polish boots really well." I looked down at mine. They had not been cleaned since I left Concord.

"Let me clean yours sir."

I was about to stop him but he had already turned back to where he was sitting and brought over a box of cleaning materials. I was embarrassed as he bent down and cleaned my boots. He took three minutes with each one. He was not only thorough, but I felt like I had a foot massage.

"Do you know about Canada," I said as he brushed the first shoe.

"No sir. I am happy where I am, sir."

"But if you weren't."

"I am, sir. I can't talk about things I know nothing about." He paused in his speech but the polishing went on as if nothing had been said. "But I can polish your shoes, sir." He started on the next shoe.

There was a confident wariness about his answers and I felt foolish presenting myself as a prospective owner and starting a conversation which could only either get him into trouble or raise false hopes.

"I hope you can see, sir, that I can help a gentleman look smart."

"Do you have a family?"

"I did, sir. Will there be anything else?"

I shook my head.

"In which case I shall bring Sloan over to you."

"Thank you."

"I hope they stay clean, sir."

Two minutes later another man of small build, forty years old, thick black hair came up to me.

"Sloan," he said.

"Thank you, I'm afraid I don't know what to say."

"Do you want a manservant?"

"No. I mean yes."

"What would you like to know? I see that your shoes have been polished."

"Thank you Sloan. I must go."

I could take it no more and rushed back to Campbell's. I entered the storefront and, inevitably, Moody was still there. We could not talk.

"Well Jack," Marylyn, or rather Ellen, said, "what did you see?"

I had planned my repartee on the short walk back from the jail.

"I'm not sure I want them."

"Why Jack? I'm sure that one of them would do you know. What about the old one?"

"He polished my boots."

"How sweet. Just adorable. You would want someone to do that for you."

"He's too old. I couldn't manage a manservant who is forty years older than me."

"I'm sure you could Jack, especially someone who brings such a shine to your boots. What about the other one?"

"Maybe," I said.

"Did you notice anything about them?"

"What do you mean?"

"Well, were they healthy? Did they look as if they'd give trouble?"

"They seemed ok to me."

"Did you check their backs?"

I looked askance.

"I bet your niggers don't need the whip."

I started to feel sick again. Ellen was not sparing the details. Her attachment to the role seemed excessive.

"No Ma'am," I said.

"Well, I've been looking at particulars for next week's sale and if you don't want those boys, maybe these will do. I've put the particulars in an envelope for you."

I took the envelope and went back to the saloon and ordered a large pitcher of beer and sat alone at a table. I downed two huge glasses in a minute flat. The envelope contained the sales particulars of five field hands.

Around the words "Lot 75" was a small pencil circle. The other particulars said "Property of Frederick Temple" with a pencil circle around the word "Frederick". 75 Frederick Street was about six blocks to the east.

I picked up the envelope. It was blank on the outside. I took out my pen knife and opened out the envelope. Inside it in pencil in small writing was "7.30". I had time to kill so I took a walk.

The posters were in little clusters around Pratt Street, each offering a reward for an escaped slave. The slaves pictured in them were usually men in their twenties, field hands mostly with relatively modest rewards. There were one or two with rewards in excess of two hundred dollars, but they were rare and were of slaves with a trade: smiths, hoopers and such like. I noticed there were no horsemen among the runaways. I counted fifteen different posters as I went round the town then down side streets and along main streets.

The rewards were to be payable upon safe return to their owners, but the slave could be returned to one of the traders in the main city. Colin Stevens and Brian Campbell were the traders whose names were mentioned most of all.

I looked at my watch. It was seven o' clock already. I had walked a bit out of town so I had to walk quickly to 75 Frederick Street.

It was seven thirty five when I arrived there. It was a small terrace house. I knocked on the door. Ellen answered and let me in.

The front door opened straight on to the kitchen. Ellen took my hand and walked me through to a small sitting room which backed onto a yard.

"I was worried you'd not look in the envelope," she said.

"Is there anyone else here?" I asked.

"I share this with a Quaker lady who looks after me. She'll not be back until late."

"I love you, but I hate Marylyn."

"I love you too Jack and I also hate Marylyn. Tracker told me about the front desk job. They come up regularly because people can't stand it too long. The money's good, though."

"How long have you been here?"

"Three months."

"So you knew about Lucy's sale before me?"

"The moment I found out about it, I wired Dr. Holmes. That's how he knew to call you back. I took the job for other reasons. Grace reckoned that it was good to have someone in with the traders. So here I am. I know she was sold out of your farm, but not where she is now."

"How come?"

"I don't know where she is," she said with a trace or irritation at my pressing her. "I'm working my source. It's hard. He's discreet."

"So someone knows where she is?" I said.

"Look, just trust me. I know how desperate you are and I'll do what has to be done."

"What does that mean?"

"Enough. I talk to people down here. I'm going to carry on talking to them until I find out." Ellen's voice had an aggressive edge and defensive impatience I'd never heard before.

"But you know about Brushes?" I said, changing the subject.

"Yes."

"How did you find out about him?"

"Do you need to know?" she said, as that hunted look passed her face.

"No." As I said that word, I felt a thread of connection between us break.

She looked relieved beyond measure and awfully alone and vulnerable. A feeling of dread passed through my heart.

"Can you at least say what happened?" I said, changing the subject as an indelible darkness seeped deep into me.

Twenty-seven

What Happened: The sale

olin Stevens had passed the word "confidentially" that Brushes could be bought in a private sale if the price was right. He had done this before with premium slaves, but not with anyone with Brushes' value. Enhancing his reputation by making Brushes a local sale at a record price would slow what he saw as a nearly unstoppable momentum behind the markets further south that were surpassing Baltimore in importance.

The first step was to ensure that Brushes was taken to an open jail so that he could be viewed by potential buyers. Traders in Baltimore typically housed their slaves in private jails, essentially warehouses where they were kept pending being put on the auction block. The best was Campbell's at 244 Pratt Street, where I had inspected Wilfred and Sloan.

Colin's plan was to visit all the trader's offices and asked their "advice" as to how he could sell Brushes. He wanted them to talk among themselves to find out whether among their own local customers anyone would be interested in buying Brushes in a private sale. Colin would not mind sharing the commission if he got an introduction which produced a good price.

His first port of call was Brian Campbell's. He had bought the slave trading business from Hope Slatter. Campbell's was just two blocks from Colin's office.

Brian Campbell was the proprietor, his younger brother William had been bought out and had left to run the associated business in

144

New Orleans. Brian was about five feet eight and of medium build. He was in his office chair behind his desk when Colin entered, as usual, without knocking. His new receptionist, Marylyn, was on vacation, so he was manning the front desk himself.

Brian saw himself a cut above Colin. Brian's family was old money But Colin brought Brian a lot of business. Colin thought that getting to know Brian would somehow overcome some of the reserve with which he was treated socially, because alone among the fifteen or so slave traders, Brian had access to Society. Colin did deals with Brian but he was never invited to his house.

Although they were competitors, there was a slave trader's club and gossip mill. They exchanged information about who was doing what and where the best merchandise was coming from and also about the market generally. Whenever they met, traders would be cagey about their own position, but you could always figure out how they were doing. If an answer to a question was "Yes the market's holding up well," that would normally mean that they were worried about a possible fall in the market. If on the other hand they said "I don't know how long this can last," then what they really meant was that prices of slaves were rising and times were good. If they announced that they were "really busy" and asked you how busy you were, then business was slow.

"What can I do for you, this fine morning?" Brian asked. The best way he could keep his distance from Colin was to engage in what appeared to be light hearted banter.

"I need your advice," the older man said as he helped himself to the nearest chair. "You aren't busy are you?"

Brian shook his head. Colin did not normally ask for advice, indeed he had taught Brian a lot about the trade. One was how best to get a better price by blacking slaves' hair to make them look younger without the dye running from sweat.

"I've got Brushes for sale and I am not sure how to market him."

Brian's tell at poker was to take a long draw of his cigar whenever he was surprised by how good his cards were. Colin was not asked to Brian's poker games and attached no significance to Brian breathing in a large amount of cigar smoke and breathing it out slowly towards Colin. He was annoyed that Neil had gone to Colin.

Brian's thought processes were exactly the same as Colin's. He would get the best price in a local sale, because Brushes' reputation was essentially local. The better society did not like to be present at the market for trophy slaves. It made them uncomfortable to be in the hurly burly of trade, whereas the making of a private sale was a gentleman's occupation.

"I'll ask around. It's not going to be long before Neil has to sell all his property."

"I think he'll have another few years. He'll get this year's crops in, but he'll have a problem after he's spent what he gets for Brushes."

"Have you got a price in mind?"

"Fifteen thousand dollars."

Brian flinched. Even with the recent price inflation for slaves you would get a good field hand for one thousand dollars. Brian could recall the most money paid for a single slave was ten thousand dollars.

"There has been nobody like him on the block in my professional lifetime."

"Your next sale's in a few days. Will you put him on the block if you've not sold him before then?"

"I think so, Neil needs money and can't wait for the Premium Sale. He should've given me more notice. But I'll do the best I can. I've got the maid who he's married to for sale, it may be good to sell them together."

"Good precaution. Let's see what the new owner wants. We do the private sale jointly and I get half commission."

Standard commission for higher end traders like Campbell, Buchanan and Stevens was ten percent.

"Agreed. I'll tell the others and give them a fee for an introduction and we split that."

"Done."

"Moody, I'm going out," Brian shouted to the man in the back office.

Moody sat down in Brian's chair as the door closed behind him. He could read "Brushes" and "$15,000" written in large letters on a piece of scrap paper. The meaning to a good desk trader like Moody was clear. Brushes was on the market and there's only one place where that price could be obtained. Captain Fleming's farm.

I had met Captain Charles Fleming when I went with Brushes to tame unruly horses. A rich man, his title was honorary and self-awarded. All my fellow cadets who were from the South knew someone who took a title like he did. Colonel was the most popular rank, Captain was the next most popular. "General" and "Lieutenant" were never chosen.

Fleming's money was assumed to be old money because his lifestyle was more lavish than his harvest would suggest. His farm was about seven miles on the south western side of Baltimore. He called it a farm, rather than a plantation. He kept horses, which he enjoyed racing at Martin Potter's racetrack in Baltimore. Fleming, with his neighbor Gerald Butler, also took pleasure in the English pursuit of "steeple chasing". Horses racing towards landmarks. Of course, there were no church steeples as landmarks, but the principle was the same.

He had a stable of twelve race horses, which he used for racing locally and at the track. The arrival of Gerald Butler's horses had made life more interesting. Fleming was into breeding and breaking horses. This meant that the farm did not produce very much, but there was always money for Fleming, his wife and two sons and their horses. The elder son Alastair was in England checking out thoroughbreds with instructions to bring back a good stallion for breeding. A Derby winner, if possible, or equivalent. He was also looking west to Kentucky.

Campbell started riding to the Fleming farm at a canter, but then, realizing that he might appear too keen and also that his horse had to make the return journey, slowed to a trot two miles from the farm. Fleming had hired Brushes many times and had come to admire him. When I accompanied Brushes, he was hospitable to us both. He was a poor rider but a good trainer. He loved horses and he had only admiration for Brushes' ability to make them do exactly what he asked of them.

Fleming was schooling a yearling colt as Brian approached.

"Captain," Brian shouted from about fifty yards away. The yearling shied and then bolted.

The sudden movement caused Fleming to lose his grip on the reins and the colt ran to the far side of the field from where the schooling was taking place and waited for the Captain to try and catch him.

"Sorry," Brian said.

"I'll catch him in a minute. He can wait. He might even come back."

"I have some news and I think you should be the first to know. Neil Ruffin is selling Brushes. He's got Colin Stevens to sell him."

The Captain wrinkled his nose at the mention of Colin's name.

"How much?"

"Fifteen thousand will close out the opposition, otherwise he goes on the block."

"I'm not sure I have that kind of money."

Brian was encouraged. The Captain did not say that the price was too high. He was not saying that he did not have that kind of money either. He was just not sure.

After a pause the Captain said, "I'll have to sell some stock."

"What sort?"

"My groom, Nathan, and perhaps his family. It depends whether they go better together. He has small children."

"If you want him guaranteed, then you best sell the lot together."

"Come, take a look at them."

Nathan, was in the stable area at the other side of the house. The farm had a round horses' school at the front. The slaves' quarters and the stables were at the back

"Nathan," Captain Fleming called.

Nathan was cleaning out the feet of one of the stallions and was concentrating on the stallion's foot when he heard his master's voice. Without any sudden movement and almost as if it was planned, Fleming's groom put the hoof down and stood up and then saw Brian Campbell. He knew who Brian was and he understood immediately what the visit was about. The only thing which would bring Campbell to his stable yard would be if the Captain was buying Brushes. His right leg almost gave way under him, but he was able to steady himself and make it appear that he had stumbled.

148

Nathan was thirty years old and had three boys aged five, three and eighteen months. His wife, Ada, was a field hand and the children were cared for by Ada's grandmother, Bertha, who was too old to till the fields and during the day looked after all the small children on the plantation, free or slave.

Now that the moment arrived, he felt powerless. He had thought many times about how he could persuade the Captain to sell the family all together. He would plead with him that he could get a better price for them as a unit. But even as he was about to open his mouth, he realized doing so was a bad idea. By making that suggestion he would be perceived as threatening.

Nathan had known Captain Fleming since he was bought, at eight years old, with his mother, who was purchased as a domestic. He had never himself been mistreated but now he was frozen with fear. Instead of saying anything, he stared at the ground.

"What would you like me to do Master?"

"Can you go get Ada?" Captain Fleming asked. "Bring her along to the porch. Mr. Campbell and I'll wait for you."

"Do you want me to bring my children, Master?"

Captain Fleming paused, as if he had an important decision to make. Surely, Nathan wondered, he would not sell them both and leave the children here? But then he might. He would not get much for children so young and indeed they may reduce the purchase price if they were sold together as the children would need to be looked after in the new place whilst Ada was in the fields.

"Let's see Ada first," Fleming said.

The pit in Nathan's stomach became a gaping hole. Whether he would keep his children would be decided in the next few minutes, or hour at the most.

The farm grew oats, potatoes and rye principally. At this time the field hands were weeding the oats crop. Nathan hoped his walk looked casual as he went towards the field where Ada was working. He did not want to frighten her.

His stomach tightened with every step. As soon as he entered the fields, and out of view of the Captain and Brian Campbell, he stopped

149

and was sick. He doubled over in pain. It was a dry heave except for some acid. His mouth felt thick as he picked himself up. What was he to tell Ada?

He knew that she would go through the same thought processes as he had, but her upset would be loud and heartrending and there would be nothing he could do to protect her. If she cried aloud, then the overseer might whip her. The overseer would have no idea that she was about to be sold and so would not hesitate to strike her if she stopped work for no reason.

Nathan resolved to tell the overseer first. That way he would know why Ada was crying and would hesitate to whip her prior to a sale.

The overseer, Douglas, was a slave himself. He was proud of his status which meant that he was no longer called upon to do the hard backbreaking work. But if he was soft on the field hands, then he would most likely be replaced and either sold or put back to work in the fields.

Nathan walked past Ada, scarcely giving her a glance.

"I must speak to Douglas," he said as he passed her.

Ada continued hoeing.

Douglas was walking up and down the rows, carrying his whip under his arm.

"Douglas," Nathan called.

Douglas stopped and turned. When he saw Nathan, he smiled. They had a connection, aside from their bondage. They both had the confidence of their master. Nathan did not flaunt his master's high regard and it was only by chance that Douglas heard that Nathan had been allowed to go to Baltimore on business. Douglas had tried to get Nathan to talk about Baltimore and the people there, but Nathan did not do so, afraid that he would be accused of painting an attractive picture of life outside.

"Nothing to see, Douglas," he would say.

"Have you come here to rest yourself?" Douglas asked Nathan. Douglas allowed his field hands two rest breaks a day. The first was due. Douglas had observed that the slaves worked harder if they had a break. He would announce that a ten minute break started when the last slave got to the end of their row. That ensured that they worked to get their break as soon as they could and fewer slaves, like Tracker's mother, would faint under the relentless hot sun.

Douglas instituted the two breaks, one in the morning and one in the afternoon, spaced two hours either side of midday.

"I've come to get Ada. Master wants to see her. Brian Campbell's here," Nathan said.

Although Douglas had not been to Baltimore, he knew who Brian Campbell was. He had bought and sold most of Captain Fleming's slaves. Nathan was a small boy when he was bought, and Douglas was fully home grown in that he was born on the Fleming Farm. They were exceptions in their longevity. There was a high turnover of field hands. On average about two or three per year were traded.

"Does that mean you're going away?" Douglas asked.

"Maybe. Brushes is for sale."

"Shall I walk with you?"

"No. I had better see her on her own."

Douglas took the whip from under his arm, passed it to his left hand and held out his right hand.

"This might be goodbye."

Nathan took the offered hand and nodded, but then added, "It may take a while to sort out the paperwork."

"He'll want you gone while that's being done."

Douglas knew about the paperwork. Bills of sale, roots of title and guarantees were part of the business. He knew because Captain Fleming spoke about it, although he never actually showed the paperwork to him. It was more by way of introduction to a new field hand. Where he had come from, with whom he was sold, whether he was guaranteed and what the potential problems were with the slave.

After the handshake Nathan walked back towards Ada, who was bent over, hoe in hand.

"Stop now Ada," he called. He noticed she stood up gradually and with effort. By the time he got to her she was looking at him with a mixture of pleasure and alarm. Her first thought was that he had been made a field hand, but she dismissed that idea when she realized that he would not have called her to stop work if that was the case.

"The Master wants to see you."

She put her hand to her mouth. The moment Nathan spoke, she knew why.

"Brushes is for sale and Brian Campbell's here," he said.

They walked back in silence sharing their unspoken wish to be sold together and with their children.

As Ada approached them, Brian Campbell and Captain Fleming were discussing how they could get the best price for Nathan and his family.

The thought that Brushes could work alongside Nathan and that he could own them both did cross his mind. The Captain had the money despite what he said to Campell, even though his wife would complain about the cost. But Brian wanted an incentive to get the deal done for him. A meaningful commission and the status which from the sale of Nathan and his family would be as good an incentive as any. The money from the sale of Nathan and his family would make sure Campbell did the deal for him and leave money over to buy the yearling at Woodburn Kentucky which he had his eye on.

Nathan and Ada arrived at the porch whilst Captain Fleming and Brian Campbell were deep in conversation.

"Master," Nathan said.

Captain Fleming looked up. "Thank you Nathan, you can go back to the stables now."

Ada stood below the porch.

"You can come up here," Captain Fleming said. He turned to Brian Campbell, "She's hard working and tractable, no handicap or vices and with three healthy young children."

"So, I could say that the children are a good investment for the future."

"You sure could."

"Can you guarantee her?"

"Of course, she's a good field hand without a stripe on her back." Captain Fleming then raised his voice.

"Ada, take off your dress."

Ada had never shown herself to anyone except Nathan. But she did not hesitate and faced the two men, naked and trembling.

"Turn around, it's your clean back he needs to see," said Captain Fleming with a laugh.

Ada turned around.

"There you go Brian." Fleming said. "Now Ada put your dress on and go get your children."

After Ada left to find her children, their conversation resumed.

"Paperwork," Brian said. "It is the bane of my life, I can tell you. Everything has to be perfect for sales like this."

A premium rate slave required careful paperwork. Title had to be guaranteed, health assured and the bill of sale had to be faultless. It was different at the lower end of the market. There some traders sold off the back of a wagon. But there were no guarantees and no proper paperwork and some people bought slaves who belonged to someone else, who might be looking for them.

"I think I know how to get the best price for Nathan," Brian said. Ada was now nearly out of earshot, but she did hear the words, "Best price for Nathan," as she walked to where she thought her children might be playing outside the quarters.

"He's not as well known as Brushes," Captain Fleming said.

"True but they've worked together and not just for you. You can be sure the market in horsemen'll now be wide open. The under bidders for Brushes will want the next best thing."

And so the strategy emerged that Brian would follow Colin's trail and speak to the other potential bidders for Brushes to see if they would be interested in buying Nathan, who may be slightly less talented than Brushes, but was more affordable.

As they talked, Ada looked for the children inside and outside the quarters. The Captain's three grandchildren had come to stay and it was likely that they would be playing with Ada's children as they had the previous two days.

"Bertha," she shouted. There was no reply.

"Bertha," she shouted again.

Then she looked towards the fields and saw Bertha with one hand on her hips holding Ada's youngest child with three white and six black children chasing each other around a small part of the edge of a field. Ada had not noticed before, but a small semi-circle had been made at the edge of the bean field to act as a playground.

When Ada reached the group, Bertha explained that they had just finished playing a game of Patty Rollers. Bertha did not ask why Ada had left the fields before sundown, and she made it appear this was the most normal event in the world. Ada picked up her youngest and then called her other two children. "We must go see the Master now." When she said this she glanced at Bertha with a mixture of fear and defeat, as she did so, her voice rose in pitch.

"Don't you worry," Bertha said, "You just bring then back and we can all have another game." Her voice was soothing.

"Can I come too and see Grandpa?" Barney asked. He was Captain Fleming's eldest grandchild.

"No son," Bertha said. "He'll want to see you a little later."

"Please."

"No Barney, now go pick up your sister," Bertha said as Ada walked slowly back to the main house to display her family to Brian Campbell.

"Hey children," Captain Fleming said as he saw them approach. The eldest, Fitz, aged five, broke from his mother's hand and ran up to Fleming and grabbed his knee. Fleming picked him up. Fitz was his favorite. A momentary flash told Fleming that he loved Fitz more than is own grandchildren. Ever since Fitz was able to walk he ran to the Captain and squealed in delight in a way that his own children never had. Fitz was naturally affectionate and worshipped "the Master" ever since he could walk. It was only at this point that Captain Fleming fully understood what he was going to lose when he sold Nathan and his family. In his excitement of the deal to get Brushes he had over-looked what the loss of Fitz from his family would mean. But he could not stop now.

"Well, how's my Fitz?"

The Captain smiled as he asked the question.

"I've been playing with Barney."

"Really? Does Barney play a good game"

"Yes. Patty Rollers. I won."

"You caught Barney then?"

"Yes Master I caught him good. He hid in a silly place."

"Well, well." Captain Fleming said. "Now Fitz, here is someone I want you to meet. This is Mr. Campbell. He'd like to see you." Captain Fleming put the young boy down. Fitz then turned to Brian and stood at attention like a soldier.

"Can you run Fitz?" Brian asked, smiling at the boy standing in front of him.

"Yes sir."

"Show me."

"Where to, sir?"

"See that fence post over there?"

"Yes sir."

"You run to that post, touch it and run back to your master and I'll count as you do."

Fitz started to run towards the post.

"He's fit and well," Brian said as they watched Fitz run.

"I take care of all my niggers," Captain Fleming said.

"Yes, Captain, you do."

The Captain turned to the three year old. "Hopp, can you run like your brother?"

Fitz was half way back as Hopp started stumbling towards the post. He fell and then picked himself up, turned to the Captain and smiled and ran on. He was much younger than his brother. Ada saw how proud the Captain was of Fitz and that Hopp did not have his brother's prowess. She wanted to say, "He's only three," but the words did not come.

"Plucky boy," Brian said, who then turned away from watching the spectacle of the boys running. "Ok," he added, "I might be able to get between three and five thousand for the lot, but I'll have to ask around."

"Five thousand." the Captain said, as Fitz arrived panting on the porch. Little Hopp was running and falling over and had not got half way to the fence.

"Ada, take these children away and go back to the fields," Fleming said.

Ada wanted to appear docile and calm to Brian with a passive and accepting demeanor. So quickly and with as little fuss as possible she took Fitz's hand and walked towards Hopp, who was not even on his way back from the post.

"Come on Hopp," she said putting her hand out to him.

"No, I run to Master." The reply was defiant. He wanted the same praise as his brother.

"Master's seen you run."

"I run to Master."

Ada was now in a quandary. Hopp could really make a noise. If she tried to pick him up, then there would be a scene and Brian Campbell might think her children troublesome and they may not be sold with her and Nathan. If she did not pick him up, then Campbell would think her disobedient and Brian would sell Nathan and not her, because Nathan was tractable and she was not.

There was nothing she could do which was right, she thought, as she saw Hopp continue to run. She stood paralyzed with fear and felt warm water running down her leg.

Captain Fleming's voice came to her rescue.

"It's ok, Ada. Come to Master, Hopp." There was a smile in his voice as if he was saying that all his slaves loved him, even the little children and they were only disobedient to their parents because they loved him more.

Ada watched Hopp imitate his brother. Then the little boy ran to his mother while Fitz went to resume the Patty Rollers game with the Captain's grandchildren.

Nathan was waiting as she delivered Hopp to Bertha.

"Master told me to go back to the fields," she said.

"You can talk to me a while."

"He wants me to go back to the fields." Ada repeated. The fear that had caused her to wet herself still gripped her.

156

"I'll walk you there," he said. Then he saw her wet field dress. His own sense of helplessness washed over him again.

"Do you want to change your dress?" he asked.

"Master told me to go back to the fields."

"I'll ask him to sell us together," Nathan said, as Ada turned and walked purposefully towards the field and he followed her.

"Don't you say nothing to him. Nothing. He'll think you uppity and then where will we be?"

Her breathing was labored. He saw her legs give way and she fell into his arms. She started to cry. Nathan held her. He wanted to protect her, but his fate and that of his whole family rested elsewhere. He always knew that. He enjoyed pleasing the Captain and the Captain's favor towards him. The good work that he did had allowed him to forget his position. Now, like a guilty secret come to life, the realization of his powerlessness and the emasculating reality of his position hit him.

"We'd better walk to the fields," he said. It was all he could say. He was in no position to bargain with his master.

"We'll be sold together," he said after a minute, as they walked. He was trying to reassure himself as much as her.

All Ada could do was nod. No words came to her.

Meanwhile Brian had mounted his horse and waved the Captain good-bye. For him it was a good day's work. If he could get someone interested in Nathan, then he could arrange the sale of Brushes to Fleming for fifteen thousand dollars. But that meant finding an under-bidder for Brushes who could then be steered towards buying Nathan. He had to work fast, he thought, as he saw Colin's wagon approach the Fleming Farm.

They were about to pass about half a mile from the farm. Brian stopped his horse. Colin drove on. Brian turned round and caught up with the wagon and Colin finally stopped.

"I've already seen him," Brian said, as Colin's two horse buggy came to a halt. Colin used his larger wagon for picking up slaves and the smaller buggy for himself.

Colin tried to smile. "So he's yours then?" Colin said.

"I guess. But he will buy. How many do you have interested?"

"Two, the Butlers and the Regans."

"I thought... they might be," Brian said. He was thinking and was about to say that he had thought that Colin would go to them first. But he corrected himself. Colin noted the correction, but let it pass.

"Sealed bids then?" Colin asked.

"I think so." Brian replied. "Will they make your price?"

Colin was not sure. He had indicated they were both interested but the price, they said, was far too high. Brian sensed the hesitation and guessed the reason for it.

"It's an awful lot of money." Colin said.

"I think we ask them all to do a close out bid with a reserve of fifteen thousand dollars," Brian said. He knew that he was indirectly telling Colin that Captain Fleming would bid as high as fifteen thousand dollars, but he saw from Colin's hesitation that the other two were unlikely to come up with that much. So if Colin wanted a sale at that price, Brian knew that he had as much as told him that he could get it.

"Will you tell him? Sealed bids in my office by noon tomorrow."

"I'll go," Brian said and he turned his horse back towards Captain Fleming's farm.

When Brian Campbell returned to Fleming's farm, the Captain was sitting on his porch contemplating Brushes and his successful stud farm and all the match races he could win.

Twenty-eight

Ellen told the story calmly and with no emotion. Even when she had finished and saw my distress she remained composed. I looked at her. This was a side to her I had not seen before.

She read my thoughts.

"Don't forget I work right by the biggest slave jail in Baltimore. I hear everything, both from Campbell and the slaves. I've worked other such places too. It makes you numb. Maybe that's why Brian can't keep his front desk people."

I was doubled over in pain.

"There's more," she said.

Fleming wanted the best bloodstock in the country and the way to do that was to have the best judge and handler of horses which you could possibly own. Nathan was excellent, but Brushes was a class apart. Captain Fleming's friend, Robert Alexander had the best bloodstock. He owned the Woodburn Stud on the waters of the Elkhorn Creek in Woodford County, Kentucky. He started Woodburn in 1852 with about 2,000 acres. By 1859 he had 4,000 acres having bought several very good horses and one champion, all of which enabled him to expand his acreage and ambitions.

Alexander told him Kentucky was the future, but the racetracks Fleming preferred were in Maryland and he felt he could make a better success of his horses at his farm there.

Fleming had traded with Alexander in a desultory sort of way. But the distance from his farm to Woodburn was over five hundred miles, and so Fleming's purchases had been "sight unseen". Alexander had been honest in his dealings, but Fleming was disappointed in his purchases through a good natured jealousy. The horses he had bought were good but were no more than that. Alexander's world-famous stallion Lexington had made Fleming ask himself "why not me"?. His head told him that you had to be very lucky to own a champion. His heart was envious.

Brushes was an answer to his prayer. There was no better judge of a horse. So he sent Brushes to Woodburn, get him to look at the horses and come back with a yearling which would turn into a champion.

Ellen's story had concentrated on Brushes.

"You want to know about Lucy. I know," she said. "She went to Fleming's with Brushes. Then ... I don't know. It seems she's not there now. Tracker went to Fleming's to speak to Brushes, but he'd left for Woodburn and Lucy had gone. She'd been sold. Something about having a Bible. But, as I say, Tracker should know where she is by now."

"Where is he?"

"He'll find you, but he won't come here for you. It's going to be hard getting her out even if you know where she is. You can't do it yourself."

"I know."

We sat together and as we did so I felt the distance between us grow and cover us like an in-coming tide.

"I wanted to be your protector," I said.

"Part of me wanted that. Most of me wanted that. But things can't be the same between us now. Not after this."

"Why?"

"We've grown beyond the storybook Jack."

"Can you kiss me anyway?" I said and pulled her towards me as I had so many times before. I felt her body freeze and she looked away from me.

"What's the matter?" I asked.

"I've a lot on my mind," she said.

Her body softened in my arms, but she still looked away from me. I felt distance between us as never before. I'd lost her, I felt. But I didn't know how and I dreaded asking her why. I stole a glance at her face by looking in the mirror on the wall. Her face was rigid as if haunted. She caught my glance and froze again.

* * *

The innkeeper poured me a drink. While I smiled, a rage that I thought would never be quenched welled up inside. Brushes had been like a father to me. He had nurtured my talent with horses. Lucy, my mother, to whom he was bound, had been sold. Brushes was five hundred miles away, guarded like a cash consignment, and Lucy - I did not know where she was.

As for Ellen, there was something lost forever. Something the streets and people of Baltimore had taken from us and she had given away for me.

I was accomplished at holding my liquor on the evenings that we cadets escaped the Academy's grounds. I would need a lot of whiskey to become really drunk. Eventually, at ten o clock, unsteadily on my feet, I went upstairs to bed and oblivion.

I was shaken awake. It was still night and the room was lit by a lamp. I had a nasty taste in my mouth and a crashing headache.

"Drink this," Tracker said and he passed me a large cup of very black coffee.

I drank as if ordered to take medicine.

Tracker stood by the door and watched. "Get dressed. Can you function?"

"How long have I been asleep?"

"You went to bed at ten. It's now two. Did you go to sleep immediately?"

"Where were you?"

"Working."

I had been half asleep as I drank the coffee. I kept the headache but Tracker's words sobered me up.

"I'm okay"

"No you're not and you've wasted time. Pick up Pierce and go out to Butler's place. Ride around it and keep an eye out for me."

He told me the plan and I listened taking it all in.

When he finished, I drained the coffee cup and placed it onto the bedside table. I looked up. He had gone. There had been no footfall and the door had closed as if it had never been touched. His silence in movement was as sure and mystifying as Grace's.

Early morning and very dark. My head no longer ached. My mind was clear. Tracker found me on the outer ditches of the Butler plantation and gave me more instructions. He had no sooner left me than he disappeared.

I left Pierce and told him to stay where he was and that I'd return. I walked a figure eight though the final cotton field at the back of the plantation and then towards the stables where Tracker said I should find Nathan.

Butler kept a bed in the stable loft for his horseman to use and I would try there first. The moon came out. I could see now, but I could be seen too. I looked back to see if I could see Tracker. I felt by now that I ought to be able to see him in the open countryside with the moon out, even if I could not see him on city streets.

There was no sign of Tracker. I had left him not five minutes before. He had pointed with his palm sideways towards the stables and then pointed to himself and did a circle with his index finger.

We had agreed a set of signs. The one with his index finger said that he was going to circle the plantation. If he saw anything to abort the mission he would send a signal. The sound of the cuckoo meant we abort the mission. No real cuckoo would be calling either at that time of night or even at that time of year so there was no danger of our signals getting mixed up with the call of a real bird.

There had been no cuckoo call as I stood at the stable door. This made me unprepared for the noise which greeted me. It was as if the horses had become guard dogs. I put my finger to my mouth. Then I felt absurd because none of them could see me and I had not yet established a link with them. I had to get in there quickly to calm them down.

The barn door was open and I ran inside so they could see me, then I closed my eyes and gestured them to be quiet. Their whinnying stopped. I listened to see if I had disturbed the household. Then came the sound of footsteps approaching the barn. There were two men speaking together in whispers.

"Someone's in there," one of them said.

"I guess," the other replied. "Sometimes they get disturbed by one of their own. It's mighty strange that they made such a fuss."

"Mr. Butler, sir, I'll lock the front door behind me and you wait outside the back entrance. Whoever is in there will have to go out the back."

"Good plan."

I could hear every word clearly. There was nowhere for me to go. If I tried to move, then they would hear my footsteps. If I climbed up the ladder to the loft, then I would be trapped. But I was already trapped. The overseer was going to see me, crouched, for no good reason, in the middle of the barn with stabling on either side of me and horses looking over at me wondering why I was there.

The man slipped silently into the barn. He locked door behind him and ignored my crouched figure. As I looked up, he walked through the passage and out the other side where Butler was supposed to wait.

"I'll just check the roof Mr. Butler, but there's no one here that I can see."

"I'll stay here in case anyone comes out."

"Thank you sir."

The man returned to the barn and climbed up the ladder. He stopped at the top and then climbed down again and then walked out of the back door where Butler waited. They now spoke with their normal voices.

"Nobody there, sir. I guess they are excited about the race. They can feel sometimes when they're going to the racetrack if you change their routine."

"I guess you're right."

"I think I'll sleep here with them in the top of the barn, just to be on the safe side."

"Thank you. We can't be taking any chances."

"No sir," the man replied.

I sat still as the footsteps of Gerald Butler grew softer and softer in the night time. and the overseer walked back into the barn and sat down beside me.

"Nathan." he said eventually, as he put his hand out to shake mine.

"Jack Ruffin. We've worked together once, remember?"

He nodded.

"We're to take the children first, tomorrow afternoon," I said.

"You've got it worked out?"

"He has." I said, referring to Tracker. "Brushes is in Kentucky."

Nathan looked stricken.

"We met for me to hand over the Fleming horses to him." Nathan said. "He and Lucy were going to escape together. Then he disappeared. No one on the farm knew where he'd gone, not even Douglas, or if he did he wasn't saying. It was just 'a long way away'. I reckoned it must have been Kentucky."

"Do you know what happened to Lucy?"

"Yes. She went to Dan Robinson's"

"How do you know?"

"Tracker told me."

Twenty-nine

The Robinson Plantation was a small farm on the outskirts of
Baltimore where Dr. Dan Robinson lived with his wife Louise.
Their house gave the appearance and aura of an old, respected
family home. Dr. Robinson stood six feet two inches in height. About
fifty years old, his blond hair was fading as grey streaks grew into
it and was neatly parted on his left side. His figure was angular. He
was a general practitioner whose patients came from about ten square
miles around where he lived. That included South Baltimore and Dick
Smith's hardscrabble farm.

Louise his wife, had come from England. The sadness in their lives
was the absence of children. Louise was well known locally and was
one of the few to visit Patty Smith. She knew Patty's secrets and occasionally tended her bruises.

Louise was forgetting things, her behavior was becoming bizarre.
In the course of his medical practice, he had seen many people slip
into senility, and, although Louise was only fifty-five, he recognized the
signs. Dinner was forgotten, or it was served late. Clothes went missing and were found in the oddest places. The latest sources of concern
occurred when one of his slaves had found Louise's old wedding dress
hanging in the barn and when Louise was found pacing up and down
the cornfield wearing only a night-dress.

Dan was desperate. He'd never bid in an auction before. He stood
on the edge of the crowd and the first thing he noticed was the smell of

sweat, tobacco and whiskey from the buyers. Melvin, the auctioneer, was brisk, or seemed so to Dan. This was a scene which made no sense to him. People were led in, there was a lot of noise and then they were led away whilst someone from the auction house ran to the successful bidder with a sheaf of papers. Everyone seemed to know what they were doing. The only people who seemed to Dan to be completely bewildered by the whole process were him and the slaves being sold. Everyone else seemed self-assured and in the know. The loneliness he began to feel, as Louise's mind started to leave her, washed over him.

He walked to 'the shute' being a roped off section of roadway adjacent to the auction square. Six slaves were walking up and down the shute. Dan saw Lucy immediately as she walked towards him. He remembered her from his occasional visits to the Ruffins. The last illness and death of Grandpa Clive had taken a lot of his time. More recently he dealt with Neil's minor illnesses which accompanied his alcoholism and drained his immune system. When Maud had visited her sister in Baltimore, he treated the flu-like symptoms which came with her depressions.

Lucy was an answer to his prayers.

"Thirty to thirty five year old woman," called Melvin, the auction-eer. "There's one thing to add to the particulars on the page. She had one child twenty years ago and lost it at birth. No pregnancy since. She's a strong domestic maid with over twenty years good service with a top local family. Who'll start me off?"

"Should I bid now?" Dan wondered to himself.

"Five hundred dollars? Who'll give me five hundred? Good local family. Four hundred? Who'll give me four hundred?"

Involuntarily Dan put up his hand and immediately pulled it down, but Melvin was too quick and spotted the bid.

"I have four hundred."

Horton Field, a regular patient of Dan's, was standing beside him and saw his hesitation and confusion.

"Five hundred'" Melvin called.

"You should have told me you were buying." Field said. "I can take care of this for you for ten-per-cent. I'll save you money."

166

Dan nodded in assent.

"Stay still and let me bid. Norfolk has topped you, let's see if anyone else comes in. What's your maximum?"

"Seven hundred," Dan whispered.

"Six hundred," Melvin called.

"That's Richmond. So far Washington hasn't made a bid."

Melvin Field looked to Dan. "That's six hundred to you sir."

Field put up two fingers.

"Mevin'll see it as twenty dollars. We need to slow this down."

Immediately Melvin said "Six hundred and twenty," and as he did so his voice went quiet. The square went quiet.

"We've slowed it down," Field said.

"Six fifty." Melvin paused and said again, "six fifty."

"Good, it's slower now. It was starting to run away."

"Should we bid now?"

"No. Wait."

Melvin repeated: "Six fifty," looking around the square as he did.

"No one else is bidding," Field said. "Encouraging."

"I have six fifty once," said Melvin.

"Now I must go to seven hundred." Filed raised his index finger.

"Seven hundred," called Melvin. The square stayed quiet. "Seven hundred to you sir." The mood in the square was that it had to be enough.

"Looks like you've got her," Field whispered.

Melvin then turned to the man from Norfolk.

"You've given me some help, sir. Can you give me a little more? On the market and selling at seven hundred dollars. Just a little more will get her for you."

The man from Norfolk shook his head. A surge of relief came over Dan.

"Seven hundred to you, sir," Melvin said looking again at Horton Field.

Then Melvin looked imperceptibly to Dan's right.

"Seven hundred and fifty."

"That's Washington, we're up. Let's walk away. It was your maximum, right?" Dan had feared this moment. He'd have to go home either empty handed or having paid more than he could really afford. The prospect of seeing Louise again caused a mixture of bravado and despair well up inside him.

"No," said Dan "You can go to a thousand."

"Are you sure?"

"Yes. Please don't lose her."

"I have seven fifty to your right." Melvin said directly to Field. "Can you take me to eight hundred, sir."

Horton Field nodded.

Dan had hoped to get Lucy for five hundred dollars. He never thought he'd be about to bid for nearly twice that.

"Eight hundred to the Field agency. A good maid. Excellent family. They don't come up very often.... Eight hundred once; eight hundred twice. Sold to the Field Agency eight hundred dollars"

Dan Robinson drove home in a single horse and cart. The anxiousness he had at nearly wiping out his savings was compensated for by his relief at having someone he could trust to look after Louise. After Horton Field had signed the sales slip for him, he said that such good domestics were rare. Robinson knew he had overpaid, but he had peace of mind.

Lucy sat in the back of the cart wrapped in the only clothes she possessed, grieving her parting from Brushes, devastated that neither he nor her son would be able to find her. Her fears of being sold and sold separately had been realized in a few short days. Bewildered at the speed at which Brushes been torn from her yet again, she sobbed uncontrollably.

Thirty

Tracker was waiting for me in my hotel room. He had returned to Baltimore quicker than I had. I knew better than to ask how. He was sitting at the table, drawing a map from memory.

"Why didn't you tell me you'd found out where Lucy'd gone?" I said.

Tracker did not look up from his drawing.

"No time. You were too hung over and we had to get going."

When he finished drawing the map, he wrote out instructions on the back, folded the paper and handed it to me.

"Memorize it, destroy it. Then get the wagon," he said.

I bought some seed samples and drove back to the new Butler place. I asked Butler if he needed wheat seeds or oats. While I expected that he would say no, I was persistent and offered him a free sack of oats. I said if he liked the oats, it could be the beginning of a trading relationship.

I told Butler that this was my holiday job for a week. This was designed to make him take pity on me, but it was far more likely that the free sample made him responsive. He pointed to the barn where I had been greeted by the horses a few hours before and asked me to unload the sample next to the sacks by the door.

I was to take Nathan's children, put them in the false bottom of the wagon and drive them, in broad daylight, to Tobin Arthur's forge and livery. From there they would be forwarded on by varying safe houses to Baltimore, where they would be collected for transport on to Boston, which would serve as the place where they would be reunited with their parents.

Nathan thought that nobody would miss them because they were not yet ready to work in the fields and there was no playgroup like the one at the Fleming's. Nathan and Ada could conceal the loss of their children so that they could get clear before their parents' escape.

I drove my cart into the barn. The horses were quiet. All fifteen of them stood with their ears pricked as Ada and Nathan put their children into the false bottom of the cart.

I gave the horses some oats as a "thank you" for keeping quiet. I normally disapprove of rewards, but the number of horses and the tension of the moment made it easy to break my habit. I gave them the oats from the sack that I had brought. I then had a story to tell anyone who wanted to know why I took so long leaving a bag of oats in the barn.

After their children were stowed away, Ada was crying. Nathan looked grim. I wanted to say they were in good hands. Whether they could see their children again depended on luck as well as the good will of the many unknown strangers in Grace's network. Reassurance would be hollow, so I gave none and handed over the map and instructions.

My mouth was dry and I sweated profusely as I drove away with my cargo.

Thirty-one

It was three days after I had taken the cart with Nathan and Ada's children to Tobin Arthur's place. I had become more and more impatient in the time as I stayed around Baltimore but it was well spent studying and memorizing maps from Maryland to Kentucky. Large and small. Broad and detailed. A few printed. Most in the careful hand of the Birdwatcher, each with due North shown, all with creeks, valleys, dips and other hiding places.

The maps had been delivered in a box by a paper salesman, I was told by the receptionist. The paper was 'on approval' a note in the package said, and could be returned if I deposited it in the telegraph office.

Tracker said he would come back to see me when things were ready. The only instructions I had, aside from learning the maps, were to take Pierce to the Ruffin plantation.

"You'll probably have may have to abandon your horse. I assume you won't want to abandon Pierce," he had said.

I was anxious to see Ellen and at the same time worried that our being seen together would compromise her. The learning of maps was sedentary and mind bending. I took walks to clear my head and on one of them I could not resist. I went into Campbell's store to find Ellen. Brian Campbell was at the front desk in a welcoming clients mode. Moody was hunched over bills of sale, bills of exchange and receipts. He was entering figures into a ledger. Ellen was not there.

"Good afternoon, can I help you?" Campbell said.

"I wonder if Marylyn is about. I'd like to see her."

"If I had a dollar for every time someone said what you just have, I'd be a rich man. She's gone. Left without giving notice, saying something visiting about an ill aunt in Raleigh. Not sure I believe her. Another girl gone. I just don't seem to keep 'em."

Visiting an aunt in Raleigh meant that she had gone into the field for the Railroad. The upset in my face was genuine.

"Don't worry, you're not the only one who's disappointed." I heard Campbell say as I left. "She's broken a lot of hearts here."

* * *

It was early afternoon. Tracker and I were in a cornfield at the back of the Robinson farm. We had circled it twice on foot.

"You'll remember all this now?" he said.

I would remember every hill, track, barn, dip and field. Front, back and side. My head full of maps was now filling with memories of topography.

"This is it where she is?" I asked.

"Yes, this is it. Now wait."

"Why?"

"Just promise whatever it is you see, that you'll stay where you are and say nothing."

"I promise."

"Watch."

Five long minutes passed. Then the back door to the farmhouse opened and two people emerged.

The first was Mrs. Robinson. She was frail and leaning on a stick.

The second was Lucy.

She looked as she always had. Though she was now in her late thirties, her face was still unlined, as far as I could tell from fifty yards distance and crouching in a cornfield. She wore a hand-me-down print dress, red with yellow and green patterns. Her hair was straight and black, parted in the middle and loose around the side of her face, with a small curl turning towards her mouth. Her nose was small and snub,

172

her arms muscular and her color a very light brown.

My heart jumped. Tracker put his hand on my shoulder. Heavily. Just as Superintendent Lee had three years before.

"They'll walk round to the front of the house and down the drive. This is Mrs. Robinson's exercise. Every day. Same time. Let's go. You've done your reconnaissance here. She leaves…you leave tomorrow night. There's one more place I want you to see."

We sat on a log in the woods. You could see the Smith's hardscrabble farm.

"You know what they're like," he said as if it were both a question and a statement. Then, as if to answer it, he told Norbert's story.

Norbert was thirty year old field hand and, like Tracker, had run for four nights from the plantation where he had grown up. He had heard a rumor around the quarters that he was about to be sold. There had been such rumors before. They came from the overseer who sometimes talked to the older field hands about what sort of slaves the Master needed.

Just then the Master needed someone to take care of the cotton gin. None of the field hands could do so and one of them would have to be sold for the cash to buy a slave who could operate machinery. The rumor was not specific to Norbert. It was just that a field hand would have to go in exchange for a slave to run the gin.

Norbert had no wife, and on the plantation only his mother remained of his family. He never knew his father and his mother never spoke of him. His older brother had been sold three years previously. Encouraged by his mother, he fled the plantation where he had grown up and took the North Star route to freedom. The North Star route was the most frequent route used by those the Underground Railroad called "freelancers".

"Just follow the North Star. Hide when it's cloudy. You'll find yourself in a place where slaves are free," he was told by his mother. The place was called Canada. That was all Norbert knew.

Norbert did not know how much time he had before he was to go to market. If he had enough time, he would have waited for a full moon. He left immediately with a small bag of food on his back, which his mother, who worked in the kitchen, had made up for him.

Norbert reached the area under the jurisdiction of the Smith Patrol. He saw the Smith farm in the distance. He had traveled about sixty miles over four nights and had survived with the food he had carried. He had filled a bottle with water from the streams which he found along the way. His bag was empty. He would have to live off the land.

It was three o' clock in the morning. The moon was full. Norbert was unable to tell whether the farm buildings, which he saw in the distance, were outbuildings of a larger plantation or whether they were the whole farm. As he had fled further north, the number of small farms increased and the size of the plantations began to shrink. The fields were smaller too. Norbert felt safer hiding in cotton fields. But the harvest was now nearly over and the cover from the crops was skimpy.

Norbert decided that he would run to the woods and try to circle the farm buildings. He did not make the mistake that the young Tracker did of hiding in a barn.

The Smith family were riding home after a fruitless night on Patrol. Norbert broke cover in full view of Dick and his two sons and he did not have a chance. Dick's Patrol was about four hundred yards away. It was Tim who spotted him and shouted, "Nigger near the woods."

Norbert kept running. He felt that if he made it to the woods then he could hide and would have some small advantage over the slave hunters on horseback.

It was Dick who got to him first. He was a good fifty yards ahead of his two sons. Norbert had reached the trees. There was still plenty of space for a horse in the woods. Dick came alongside Norbert. Norbert thought that if he could pull this old man off his horse, then maybe he could grab the reins escape on horseback. He pulled at Dick's right leg

Dick did not have a good seat. He had no balance and any horse with good balance lost it with Dick in the saddle. One pull of his right leg and Dick tumbled off. Norbert tried to grab the reins, but, freed of the weight on her back, Dick's mare started to run. The reins slipped through Norbert's fingers and a shot rang out. Norbert fell as he grasped for the reins which might have given him a chance of freedom.

Jake had fired. He was about fifty yards away, sitting on his horse with his gun pointing in the air. Tim was the first to arrive.

Norbert looked up at Tim. Norbert said to Tracker that he wished that he had tried to pull Tim off his horse and brave Jake's shots.

"At least it would have been quick," he said.

Norbert's right leg was struck by Tim's iron bar. Pain from his shattered leg remained with him for the rest of his life. In the cold of winter he felt a dull ache in his leg and forever after he had a limp. But, right then, he felt the overwhelming and unbearable pain caused by the iron bar.

"You want to run nigger?" Tim yelled as Norbert screamed while he writhed on the ground. Tim raised the bar to hit him again. Norbert sensed that if he did not say anything, the bar would come down on his head.

"No, Sir!"

At that point Dick said, "I guess he can't run now Tim."

Tim hit Norbert's leg again anyway.

The brothers put Norbert in a cart and Dick took his captive to Leon Bott's store in Baltimore.

Tracker and I were sitting right where Norbert was caught and crippled by Tim.

"He can scarcely walk. Robinson didn't set his leg right. Probably because Field told him to and he was sent back to his 'home' as an example to anyone thinking of leaving."

Thirty-two

Tracker and I tied the horses about half a mile from the Robinson's farm. Nathan and Ada stayed mounted, holding our horses and the spare for Lucy, as we walked the rest of the way. There was a dusty path and there were a few ditches. We used them only a couple of times. Tracker would drop to the ground. As he did so, I did as well. Tracker then listened.

Occasionally he held his palm ostentatiously to his ear. I was not sure whether he was smiling or straining to hear. He dropped again and then motioned to me to come close to him. I started to stand up, but he signaled to me to stay prone. I crawled about twenty yards before I reached him.

"Can you hear them?" he whispered.

I shook my head.

"Must be the Smith gang. They're waiting for us."

I had heard nothing.

I got a sudden knot in my stomach. If Robinson's place was being guarded, then our plan had been compromised. If it was the Smith gang, then it was to Horton Field's order.

We had come all this way. Would we now turn back? If we did, would we have another opportunity? If they were expecting us then they could just pick us up anyway. Even if we slipped away, would Lucy now be sold? If she was, would I be able to trace her?

"You stay here." My whisper was far too loud. I had still heard nothing. I had tears of rage and frustration in my eyes as I signaled Tracker to stay down or even leave. Whether I pointed to the ground or pointed back towards the horses I cannot now say. I was not going to let anyone hold Lucy prisoner for a moment longer.

I again gestured to Tracker to stay where he was or go back to the horses. His face seemed relaxed, almost amused. His response drained my anger as I walked towards the house. Exposure and disgrace did not matter to me then. I was committed and would not turn back.

Without Tracker, I was slower and more cautious. But the small hiding places and ridges in the ground were exactly as I had memorized them.

I was a hundred yards from the slave quarters when I reached a small dip in the ground. Robinson only kept five slaves, so the hut in which they lived was small. I looked up. Lucy was waiting by the door of the quarters as Tracker had asked her to.

She ran and dropped down beside me. I gestured her to follow me back to the horses.

I wanted to embrace her. She put her right hand to my mouth and her left index finger to her lips. There was no joy in her expression. Just fright. Tracker was right. I could sense other people now. I could not hear them. I could not see them. I knew they were there. She pointed to the front of the house. The Smiths must be watching the front and the far side. If, as was likely, they were guarding the other approaches to the house in rotation, it would not be too long before they circled and found us. We had to run back quickly.

I signaled to Lucy to follow me. Her expression was solemn, the fear had gone from her face. There was now a look of determination. I felt the same. The time for caution and calculation was over. We had to run. I looked up and saw the outline of a horse in the darkness. To run back the way I had come would take us right into Dick's Patrol.

I signaled for us to turn and we ran a hundred yards away from the figure, then caught our breath under cover of a dip in the ground. We were lying face down. She looked at me and I saw she was ready. We got up and then ran another fifty yards towards the cover of the corn field from where I had seen her the day before. We were three hundred yards from our horses.

I wanted to break from the cover of the corn field and run sideways for our horses. We were about to do so when a hand grabbed me. It was Tracker. I gestured towards the horses. There was a smile on his face. He pointed us in the opposite direction, through the corn field. Then pointing in the direction of the horses he shook his head.

We would have escape on foot by the alternate route to Simpsonville which Tracker had shown me. I had memorized the two ways to the safe house, which was owned by teachers called Clutterbuck. This meant going west over unfriendly and swampy terrain. The perils were less certain than the Patrol guarding our horses, but they were no less real. This was our only route out. If that became blocked, we were finished.

I was glad that Pierce was away. I could not have left him with the Patrol. I wondered about Nathan and Ada and hoped they had got away.

We ran. Terrified.

Either Lucy was fitter than me or she was impervious to the exertion. We had gone about two hundred yards when I realized that Tracker was no longer with us. I stopped. Lucy ran on. She turned towards me and gestured to me to follow. The gesture was authoritative and impatient. I ran towards her. She continued running. I could hear men's voices now loud in the night.

"Where are you, Boy?" I could hear one shout. The night air and the flat ground carried voices a huge distance.

"We've got your horses. So you better come out," another shouted. I was paralyzed between the need for flight and fear for Tracker. He had remained behind to face them and give us time to escape. We had to run on. My forlorn glimmer of hope was that Tracker never made mistakes.

I had caught up with Lucy and gestured to her that we should keep running. She did not need it.

She was running as if she would never stop. I shall never forget the expression on her face and the look in her eye as we ran through that cornfield. Her eyes were fierce and her jaw was set in determination and desperation.

Then a chilling scream pierced the night. It must have carried miles. It was as loud and awful as ever I had heard. Tracker must have been caught by the Patrol. I shuddered at the thought of that iron bar.

We ran on.

Thirty-three

The cornfield was about six hundred yards in length and at its end was a wood. We had gone half way through the field when we heard Tracker's blood curdling scream. I was leading Lucy when, out of breath, we stopped some four hundred yards into the wood. Where were we to go from here? Then I remembered from one of the maps. Dorsey's Swamp.

The dogs would be searching for us soon. Our scent would be smothered by the swamp. I caught my breath. Lucy looked at me with impatience.

"Dorsey's Swamp," I whispered.

"You know where it is?" Lucy asked. Her whispered voice was very small. "We don't have long before sun-up."

"We'll get there."

We had run south. We had to start going west once we were five hundred yards into the woods.

"We'll walk," I said. I could hear no one chasing us. I wanted to walk so I could listen for the Patrol and catch my breath. The terrain was awkward. We would be lucky to get to the swamp by sun up. The earth was clumpy, the wood dense. Every one hundred yards or so we tripped and fell. No horse could have gone through these woods without difficulty. Anyone following us would move as slowly as we did.

Lucy seemed in much better condition than me. We went due west, which took us through the woods across a small stream, through half a mile of open country and then through another cornfield.

As we passed each landmark, the woods, the stream, the open country and the cornfield, I thanked the Birdwatcher for the accuracy of his maps made years before. I felt admiration for Tracker and ashamed of myself. We could have returned for Lucy after the Patrol had left. Instead I insisted on going ahead and he covered our escape.

I forced myself to recall the maps and the topography the Birdwatcher had drawn. As we approached the last cornfield I looked behind me to check where Lucy was. I could see the redness in the eastern sky behind us. She was wearing a dark brown wool dress and no shoes. Her hair was tied back. Her feet were bleeding. But she had the same look of determination that I saw as we ran from the Robinsons.

The sketch showed the land at the west end of the cornfield dropping into a ditch. Beyond the ditch was some ground, which was firm in the dryness of the summer but boggy after rainfall. It was boggy. Our legs dragged. Our pace was slow. The sun was rising.

It felt like Dorsey's Swamp came to us inch by inch. When we got there we were up to our knees in warm fetid water. Insects surrounded us in seconds. Nevertheless, compared with the ground we had just covered, this was easy.

There was a wooded area in the middle of the swamp. The Birdwatcher had drawn a small duck egg in the middle. His joke aided my memory. We waded through the water. I could see a road at the other side of the swamp. Forty yards before the road, just as he had sketched, was a tiny island. If I had not remembered it and the duck egg on the map, I would have dismissed it. It looked as if trees were sticking out of the swamp. I climbed up and beckoned Lucy to follow me. She waded towards me slapping herself to get rid of the insects. I reached out my hand and helped her up.

I set about making a hiding place. If we lay down and covered ourselves then we would not be seen from the road. The sun was up and people would soon be passing. There was no time to lose. I gathered reeds and wood and Lucy, watching me, did the same.

181

It was a long day. Dogs bayed near us but never came to the swamp. When they seemed to be close, which seemed to be almost constantly, we were utterly helpless and tensed with fear. I was grateful for our water bottle. We took small sips from it every hour.

By the afternoon the dogs had gone home. That meant that the day's search for finding a known escapee would be finished. My experience with the Stimsons in Lynchburg made me think the Patrol would not be able to stay out for an entire second night

Darkness finally came andI fell asleep. When I woke I could see the moon. It was three o' clock in the morning. The Patrol would be on its way home, I reckoned. We had two hours to sun up. Tracker said we should walk into Simpsonville on that road from due south and approach the village just before sun-up. No earlier and no later, whatever day we came.

We needed shelter and food. Lucy needed shoes. I had Tracker's maps in my head and the possibility that we would have to live off the land. That only had its attractions as a military exercise and in the classroom. I was bedraggled, fearful, wet and afraid. I was discovering that fear both eats at you and hangs over you.

Lucy was awake. I signaled to her that we should leave. She nodded and smiled. She seemed fresh. While my face must have shown the fear I felt, hers only reflected hope and confidence.

We waded across the swamp to the road and started to walk. The moonlight gave good visibility. We had walked about half an hour when I got the same feeling I had in Philadelphia. We were being followed. But I could not see how. Every five minutes I turned around and looked, but there was no sign of anyone. Lucy made no comment, but I must have seemed deranged as I searched for a shadow I could not see.

Within an hour and a half we had arrived at the intersection with the road going to Simpsonville and fifteen minutes later we got to the road approaching from the north. So far we had not met anyone else. Since the roads were straight, we would have seen anyone coming in the either direction from a long way off and could have hid in a field or a wood. Although the feeling had not left me, I felt re-assured that if anyone was following I could have seen them.

It was apparent that my fear of being followed had begun to torment me. My instincts were now useless. Without them I would have been no more than an average cadet and a poor escapee.

As we approached Simpsonville I could see a sweeping bend in the road. It was the first bend we had come across. To our left was a plowed field, to our right woods. I thought that I heard voices coming towards us. I took Lucy's hand and we ran into the woods. No tree gave us complete shelter from the road. We dropped to the ground and hid behind two trees. Again we were exposed. If this was the Patrol, we had no chance. This wood was not dense. Dogs and horses could run through it easily.

I could hear a man's voice. I expected to hear a second making a conversation, but I heard only one. I guessed it was two hundred yards away. The voice was not moving. The man must have stopped and he was reading aloud. I could not make out the words. I looked east towards where the sun would be rising and could see the purple line of light on the horizon. The man resumed walking. The words were indistinct. His voice sounded like a preacher's.

Finally I could hear that he was reading from a Bible. By then our chances of reaching the safe house before sun up had disappeared. We had to stay still until he passed. The thought of another day without food or shelter filled me with dread. I looked around and could see little cover from the woods. It was too late to return to the swamp. We were exposed.

The preacher would walk twenty five yards, stop and then read from his Bible. When he was seventy yards from us he stopped again. I could see that he was wearing a preacher's hat and a long black broadcloth coat and at last I could recognize the words. He was reading from the Book of Exodus, the part where God punished Pharaoh for not letting the Israelites go. He read five verses and then he intoned: "The house of Egypt is no longer safe." He closed the book and walked on.

I now knew why I had to approach Simpsonville from that particular road at that exact time. It was so we could receive messages from the preacher. The message was as simple as it was unwelcome. The safe house was compromised.

I ran out to him. Lucy followed. As we approached he looked at us with sadness in his eyes. "So you are the young man," he said to me. He then took off his hat to Lucy and smiled like a welcoming host at a party.

"The house was raided yesterday afternoon. They didn't find anything. The people who were to take you in think they are still being watched. Field's Patrol watches suspect houses for weeks on end."

I sighed with relief for them and despair for us. There was to be no respite. I had slept a little in Dorsey's swamp, but it had not refreshed me and I started to feel the dull ache of exhaustion.

Lucy's face contained only hope. We would have to take the route west to Frederick and then north to Hagerstown, which would be our first stop. To get there we would have to manage without supplies and keep moving.

The preacher put a hand into his coat pocket and pulled out a piece of paper. "I was given this by a man you know. I was told to hand it to you if the house was compromised."

I snatched the paper from him and studied it. It was a map. It was in a different hand to the Birdwatcher's, more detailed and was cleverly drawn. I ignored both Lucy and the preacher as I tried to make out the codes within it and the secrets it might give me. I studied it for a full minute and gradually became conscious of the preacher watching me as I was absorbed in the details of the map.

"He means to say thank you and you're a good man," Lucy said to the preacher. "That's what he means to say to you. He's sorry he's forgotten how to be polite and thank people for their help."

I felt myself flushing to the roots of my hair.

"I'm sorry," I stammered. "I needed to look at the map."

Lucy was about to speak. I knew she was about to reproach me directly, just as Maud had occasionally when my direct concentration, on what I saw as a job in hand, made me rude to people. Instead it was the preacher who spoke first.

"Bless you both and be free." He then turned back towards Simpsonville.

I covered my embarrassment by looking around and at the map. It provided directions from a starting point marked on the road at about where it curved to a spot a mile deeper into the woods. After half an hour we arrived at the small clearing shown on the sketch. A large bag was on the ground. In it was a cooking pot, bread, sweet potatoes and chicken. There was also a smaller bag. I opened it and took out the contents and handed them to Lucy.

There was small key with a hollow round base, its business end was in the shape of a small hollow octagon. There were two small clasp knives. Then a blade four inches long with no handle but a round coin-like butt end.

"Is that all?" Lucy asked.

"I think so."

"Give it to me."

I passed her the bag and she rooted round the bottom of it and finally came up with a needle and thread.

"Give me the blade."

I passed it to her. She then sat down on the ground and cut an inch from the stitching on the hem of her dress.

"What you doing?"

"Watch."

She then pushed the four inch blade into the hollow of her hem.

"Keep the key in your shoe," she said.

I put the key into my shoe and felt for my ankle knife. It was so much part of me that I had forgotten it was there.

She sewed the blade into the hem of her dress and picked up the two clasp knives.

"One for me and one for you," she said. I put the knife into my pocket.

"How did you know about the needle and thread?" I asked.

"You hadn't looked thoroughly so I checked. Now what have we got here?" she said looking at the contents of the larger bag.

It looked like two days supplies. We were hungry, but Lucy took just a small portion of sweet potato and chicken.

"How many days travel have we got?" she asked.

"Ten days ," I replied. I was guessing. Our objective was Hagers-

town in the most northern part of Maryland. The landmarks I had figured out were small towns on the way. First we were to go past Clarksville and head west towards Neelsville and then we were to shadow
the road to Frederick. After Frederick, we were to travel northwest
to Hagerstown. The terrain was uncertain. Some roads I thought we
could take. However good the maps were, I could not tell how sticky
the ground would be when we were off the road.

"We eat the chicken today and save the rest," she said.

I showed our route to Lucy, drawing a map as I did so on the back of
the paper the preacher had given us. We were sitting on a thick fallen
tree branch.

"You remember all that?" she asked.

"Yes. I learned to remember maps in Mahan and Weir's classes."

"I am so glad you went there."

"Why?"

"So you can remember maps," she said laughing. Her laugh was
always soft, but this was silent. Her eyes flashed in humor at me as she
said it. There had always been a certain watchfulness or tension about
Lucy, even when we were alone talking about my time at school. But
now tension seemed to be leaving her. Her shoulders relaxed.

Then I explained the plan. We were to got to a safe house in Hagerstown, then, after a change of clothes, take the train, as master and
servant, to Cincinnati. We would both go south to Ripley in Ohio,
where there was the Rawlins House. I could leave Lucy there and then
go south to Lexington Kentucky to collect Brushes and then Brushes
and I would meet Lucy in Ripley and then we would go on to Canada.

I had discussed this plan with Tracker. We had both agreed that
Lucy should stay at the Rawlins House, which was as safe as any safe
house in Ohio and wait for Brushes and me there.

"I want to go to Lexington," she said.

"It's too risky, you'll be safe in Ripley," I said.

She did not reply. I sensed that she did not want to stay in Ripley
whilst I went south to Lexington for Brushes and was looking for a
way to say so.

186

She put her hands up, covered her eyes and rubbed her face. We could have been sitting in the parlor at the Ruffin plantation, or talking where she did the washing. I looked at my watch. It was nine o' clock in the morning.

"We sleep here today," I said. "Then we shall do our first eight miles at night, which should take us Clarksville. There are some woods near Clarksville and we'll stop there."

"No swamps?" she said, her eyes shining.

"No. Just the Hawlings River as we go towards Neelville. But that should be low. Now we need to sleep, One of us sleeps and the other keeps watch. Do you want to sleep first?"

"No. I'm too excited."

"Wake me up in four hours." I said and handed her my watch. "You should be ready to sleep by then."

I wanted to apologize for being rude to the preacher. When Maud had upbraided me I used to sulk and retreat to a defensive defiance. That I did not know how to apologize to Lucy was the least of it. I felt a pang as I realized I had lost the years she could have parented me.

Exhaustion seemed to drain me. I felt I was being watched but that could only mean that my sixth sense was deserting me, just when I needed it.

"Son," she said.

Her face was alight. This was the first time she had called me that. These were her first moments of freedom when we could talk and I felt their enormity.

"I can call you 'Mother' now," I said.

"I've waited so long for this," she said.

"You waited so you can sit in a clearing after two nights in a swamp?" I was trying to disguise what I felt as her words hit home. The tears in my eyes gave me away and she held out her arms for me.

We held each other close and then I lay down to sleep, trying to get the sound of Tracker's scream out of my mind. At least, I thought, I had not heard a shot and he might be alive. Though I could not summon words to say to Lucy, I felt joy through my exhaustion as she stroked my brow.

Thirty-four

When I woke, I reached for the water bottle. As I rinsed my mouth I reflected that there was so much that I wanted to ask Lucy, but the urgency of our flight and my exhaustion had prevented it. The feeling of being watched had left me. Sleep had done its work.

I looked around for Lucy. I could not see her. The bag of food lay where we had left it. I closed my eyes in case I could "see" her in my mind's eye. I could not. A sinking feeling hit my stomach. I had lost Tracker. Now Lucy must been taken as I slept.

I walked in wider and wider circles looking for tracks. Just thirty yards from where I had slept, I saw some logs stacked as if ready for a fire. Leading from there were two sets of feet, both small, going up a ridge. I oriented myself to where the food was and where I had slept and noted that direction in my mind following the footsteps up to the top of the ridge. Whoever had taken Lucy had done so quickly and silently. I cursed myself for not following my instincts about being watched and not having Lucy sleep first.

At the top of the ridge there was a drop down into a punchbowl and two people sat opposite one another in the base of the punchbowl. One was Lucy, who was facing me. The other had his back to me. I could only see a green-grey jacket and black cap. The jacket gave excellent camouflage in the woods. They were talking intently and looked to be talking as friends, but I could think of no one who could be friendly to us in that county. Tracker had repeated Professor Mahan's advice to me that to stay alive in the field you must assume that nothing is as it seems. I reached for the ankle knife.

"Put the knife away," the figure said in a voice I would recognize all my life, whatever disguise she wore. Nothing was as it seemed. It was Grace.

I walked towards them.

"What are you doing here?" I asked.

"Following you."

"So it was you."

"You were real jumpy."

"Because I was being followed."

"Tracker told me you could tell."

"You're not supposed to be in the field. How long have you been down here?"

"Not long," Grace said. "I had worries about the safe house and cleared it out before it was raided and followed you after you met the preacher. I took Lucy here for a talk."

"Did she tell you about Tracker?"

Lucy nodded. I felt nothing but despair.

"I'm so sorry," I said.

"From what Lucy told me, there was nothing you could have done."

"I've lost Tracker. It was my fault, going on when they were waiting."

Grace listened as I told her of Tracker's sensing the Patrol and my insisting on continuing.

"There was always the chance they'd be there," Grace said.

"I'm sorry," I said again.

"Quiet, Son. Tracker can look after himself. He's my best man."

"I lost him."

"No you didn't. Tracker always knows exactly what he's doing. You've got away. The best thing you can do for him is to make sure you get your Mama to freedom."

Her words did not make me feel better.

"If I know Horton Field," Grace said, "he'll get those Stimson boys from Lynchburg after you, which is why I got you to meet them. I've arranged for my precious Ellen to give you a set of clothes when you next see her."

"Ellen Emerson?"

"Yes, Ellen, young soldier. She's stuck on you."

I blushed. Lucy smiled. Grace laughed.

"Well," said Grace. "I guess you're stuck on her. She's one of my best people."

Grace then turned to Lucy. "My sister was called Vallie when she disappeared, she's the same age as your mother, Sally."

Tears came to Lucy's eyes. Her face showed not sadness but hope and a longing. Grace continued. "I'll go look for her. The drawing you gave me is pretty good."

There was silence between us. I had heard from Tracker about the sister Grace had been looking for since she started her branches of the Railroad. Then Grace spoke.

"This boy'd better get back to West Point when he's done."

"Where're you going?" I said.

"First east to get sighted. That should take some pressure off you. They'd rather capture me than you. My reward's still fifteen thousand dollars. They'll chase me for a while and you can get clear. Meet me in Philadelphia when you've got Lucy free. We can talk about Tracker then. Meantime just go on. You did the best you could and think how good Tracker is. He's been in worse places before"

Grace's calm optimism was reassuring. The loss of Tracker would never leave me. But, right then, I remembered how good Tracker was. Maybe he was okay after all.

Grace got up. Lucy rose with her. Grace held out her arms. Lucy fell into them and clutched Grace. She could scarcely hold herself up as Grace held her tightly.

"Don't worry, child," said Grace. "This is part of a long road for me, but the start of a new one for you." Grace's voice was light, but I saw tears running down her cheeks as Lucy heaved with emotion in her arms.

"You take care of your Mammy," Grace said to me. Her face was covered with tears, but her voice carried command. "Then you go back to West Point, you hear?"

"I want to help the Railroad."

"I want you to be a soldier, so go back. You can best help us as a soldier."

By this time Lucy had left Grace's embrace and was standing beside her. Then Lucy said, "I want you to be a soldier too."

"I thought you'd quit the road," I said to Grace, trying to change the subject.

"So did I child," said Grace. "So did I. Now y'all had better get going. You remember Patrick's maps Jack. Thank him when you next see him."

"Yes Ma'am," I said.

"Your Mama tells me you don't say thank you."

I blushed in embarrassment.

"You got the knives and the key?"

"Yes. What's the key for?"

"In case you get caught. Leg irons in these parts all use the same key."

I must have looked surprised.

"Yes, the same key from the same makers. They'd have too many different keys otherwise."

Grace turned and walked away. I looked at Lucy.

"I guess we're equipped," I said.

Lucy nodded.

I looked back at Grace, but she had disappeared. I'd not looked away for long. This was uncanny. It was like she was a ghost that had evaporated. I tried to regain my composure by setting out the places we were to go to on the first part of our flight.

"Clarksville, Dayton, Laytonsville, Neelsville, Frederick and then Hagerstown," I said. They were all towns in Maryland. Hagerstown was where our night marches together would stop and we could take the train to Ohio.

We walked all night.

As we sat beside the fire after that night's march, with the sun coming up in the East, Lucy told her story as he had told it to Grace.

Thirty-five

Lucy Ruffin's Slave Narrative

I was born on a plantation in New Bern, North Carolina. My mother, Sally, worked as a farmhand and my elder brother and I, the Master's daughter, were the Master's property. Sally was half white and half black so that made me one quarter black. But I was still a slave and one of my of half brothers or my half sister, being white, if all went to plan, would inherit me.

The world in which I grew up did not acknowledge the blood tie. But, until I was old enough to go into the fields to work, I played with all my brothers and sisters.

When I was ten or eleven years old the difference between the kin with black blood and the kin without it came home to me. You would have thought that the differences in our existence, like living in the quarters as opposed to the main house, would have upset me, but they did not. It was the difference in learning which did. Slaves were not supposed to read and write.

At sundown one of my brothers came to the quarters to play "Patty Rollers" with me and he told me about his lessons. I asked him if I could learn from him what he was taught and he agreed and started to teach me.

After each Patty Rollers game my white brother Ben, and I would spend fifteen minutes with his reading book.

It was then that I first had the dreams.

There was nothing scary about them. Sally had the dreams too, but *hers were more intense. My visions involved being able to see what members of my family were doing and where they were at any particular time. What would happen was that I would lie down and close my eyes and think of my family member I wanted to know about.*

I first discovered this gift when I was ill and wanted my mother to come to me. I was alone and scared. I had a high temperature and felt sick. I shouted for Sally. But it was late afternoon in the summer time so she was in the fields and far away from the slave quarters. The quarters were about one hundred yards from the main house, so nobody heard me there. Besides I did not want anyone from the main house to come to me. I wanted my mother.

I had thought of my mother before at different times in my childhood. Up to then I thought she came to me by chance. I had got used to the idea that when I thought of Sally I would see her in the flesh.

I saw where she was in the fields. As she looked up, she stopped hoeing her row of cotton. There was no overseer where she was working and she was able to stand still without being noticed. I felt that she knew I was calling to her.

"Mom, come to me I'm too hot," were words that came into my head. She had stopped a fever of mine before. She was able to make medicine. I saw her put down her hoe and then walk away from the quarters. This disturbed me because she was going away from me.

"No Mom, come to me, I'm hot." I called out.

I then saw my mother stop, look up and call out, "I must get the medicine first." She walked towards her plot and picked some herbs and turned back towards the slave quarters.

When she got back to about where she left her hoe, Joe the overseer, who had by then got to near where she had been working, called to her. "What are you doing Sally? Sundown's not for a while," he shouted to her from fifty yards away.

She did not break stride. "Lucy's ill. I must nurse her with these plants," she replied. Her firm tone meant Joe should not try to stop her.

In my vision I followed her progress almost to the door of the quarters when the vision stopped and she walked in and I opened my eyes to see her.

"Mom, I called you."

"I know, that's why I am here, child." she replied. She did not go to me immediately. She took the herbs and pounded them with the pestle and mortar and then added water and put the medicine into a cup. She had done this every time I was ill.

As she was preparing the medicine, I said, "Mom, I thought that Joe was going to stop you."

"Why you say that?" she replied.

"I saw you stop hoeing after I called you and go to the patch for the medicine and as you walked to the quarters he called to you and you told him you were going to nurse me with the plants. I saw it all with my eyes shut."

As I was saying that, she mixed the pounded herbs and water in the cup for me to drink.

"You got the gift too Lucy. You can see when you're not there like I can." she said. "Drink this. Tonight I'll tell you about the gift. Meantime you tell no one, you hear?"

I drank the medicine. My mother returned to the fields and I fell into a deep sleep, which must have been where the medicine sent me.

I slept the whole night and most of the following day. It was in the evening of the next day before Sally could talk about what she called 'the gift' and I called 'the visions'. She had them since she was eight years old. Her mother told her about hers much as Sally told me. You think hard about someone in a quiet place and then sometimes, only sometimes, you get to see where they are and what they are doing. I don't get them much now I'm grown.

"Just you and I know about this," Sally said to me. "Nobody here else knows I can do this. You tell no one or they get frightened of you or you get sold."

It did not take me long to see that I could learn to read by attending Ben's classes in my visions. You can imagine what it was like for such a young girl to become part of what your brother was doing and what his classes were learning was exciting. The first time it happened, Ben was learning "I am", "He is" and "You are". He sat with his brother

194

and sister beside his mother in the big room at the main house learning the letters as well as the words. I concentrated through the whole of the lesson, so when Ben came to play "Patty Rollers" and teach me afterwards, I knew what the lesson was about. I was a quick learner.

Sally warned me again I had to keep the visions to myself. It would scare people. It would scare Ben and his father the Master. It would not be possible to know how they would act if they learned about my gift.

We talked on the plantation about being sold "down the river". It had happened to people on other plantations, but nobody had been sold on ours. Next door the mistress of the house told her maid, Alicia, that she had better behave because "I can put you in my pocket." She meant that she could sell her and put the money she got in her pocket.

We heard what the mistress had said from Alicia herself who was walking out with one of our field hands. Alicia would visit him on Sundays and at Christmas. She asked what her mistress meant and Sally told her. It was a frequently used expression with some slaveholders.

Alica did not want to be sold away from the people she knew and her family and promised to behave, but all it did was make her frightened because she did not think that she had done anything which could be seen as misbehavior. She worried about what she had said and done. It caused her to sit with Sally on a Sunday and describe her days to check that she had not misbehaved so as to be sold away.

I knew that might happen if I scared Ben or anyone about the visions.

The summer after the coming of the visions, I was put to work in the fields. I was eleven years old and large for my age. I had broad shoulders and the overseer thought that I could work rather than spend my days running around the plantation with the other children.

The start of work did not alter my routine with Ben. After Patty Rollers the reading and writing lessons would begin. Writing involved Ben smuggling in paper and ink into the slave quarters.

I knew how difficult it was for Ben to learn, since I saw his lessons. I made sure that I was as slow as he was after I saw how upset he became at the speed I had learned.

Having the gift helped in the Patty Rollers game. If Ben went off

195

to hide and I was with the others trying to find him, I could split off from the other children, go to a quiet place and see where he was. Then I could suggest that the team looked in the place where he was hiding and Ben would be found.

After a few games I could see that Ben was getting discouraged because he was always caught before anyone else. Revealing Ben's whereabouts was doubly unfair because Ben's hiding places were clever and much more inventive than the others.

After five games when Ben was caught quickly, I could see how upset he was and I knew he would stop playing. So I stopped cheating at Patty Rollers and Ben won again. Ben was a good player. You had to catch the "Scaper", that is an escaped slave, and bring him home. That involved someone hiding anywhere on the plantation or on the adjoining one and then the group had to find him. There were barns and ditches and when the cotton and tobacco plants were high there was plenty of cover in the fields. So we usually managed to catch just one "Scaper" each time we played, which was from Spring to Winter every Wednesday.

What made me do it, I do not now know. I think it was because I knew I could do something nobody else could. After a while it was not enough that Sally knew and I could talk to her about it. I would have to tell Ben about the visions. Maybe it was a thank-you for him teaching me to read, maybe it was because I wanted to show Ben that he was good at Patty Rollers and he was caught a lot because of me being able to see where he was hiding rather than any fault of his. He had a lot of pride and was a good tracker. I just wanted someone else to know and for him to be impressed about what I could do.

I did not tell him that Sally could do it as well. I thought that it would be our secret. When I told Ben, he did not believe me.

"I saw your lesson and it was about paragraphs."

"You saw? Where were you?"

"Here, with my eyes shut."

"No you must have been under the schoolroom window. You heard my lesson. You shouldn't do that. Niggers are not supposed to learn these things. If my Pa finds out, I'll be in trouble and you'll be sold. Pa does not want you people learning to read."

I had not thought about being sold away if I learned to read, although I knew it would be trouble. I explained about closing my eyes and knowing where he was. He still did not believe me.

"You know when we played Patty Rollers and you kept getting caught?" I said.

"Yes, that was bad luck, nothing wrong with my hiding places and the trail finding was not good," he said.

Patty Rollers had two parts to it. One was hide and seek, the other was trail finding. You would look for footprints and broken twigs and plants to find the Scaper. Getting the Scaper meant you won, but you could still get points for the trail finding. Ben noticed that although he was caught, we did not find a lot of good trail clues.

"That was because I knew where you were. I shut my eyes and looked for you in my mind."

"No. You're dreaming Lucy," he said.

The argument went on and he did not believe me. The next time he had a lesson and I watched, again I told him what had happened in it and again he said that I must have been hiding outside the schoolroom window.

But then it was his turn to hide. You have to give the Scaper a start. Sometimes it was counted, sometimes it involved all of us walking round the near field if the Scaper had gone off in the other direction. Either way I had the chance to go to my hut and look for him in my mind.

I found him and then ran back to join the others, who were counting. Only the white people could count to one hundred. We had to follow their count, which was why we preferred the walk round the field. Ben had gone to the hayloft and was hiding at the top under a whole lot of hay. It was hard to climb up to the top. Nobody had done it before.

"I know where he is. He's in the hayloft." I called out.

The hayloft was in a barn, which was across the fields on the border between our plantation and that next door. That was so that both masters could share the barn. Because it was a distance away, they all shushed me and went looking elsewhere.

"He's in the hayloft", I kept saying as they looked in place after place and not finding any clues to his trail.

Finally Ben's younger brother Sam, said that we ought to look in the barn. When we got there, I shouted out that he was in the loft right at the back underneath some hay.

We found him.

Ben was upset. To be around the hayloft would be fine. But he was hiding in the roof and at the back and nobody had been there before except him. He had heard me shout out.

That was the last game of Patty Rollers that I played. Ben told his father about what I had said about the lessons and what had happened about the hayloft. Something told me that he would do that as he emerged from the hay. It may have been because he said nothing to me. He just looked at me as the others congratulated me on finding him. He climbed down from the loft ladder and walked through the fields to go home.

It was not the visions which did it for me. It was the reading and writing lessons, because Ben told his father about them and they found the paper and ink.

Sally was called to the house. Her scream could be heard throughout the whole of the plantation.

I felt that her terror had something to do with my telling Ben about the visions and the reading lessons. But I did not know for sure what it was about. I just heard Sally's screaming and then there was silence. She did not return to the slave quarters for a long time. It was dark. I did try to find out what had happened. I shut my eyes and concentrated and tried to find out where she was and therefore what was going on. But I could see nothing.

I had never seen my mother cry before. That she had screamed made me guilty and fearful at the same time. I did not know what would happen, but whatever it was, was enough to make my mother scream and I was responsible.

At the quarters there was silence. Nobody spoke. They all knew the scream came from Sally. Although they did not know exactly why, they thought it meant that she was to be sold. As they said that, I was silent. They tried not to look at me. I looked down, hoping that they would never know what I had done.

I lay down on the floor where I usually slept and waited. It was dark but my eyes were open and I was full of dread. I hoped that by lying down and pretending that nothing had happened, somehow it would turn out that nothing had happened.

"Lucy, get up." I heard Sally say.

I got up and followed her out of the hut. She walked away, towards the first field. She did not say a word, until she came to the bench where the overseers sat. There was no cloud in the sky, there was a full moon. We could see each other clearly.

"Sit Lucy," she said. "They're selling you."

"Why?"

"You know why, girl."

"The reading? Ben?" I asked.

She nodded slowly.

"When?"

"They are taking you tomorrow."

"I shouldn't have told him. I just wanted...."

She knew that I wanted to impress the boy. There was no point in saying anything more about that. She had only a short time to tell me what she needed to say.

So far as I had known up to then, Sally was brought up on a plantation in North Carolina. Nobody discussed any other life. The life on the plantation seemed the only life there was. But she explained she was born the free daughter of a free maid in Boston. She was five years old living near some wharves. Her name was not Sally. She no longer remembered it except she knew that it rhymed with 'Sally'. Her older sister, Aysie, was about ten years old.

Her memory was sketchy of her life as a free person. But she did remember the end of it. It was a Sunday. Aysie was at a friend's house.

Sally wanted to be there too, but she was told she was too small and had to stay home. She wanted to see Aysie and her friend. Quietly, and without being noticed, she went out into the street and started walking to her sister's friend's house. She was the only black face on the street and people were looking at her.

She smelled the dirt in a man's hand as it went around her face stopping her scream. She was lifted up and put into a buggy and then passed from coach to coach with bewildering speed. She was paralyzed with fear. She tried to scream, but was hit hard in her face and told to shut up.

The journey from Boston to Wilmington, North Carolina, was terrifying. Again and again she called out for her mother. In the cart there were two other children of her age, a boy and a girl and a man and a woman, both in their thirties. All wore leg irons. Even five year old Sally.

She did not tell me how she was sold off the block in Wilmington North Carolina and how she ended up at the plantation in New Bern. It must have been to spare my feelings.

"I was kidnapped," my mother said to me. "You will be free one day. But now they are selling you away." I did not know what she meant when she said that I would be free one day. I did not think it possible.

Suddenly my mother started to sob. It was not the blood curdling scream that I had heard a few hours before. It was just a quiet sob of sadness and pain.

I felt nothing, except the tears on my cheeks and my mother's embrace as she held me in her arms to her. I knew I was going away, but I did not know where. Some place far from Sally and my friend Ben.

"I'll – watch – for - you." my mother said through the tears. Each word was separated by an uncontrollable sob. I knew what she meant and nodded even as she held me. I said nothing in reply. I wanted to say that I would watch for her too. But I did not have to.

The sobbing stopped. I came out of her embrace and she said, "I know you will."

"I asked that they sell you to the North. They want niggers who can read up there more than down South, I told them they would get a better price. Promise me one thing"

"What?" I asked.

"Just remember what this place is like. One day someone will ask you to draw it on paper and you'll need to remember it. If you do that I'll see you again. Remember the house, the barns, the fields, everything."

And I did.

Perhaps Sally's master, in seeing that all slaves who learned to read would be sold away, thought that some mercy could be shown and that I should be sold north. I shall never know. But I made the drawing exactly as Sally asked me to do and kept it with me, hidden in my clothes.

Thirty-six

By the time Lucy finished, we were both exhausted. She from the telling for the second time. Me from its horror. We sat in silence. The sun was high. The fire had burned itself out.

"What happened to the drawing?"

"I gave it to Grace. I can't talk any more."

Lucy's face was crumpled. I felt hollow and tried to speak. Eventually I did, but my voice sounded strangled. I wanted to ask about her journey north but instead was only able to say, "I'll keep watch."

Lucy's face changed when I said that. Her smile lit up the day and the look of defeat and loss disappeared and she made up a bed from leaves and moss.

I climbed up a look-out tree. I could see Clarksville. A small sleepy village that did not know that there were runaways waiting for the night to fall; two people on their way to Kentucky. To Woodburn and to Brushes before swinging back north to freedom. I had, by then, realized that I would not be able to talk Lucy out of going to Woodburn with me and I would not be able to persuade her to wait in a safe house.

* * *

Dogs.

They are a distance away. I cannot not guess how far away they are. My ears are not working. Are they one mile away or two? I do not

202

know. I am sweating. My brow needs mopping. I look for Lucy. She is behind me. She smiles at me. I am re-assured. Maybe there are no dogs after all. If there were, she would hear them. We cannot outrun dogs over a long stretch if they have picked up our scent. Maybe we should run for the river.

The Hawlings River. That's the place to go. If we cross before the dogs see us, then we'll be clear and the river will wipe out our scent.

"We've got to run on to the river," I say to Lucy. She has the same determined look in her eye she had when we ran through the corn-field. This time the terrain is easier. We almost float over it. But the dogs are near. There are four of them. I can hear, just like Tracker. He can even know how tall someone is from their tread. I can hear them getting closer.

I can see Grace's face in front of me. I see the sadness in her eyes and can hear her laugh. We run on. The dogs are in a pack but one is faster than the rest and is ahead of the others.

The river has branches sticking out just south of Unity. If we get there we can do a double cross and the dogs will have a problem. That means running south east towards Brookeville. I can see the map in front of me as we run.

We run towards Brookeville. My ribs hurt, my lungs are heaving. The Hawlings river makes a noise and the wind is coming from it. Lucy runs on. Nothing is going to stop her.

Lucy is half way across the river. It is at medium torrent. If you lose your footing you could be swept down river. I float downstream so the dogs will not pick up the scent directly on the other side. I am shivering in the cold of the river and am sweating. I feel like something is mopping my brow and I push it out of the way.

The lead dog is within fifty yards of me. The others are about three hundred yards behind. I look behind me and see two people. One is running just behind the dogs and one is standing at the top of the ridge training his rifle in my direction. I swim downstream. I look back and the dog is almost at the river. Lucy is as exposed as me but near the other side.

"Go on," I shout to her. Where I get the breath to shout, I do not know. Again I feel something touching my brow and push it away.

I have to stay behind and slow the chase for Lucy. But even if I manage to fight the lead dog, the others will follow and their master will catch us, and if the man with the rifle is a half decent shot I'll be killed by him. It's strange he hasn't shot before. Maybe he prefers the dogs to do his work.

The lead dog jumps into the river. It's a much faster swimmer than me and I can hear it growl as it swims. It swims across me and before I know it. It's facing me. I think it's either going to get me in the water or on the other side. But then I see there is no need for that. It's in front of me. The others will follow and I'll be trapped. But the dogs attacking me give Lucy a start. I must fight as long as possible.

"Run." I shout at Lucy. If I could kill at least one dog, I then at least the others might think twice or at least be slowed in their chase for her.

Lucy is on the shore. She hesitates.

"Run," I shout again. "Run for me."

She runs. I swim towards the lead dog and it paddles back, growling. Then I hear the splash of the other dogs jumping into the river.

A voice calls from the distance. It comes from where the gunman is standing.

"Call your dogs off or I'll shoot them." It's an eerie voice. Slightly disembodied as it reverberates in the moonlight. The dogs behind me get closer. The dog in front looked relaxed. He's done this before.

"You're not hearing me, call 'em off or I shoot," the eerie voice shimmers across the water. I feel like something is licking my brow yet the dog has not got to me yet.

The lead dog bares its teeth and moves towards me as the others get even closer. The lead dog is in front of me and the others are behind. I swim sideways but the lead dog follows sideways. I stand no chance. Something is touching my brow again and I push it away again. The dogs have not got to me yet. I see Lucy's face come into view. I must be hallucinating. My teeth are chattering. The cold is killing me.

A shot rings out. In the small space of one yard between me and the lead dog there's a "plop".

"Call 'em off," the disembodied voice says.

There are four dogs behind me and one in front. The shooter has missed. Then a shot ring out again and the lead dog's head becomes a sea of red.

"Call'em off or I kill the rest."

A high pitched whistle pierces the night-time and the four remaining dogs turn back. The lead dog floats down the river leaving a trail of blood like a shooting star in reverse.

"Go on," I shout hoping Lucy will hear. "Go on for me," and I black out.

I think I must have pulled myself up onto the shore as I woke up, exhausted, with Lucy mopping my brow which is dripping with sweat. I sit up and look for the river. There is no river. We are outside Clarksville under the look out tree.

"It's okay," I hear Lucy say and I black out again.

* * *

I could feel my clothes were wet with sweat. My mouth tasted like Dorsey's swamp. I tried to sit up but fell back. I tried again and was just starting to fall back again when Lucy's hand stopped my fall.

"Sit up," Lucy said. "You've been down for two nights."

It was sun up. Lucy had that look people had when they were trying to appear as if they were not worried. I felt weak, my tongue was dry and big in my mouth.

"The dogs?" I said, through a sore throat. I still had a temperature and felt dizzy.

"There were no dogs Jack. Just a lot of dreams and a lot of sweating."

"Did I talk?" I asked.

"You shouted like a proper young Master. You said: 'Run' a lot."

"We were being chased by dogs."

"You got a fever, Son. Must have caught it in the swamp."

My teeth were chattering.

"I'm thirsty Mama."

Lucy picked up the water bottle and handed it to me.

"Just take two sips," she said.

I took the two sips and handed the bottle back to her.

"Now I'm going to make something."

Lucy picked up some leaves, which were in a small heap beside her, and tore them into small pieces, dropping them into the water bottle. She then put the top on the bottle and shook it.

"Now you drink this bottle dry," she said.

I drank what must have been half a pint of water tasting of mint and almonds.

"This is something my Mama taught me and I'll teach you after you're better. If your men get ill in the field, you can mend them. Now you'll sleep and when you wake up you'll not be hitting anyone trying to mop your sweaty brow."

When I awoke the sun was setting and the fever had gone. I saw that Lucy was sitting under a tree ten yards away rocking herself back and forth with her eyes shut and singing quietly to herself. I could not make out the words. They were not English and I had not heard the tune or anything like it before.

I stood up and felt as alert and fit as I thought I was before the fever came. Lucy stopped singing.

"Medicine worked then?" Lucy said.

"It did."

"Hungry?"

"No."

"Good. We need to go. You won't be hungry until tonight. We'll have lots of breaks as we go."

"Lucy...Mama. Thank you."

Through the night we had whispered talks as we rested between short bursts of running and quick walking. I spoke of my schooldays and my friends in Boston, about growing up and learning.

The following night, she talked of her sale from Fleming after Brushes was sent to Kentucky. She had kept a Bible in her pocket, the one she felt for as she was dragged away to be sold to Neil's order. On arrival at Fleming's she had been given a spare dress to wear.

No one told her that the housekeeper picked up laundry from the quarters on Thursdays. Lucy's old dress was in the quarters. The Bible was in it. The Bible was discovered and Lucy was sent to Campbell's for sale.

"We planned to leave Fleming at the first full moon. Then Master Fleming sent him to Kentucky," she whispered as we rested up. "We weren't going to stay down south after we left the Ruffins. There was no point any more."

I knew the point of her staying was me and I was overwhelmed at its enormity.

"It's okay," Lucy said. "We wouldn't have had it any other way."

"We?"

"Brushes and I. We saw you grow up. You're free, son. That's all we ever wanted."

I was about to speak.

"You never have to thank me for that. I'd do it again."

I could not speak and instead got up and we walked on.

Daybreak was an hour away when I saw the shadow in the distance.

It was a shape I had not seen before and did not expect. It looked as if a bridge was crossing the road, but I knew that there were no bridges in this part of Maryland going over these roads. The moon was up and the shadow became larger and larger as we approached.

I pointed at it. We were a good two or three hundred yards away, yet the shadow was becoming more and more distinct. It was as if someone was holding something over the road.

It was still, black in the darkness and less and less obscure as we approached. Lucy was the first to recognize what it was. She stopped, turned away from me and was sick.

The noise she made carried in the night. I wanted to ask her if she was all right, but it was obvious she was not. She stopped walking and turned away. I walked on and the shape became more and more distinct.

When I was one hundred yards away, the only thing which prevented me from throwing up was disbelief. Then I froze. The body, which was hanging from a tree, had been there at least a week. The smell was unbearable. I looked at the clothes. They were horseman's clothes. But they were shredded, as if cut to ribbons by someone with the skill to make sure they stayed on and the cutting did not make any of them fall off or pierce the skin. Then I looked at his back and saw slash marks on each shoulder, caked in blood. The head was a mass of bruises. It was difficult to make anything out about the face except that the ears had been cut off.

The legs were held together with leg irons. The thigh to the right was gashed and the trousers were soaked with blood. It was a neat cut, almost surgical. Given the amount of blood which caked the trousers, the man had bled out before he was hung. The hanging was for show.

I climbed the tree and, with the knife which was strapped to my ankle, I cut him down. There was a poster pinned to his back, which I had missed when I had first seen the gashes in the shoulder.

The torture must have been long, with slash after slash making no cut to the chest as the runaway wondered when blood would be drawn. Whether he felt the blood on his back before he saw the blood to the cut to his leg or the other way round, there was no way of knowing.

From the bleeding to his head, it was clear that the ears had been cut off before he had died. It was almost by reflex that I pulled his mouth open. As I did so, his head fell to the side and the ears came out.

This was a lesson, more terrible than Norbert's by a Patrol, which enjoyed its savage work, giving a slow death of fear and blood and a sight to all who passed by.

I pulled the body to the side of the road and turned it over to look at the poster. In large letters made indistinct by blood and dirt, it said 'RUNUWAYE'.

As I looked at the poster, Lucy stood beside me, shaking.

"We must bury him Mama," I said.

We had no spade, but we did have urgency, fear and hatred. We made a shallow grave with our hands and covered him over with earth, moss, leaves and tree branches. To this day I am haunted by the hanging figure. At evening times when I walk in the woods, I look at the trees, hoping that I see no such shape again, but fearing this outline or that shadow will show me another body and another trophy of a skilled sadist carving away at a man paralyzed by helpless fear. Until then I had seen the woods as a place of shelter. A place to hide. Now, to me and forever, they are a place of shapes and nightmare.

After the burial, we speeded up. I sensed more urgency in Lucy and that was transmitted to me. I had planned eight hour marches, but she now insisted that we go for a full twelve and eat into the daytime. When the sun was up one of us slept and the other kept look-out. My sleep was interrupted with nightmares about the Patrol. Occasionally when I was look-out I saw that Lucy's sleep was disturbed and it felt like her nightmares were the same as mine.

It seemed each day gave us less sleep and more fear and exhaustion. At night we ran, then walked, then ran. There was no 'safe house' until Hagerstown.

Thirty-seven

Hagerstown, the paper capital of Maryland, was our transfer point. It was from there that we could go to Cincinnati and then Lexington.

We were greeted at the safe house by a man who identified himself as Neville. He gave us a change of clothes. There was a parcel waiting for me. It contained a gun. It was my father's. 'Neville' told me it was a present, from a Boston doctor,

I did not believe the householder was called Neville and nor did he believe that the gun came from a Boston doctor. Whether it was Ellen or Tracker who had arranged it, I did not know. If it was Ellen, then she knew our route. If it was Tracker, I felt keenly that was the last bit of fixing he had done before that awful night at the Robinson's farm.

"You both look exhausted," Neville said.

"When's the next train to Cincinnati?" I replied.

"Half an hour," Neville said.

We had been up all night and had scarcely slept for the previous four days. Whether it was exhaustion or urgency I was keen to take that train. I looked at Lucy whose eyes flashed in assent.

"We'll take that one." I said. The need for speed pressed into me. My fever had slowed us and I remembered Tracker's advice: "You can't out-run a wire."

I feared that Fleming would probably send someone to take Brushes back to Baltimore after Lucy's sale or maybe after her escape, or he might have sold him in Lexington. I had these fears throughout our flight overland but kept them to myself. For no reason at all the fears came back to the forefront of my mind and I must have looked as preoccupied when looking at the map which the preacher gave me.

"He means, 'thank you'," Lucy said to Neville. "He means 'thank you'. He's forgotten his manners."

I stuttered an embarrassed "thank you" and we left for the station. No one had followed us in our marches through the nights and, whilst we had been seen in the street on the way to the safe house, there had been no particular attention given to us. I took it to mean that we looked like people from the shift from the paper mill. Our clothes were ragged, my shoes broken and Lucy's bare feet bleeding but we had fitted right into the dawn chorus of early risers.

Now we departed for the station, dressed as master and servant and unrecognizable from the bedraggled couple who had snuck in the back door of the nondescript house.

We looked conspicuous and I made Lucy hurry, ordering her in a preemptory way, but only succeeded in drawing further attention to us and getting a gathering feeling of being chased.

There were four carriages to the train to Cincinnati. As we stood waiting for the train, the crowd of passengers gathered and I saw a someone at the edge of a group waiting for the train. Coat, dress, bonnet familiar. Figure demure and alone. My heart jumped.

I looked straight ahead, trying to ignore her and gave no more attention to the crowd beside us. The engine whistled and chuntered slowly into the station. I looked back and could not see the woman, who had slipped from view.

Instead, I saw Jess, Wade and James Stimson. They were thirty yards away. The train had stopped and people were getting on. I pressed Lucy to climb up into the carriage. She sensed my anxiety and climbed the steps, one hand holding the rung, the other my suitcase.

I was about to follow her, when I looked again and saw Jess Stimson waving at me. I waved back and climbed into the carriage. Flight was hopeless, I reckoned. I felt for the gun which was tucked into my belt.

I would have to play my part with Lucy as my servant, hoping that they had not got news of her escape and, more importantly, her description. I hoped the picture of her would be as bad as most runaway pictures. Then the hard and obvious thought came to me. They were sent to collect Brushes.

The Robinson farm had been a trap, but with more points of exit than the Smith family could cover. As far as I could see, this train had no escape route. Three patrollers and a runaway on a moving train were trapped. My first thought was that we'd have to jump or shoot our way out, that was impossible.

Once I was inside the carriage I looked down towards where the Stimsons had been waiting to get on and could see them in the crush of people. Jess waved. I waved back. He seemed friendly and excited. I tried to seem so too, as anxiousness and despair returned to me.

The carriage was elegant, with tables set with fine linen. I looked round for Lucy and saw she was already seated facing a woman travelling on her own. It was the woman whose coat, dress and bonnet were familiar. Somehow Ellen had managed to get to our part of the train without being seen.

"I'm Marylyn," the woman said. "I'm right pleased to meet you. Do you want to join us, sir?"

"Jack Ruffin, the pleasure's all mine."

"I was just saying to my Lucy here that this carriage is just fine and almost as good as the ones we have in Wilmington. Lucy will you be a dear and ask the trainman to come see me and bring my case."

Lucy looked at me alarmed.

"Well child, don't look at him." Ellen said and then looked at me herself. "These girls are so simple sometimes. Never mind dear, I'll have to do it. I'll just wait until the train gets moving and then I'll get my case. Will you join us sir. Now Lucy, you make space for this gentleman."

I looked down the carriage to where the Stimsons had got on.

"Excuse me Ma'am," I said. "I've just seen some friends."

"Don't y'all leave like that. We've just got acquainted"

"I'll come back, Ma'am," I said. "I promise."

Our only hope was for Ellen to travel with Lucy and for me to occupy the Stimsons.

Professor Weir and Tracker had both said to me that in the field you needed to improvise. In Tracker's case it was as part of the work of the Railroad. In Weir's case it was war. It felt like both as I walked down the carriage towards Jess, Wade and James Stimson.

They greeted me like a long lost brother. I ordered beer and we talked of snakes and horses. I said I was going to Lexington to look at horses. An inner voice told me not to mention Woodburn.

They spoke of their journey north. They had just got back to Lynchburg from Maryland, they said, when they got a wire to send them back north.

RETURN JOB LEXINGTON. ORDERS CINCINNATI. SOON-EST. FIELD.

"Quite a co-incidence," Jess said.

I could not judge whether Jess's smile, as he handed the wire for me to read, was menacing or merely felt so. Lucy's instincts were right. There had been no time to lose. The 'Return Job Lexington' had to be to take Brushes back to Baltimore after Lucy's escape.

Maybe I could out-run them, I wondered. I reckoned that if their orders in Cincinnati mentioned me, then they would wire the Patrol in Lexington. But however fast my horse, I could not out-run a wire. Yet, I wondered, why would their 'Orders' mention me? At least Lucy was safe with Ellen. If Ellen took Lucy to the safe house in Ripley, Ohio, I could bring Brushes there. Somehow I would have to get clear of the Stimsons and ride in the night.

The train ride was ten hours. I tried to think of what I could do if I could get back to Ellen and Lucy and at least explain things to them. But there was no way I could do so without compromising them. The Stimsons might know about Lucy's escape, but they would not suspect her as the servant accompanying Ellen unless they had a picture and it appeared they did not.

Thirty-eight

The early evening sun was still bright, as the train moved into Cincinnati, I felt desperate. I had been laughing and joking with the Stimsons and found my false amusement harder to summon. I tried to cat nap, but found it impossible. Fear and fatigue overwhelmed and exhausted me.

I wondered if it was they who were responsible for the death of the runaway who had been hung up and cut to ribbons. They had been in the area. They were the roving Patrol. It had to be them, I thought.

My eyes wandered towards the end of the carriage. I could make out the top of Ellen's head. As I stood up, it seemed like the rest of Ellen's carriage did too and I lost sight of her in the crowd.

"Do you have a case?" Jess asked.

I had brought one and Lucy had carried it.

"I left it back there," I said indicating in the direction of Lucy's carriage. I flushed as I said so. Gentlemen would not travel without a case, yet admitting to having one in the other carriage would endanger Lucy.

"Why don't you get it and then come with us. We're all going to Lexington. We might ride together," Jess said. His voice was friendly. I searched for menace in it but felt none. Exhaustion was taking its toll, I thought.

I thought I could say that the case had been stolen. It had a change of clothes for Lucy and me and nothing else of value. It was a stage

214

prop of no practical use, except that Lucy's clothes would look strange if the case was opened in front of anyone.

I looked out of the carriage window. If the train was full, the station was even more crowded. People were waving at the train as it halted and shouting. It was a carnival atmosphere, which was strange for an evening train. It gave me hope for the 'lost' suitcase story as being credible.

"Hey, it's crazy out there. We'll wait here for you."

As I walked towards the carriage where the suitcase may or may not have been I realized that there was nothing I could do except go along with the Stimsons. Whilst I realized that I could cheerfully kill them, the carnival in Cincinnati made that impossible.

The suit case had disappeared. I turned around to go back to the Stimsons with the news of the theft of my case when I saw a black one on the floor of the carriage near where Ellen had sat. The scuffs and wear and tear of my father's 'Court Case', as he called it, were familiar as were the hand tooled initials 'JR'. I picked it up and hurried back to where the Stimsons were waiting. It was heavy.

We walked together towards the station entrance, pushing through the crowd. When we got outside I saw flags and bunting and the reason for the crowd. It was the opening of the Cincinnati to Lexington railway and they were waiting for the Lexington train.

The telegraph office was close to the station and Jess went in. I was trapped, but Lucy and Ellen had escaped.

Wade, James and I waited outside. This was the moment they would get their information. As we waited, it seemed like a burden had been lifted from my shoulders. Lucy was not with me. This might be Field's mobile Patrol, but the connection between Brushes and me must have been tenuous to the Stimsons. If I went with them, I could stop them bringing Brushes back in chains. I could kill them en route, unless they killed me.

Jess emerged from the post office. He carried an envelope with a wired message. Jess's greeting was re-assuringly familiar. I felt a shudder of relief.

Jess showed me the wire.

ALEXANDERS WOODBURN. FURTHER ORDERS AWAIT.
SOONEST. FIELD.

"You know Woodburn?" Jess asked.

"Yes."

"You can show us the way."

It was a night's ride to Woodburn from Cincinnati. I wondered that if I travelled overnight as they slept, I could out-run them. Brushes and I could go north to Ripley and we would be free and clear.

"That fat bastard always says 'Soonest'." Jess said. "I reckon we stay the night here and take the first train in the morning and pick up horses in Lexington."

"It's a pleasant ride down," I said. "I'm not sure I can stand another train."

"You know the way soldier," Wade said and we agreed to ride down to Lexington the following day.

We checked into a roach-infested inn. I looked carefully at the horses for hire in the Inn's stable and picked out a large heavy one, which would stand the long and steady eighty miles to Lexington.

The Stimsons chose racier horses. I wondered how they would stand the journey. All to the good if they could not make it in a day.

I took a room to myself. The Stimsons said they would share. I was sick of their company and dreaded an evening with them. They must have felt the same and, after a short dinner and drinking session, we agreed to part and meet at eight the following morning.

It was ten o' clock and at least eight hours of sleep beckoned. My head was starting to pound with fatigue. If I slept, the journey would be easier.

I opened the door to my room. I could see from the entrance that the bed was not as I had left it. I looked around, with a strong feeling of someone being there, yet I could not see anyone as I stood in the doorway.

"Shut the door, Jack," a voice said from behind the door.

It was Ellen.

"Good grief Ellen," I said as I shut the door.

"You're jumpy," she said.

216

"With good reason. The Stimsons' orders are for a 'Return' from Lexington. Jess talks friendly, but I can't make out whether he's onto me or not."

"You did a good job keeping them away from us," she said.

"How long have you got?" I asked.

"You need sleep."

"I know. I'm bone tired. I haven't been able to sleep properly since…"

"Since the sliced man?"

"Lucy told you?"

"Yes. That's the little Stimson's party piece."

I must have looked shocked.

"Yes, the one who looks so innocent. I heard all about him at Campbells'"

"Tracker," I said. "Tracker…"

"Lucy's told me."

"They're riding down to Woodburn tomorrow morning. Can you get Lucy to Ripley?"

"That's what I want to do, but I have a mutiny on my hands."

"What do you mean?"

"Lucy says she won't go to freedom without him."

"That's crazy. I can get Brushes to Ripley and we can all go to Canada together."

A flash of worry crossed Ellen's face. It was the same expression she always had when she did not want to tell me something.

"What's the matter?"

Ellen's face recovered.

"She won't go without him so I'll go down with her. Brushes spends Sundays mornings and evenings in the Thoroughbred Yard whilst the Alexander's people are in church. The services are at ten and six. Everyone's there except the mad Mrs. Buford. She shoots rabbits as they pray. We can meet in the yard."

"And the Stimsons?"

"There are three of them, all armed. When are you leaving?" she asked.

217

"I've agreed to meet them at eight this morning."

"That'll give you time to be in the yard at six o clock for the evening service. It's a steady ride. If you haven't dealt with them on the way, try and make sure they don't get there before six. Then we'll all be there to outnumber them."

"Ellen."

"I love you too Jack, but I have a very agitated package at the safe house. She's insisting we leave now."

"Should I go and see her? I did abandon her on the train."

"You didn't abandon her, though that's what she thought for a moment. No, there's no need for you to know where the safe house is and you're exhausted."

Thirty-nine

I could not sleep. I had no plan to deal with the Stimsons on the journey down and that bothered me. My mind was spinning as to how I would manage the following day.

At midnight I went to see my horse. I was thinking that maybe he could calm me down. He was a steady soul. When I got to the stables I could see that he was happy. But the Stimsons' horses, which were in the boxes next to him, were no longer there.

I rushed back to my room. The suitcase Ellen had left for me had a change of clothes, boots and a field dressing kit. I picked it up, strapped the gun into my belt and took the Lexington road. I did not know where the safe house was, so I could not alert Lucy and Ellen.

Nor did I know how much of a head start I had given the Stimsons. It would have been no more than two hours. I reckoned their horses were suited by the occasional gallop but not a long trip. My horse was exactly as I expected. Slow and steady. A little humorless and not as much fun as Pierce.

The moon was up and the road was clear. It was unlikely they would be expecting me to follow them. After all, they had left early to avoid me and had agreed to meet me in the morning.

If they were around two hours ahead of me, they would leave with their prisoner at around the time I was arriving. It would probably take then that long to chain Brushes, change their horses and arrange for a cart to take Brushes back to Baltimore.

Because there was no telling what route out of Lexington they would take, my only chance was to catch them at Woodburn - unless I could catch them on their journey.

I was an hour out of Cincinnati when it started to rain. This was not a light soft rain but a hard monsoon where it seemed each drop soaked through your coat to the skin and lashed at your eyes.

My horse slowed to a walk. I squeezed him with my legs trying to coax a trot, but he was not prepared to go any faster. The rain was lashing at his eyes. He sensed my urgency but could not see clearly because of the rain hitting his eyes. I dropped the reins and let him go on at his own pace. At least he was going forward, I thought. I wondered how the Stimsons would cope. At least one of their horses would stop, I thought. If that happened and the others waited, then I would catch up with them.

At last the rain stopped and we started to trot, then canter, then trot. We kept a rhythm to keep the pace up and keep me awake. Fatigue pulled at me, then fear woke me as I half-expected to catch up with the Stimsons whilst sleeping on my horse. Sometimes, as I shook myself to stay awake, I wondered how Grace managed on the road for so long.

Sunrise came as we travelled through the rolling hills of Kentucky down the Frankfort Pike towards Woodburn. It had been a long night. My horse was exhausted. I was beyond exhaustion. Just one more day, I said to myself. One more day. Then I could sleep. Maybe Brushes could drive me north in a cart. I was in a sea of maybes. I had to face the Stimsons alone, with Brushes unarmed and without even the knowledge that Lucy was safe in Ripley.

Forty

I remembered the lay-out of the farm. It was over a thousand acres and the size of a small town. The buildings, which included a disused ironworks, were well spread out. The farm raised horses cattle, pigs and sheep on a large scale.

The main house itself was made of wood and was long and wide. Its outbuildings consisted of stables, a milk house and sheds for cattle and other livestock. There were six superintendents' houses on the estate and there was a larger building for the Alexanders' racehorse trainer. Each house had its own grounds, none of the buildings crowded the other. The slave quarters for the grooms and stockmen were scattered around the site.

Most of the buildings were wooden. But the stables were made of brick, as was the church. The main house was off center and occupied by the eccentric Mrs. Buford who refused to vacate the house even though she had sold the farm.

In Maryland and Virginia the main houses stood at the center of the plantation buildings, but here the church was at the center and everything else radiated from what must have seemed like the spokes of a wheel from the hub of the church, with the occasional scatter of eccentrically located out-buildings.

Visibility was good as I rode toward the stud. From a distance I saw people outside the church. I rode towards the Thoroughbred stable yard. It was eerily quiet as I reckoned it would be if only one person was working in there. My horse was about to drop with fatigue. I jumped off and led him into the yard.

Jess Stimson emerged from the stable. I was about to reach for my gun and a hand came from behind and restrained me. One arm was around my throat and the other took the gun from my belt, patted me down and took the clasp knife, which Grace had given me.

Wade Stimson released me and threw me to the ground. As I tried to get up, I saw Lucy and Ellen propped up against the entrance wall, hands tied behind their backs and shackled together with a pair of leg irons. Brushes was standing beside them unshackled but guarded by James.

"We're about to get started on this nigger here," Wade said. "We hoped you'd be in time to see it all, like these two ladies here.

James pushed Brushes into the center of the yard.

I stood up. Ellen and Lucy were tied up and immobile. Brushes and I were not. As I wondered why, I got a sickening feeling. Then Jess hit Brushes in the stomach with the barrel of his rifle. He doubled over in pain as the wind was taken out of him. Jess then did the same to me and I fell to the ground.

As I was trying to get up. James kicked me in the face. His shoe was soft, but the force of the blow was not. I lay in shock for what seemed like forever, but could have been no more than a minute. I tried to get up but fell back again.

Wade was standing behind me and Jess in front. James was to the side holding his knife. It had a small three inch blade. Brushes was on his feet.

"This boy wants to leave," James said in the direction of Ellen and Lucy.

Then he slashed across Brushes's shirt. The tearing sound was slight. The blade was sharp. No blood was drawn and the precision was awesome.

I moved towards James, but he took another slash at Brushes and Jess raised his gun at me.

"You die or you watch and live," Jess said.

I had my back to Lucy and Ellen. Wade was behind me. James took another slash at Brushes's shirt. Then another. Each slash tore the shirt so it started to look more like ribbons than a shirt.

Brushes was sweating. I felt that he might be resigned to death but his standing still as the blade slashed his shirt, together with his watchfulness suggested something else.

"Hey Wade, you're blocking their view," Jess said.

Wade walked round to give Lucy and Ellen an uninterrupted view of the coming mutilation. The blade swung again and Lucy screamed.

"Quiet or he'll kill him now," Jess shouted. His voice was hoarse and he was panting with excitement.

"Draw some blood, James," he said.

James slashed across Brushes's right shoulder.

"Give him the irons," Jess said.

Brushes was sweating. He was looking at the Stimsons with a poised wariness.

I heard singing. Reading my thoughts Jess Stimson said, "They're all in church, all except you, this nigger and those girls."

I heard the clank of the heavy leg irons of the type I had seen on the hanging body. It had the familiar sound I had heard many times in the slave jail; the same noise I heard when I inspected Sloan and Wilfred. My head was swimming with fatigue and ached from the heavy blow James had given it. Then I saw that Brushes's watchfulness was aimed at me and reminded me of the many times we used our silent language with each other as we trained difficult horses.

"The boy can put them on himself." Jess said, leveling the gun at Brushes.

"I'll never wear those," Brushes said. He was winded and the words came out in a wheeze. He meant it. My head cleared a little.

"You will nigger and you'll put them on yourself," Jess said.

I remembered Professor Weir's words in the hand-to-hand combat class. "There is strength in nothing to lose. Give your opponent a way out or his desperation will kill you." I could tell from Brushes's face that he understood the fate planned for him by the Stimsons. I had seen it and would die rather than see it again.

"Yes you will nigger boy. You'll put them on," Jess said.

"I will not wear chains," he said.

Our communication had always been instinctive and without gesture. He was ready to spring, I felt. I had to do so at the same time. I had to give him a sign.

The Stimsons were surrounding us now. Jess and Wade with guns. James had his knife. Our choices were to die or use the unspoken communication as we had during the years I was growing up. Brushes was wet with sweat and blood. His right leg moved slightly. I gave the faintest nod in reply.

The irons were at Brushes's feet.

"Pick them up," James said. "You will wear them."

James slashed Brushes's leg with the knife. James's face was not twisted in hatred. It was calm and open but revealed a desire to show off in front of his brothers and please them with a long-practiced demonstration.

"Will this make it any easier?" James said as he picked up the leg irons by the chain with the bloody knife and held them in front of Bushes, jangling them making their familiar sound. Brushes's trousers were crimson.

I made to look as if I was falling down. I lifted up my right leg to take hold of my ankle knife. As I did so Ellen screamed. All three Stimsons looked startled. Brushes picked up the leg irons. I threw the knife at Wade, hitting him through the heart. At the same time Brushes slashed at Jess with the leg irons; surprised Jess dropped his gun as I charged him. I would have lunged at him anyway. James was for Brushes to deal with. Jess was my quarry and I would take him armed or not. It was the two brothers' shock of seeing Wade fall and Ellen's scream which gave us the second we needed.

My desperation was my strength. I gripped Jess's throat. I was on top of him and he was gripping my throat too. We were locked together. His grip was stronger than mine. My head swam. The clarity I had a minute before was gone. Fatigue was overwhelming. It would be me who gave up first. We had both been out all night, but I had the debilitating fever, the long marches with Lucy, the nights with little sleep and James's kick to the head. I felt my grip weakening. Jess was fresher than me.

Then one hand was pulled off my throat and, after that, the other. Brushes had pulled Jess's hands above his head and stood on them as he gripped his wounded thigh. I heaved in a gulp of air and squeezed Jess's throat harder.

Brushes's hold on Jess's hands could not have been more than thirty seconds. He fell backwards. The loss of blood was weakening him. His blood lay on the ground beside him.

The thirty seconds respite and the sight of Brushes bleeding made me grip harder. Jess's hands waved in the air and then tried to grip my throat again. Gradually and slowly I felt no more life in the body underneath me.

I got up. Brushes must have hit James with the leg irons However he was coming round just as Brushes was slipping away. I gave Brushes Jess's gun.

"Watch him," I said and ran to the field dressing kit in my case. I picked out the bandages and a ligature.

"How long's the church service?" I asked.

"At least another hour," Brushes said.

"He'd have killed me if you hadn't taken his grip from my throat," I said.

Brushes pointed at James, who was starting to get up. I kicked him and he fell down again, moaning.

"Let me see your leg." I said.

The trousers were soaked. He did not have long unless I could stop the bleeding. The wound was deep. James knew what he was doing when he slashed Brushes, just as he knew what he was doing when he killed the runaway. I made a tourniquet and tied it as hard as I could. I then cut away his trousers so that I could see the wound.

I had stopped the bleeding. Relieved, I made a field dressing.

"Where are fresh horses?" I asked.

"Paddocks," Brushes said and then relapsed into unconsciousness.

James was trying to get up, as he recovered from my kick and saw his dead brothers. He was confused and disoriented. He was looking for the guns, but I had put them beside Brushes.

I kicked him again and then with the key Grace gave me, undid the leg irons and, with James's knife, cut the rope round Ellen and Lucy's wrists. I gestured them to look after Brushes and went over to James who was trying to get up. I pulled him to his feet. My head was clear again. All his life James had his older brothers to first follow around and then try to impress. Now in a few short minutes, they were gone. I expected hatred in his eyes, but all I saw in his face was a mixture of defeat, confusion and loss.

"You take Jess and I'll take Wade." I said to James nodding towards the stable using the same manner of command I had in Lynchburg.

James and I pulled the bodies by their feet into the stables and laid them in an empty stall. I laid Wade along a the wall at the back of the stall and I gestured James to do the same with Jess. As James let go of Jess's feet, he looked up at me as if to ask what to do next. I felt like he was surrendering to my command with an acceptance that there was someone else to please now and his loyalty would be as steadfast to me as it was to his brothers.

"Cover them with straw," I said.

James walked out to the passageway outside the stall as I pulled the knife from Wade's chest. I hoped he would make a run for it and then I could have an excuse to kill him as he tried to escape. But that was a false hope and he brought a bale of straw into the stall. I nodded towards the bodies. He nodded back and loosened straw from its compressed bale. He covered his brothers, looking up at me as he did so.

"That's good," I said. "You're doing a fine job."

There was no trace of sarcasm in my voice. This was what he wanted to hear. He was pleasing the new master in his life and I was re-assuring him that he was doing so. I reckoned that then, until shock came over him, he would do anything I asked. Just as he did anything his brothers asked him to or what he thought would please them. His cutting of captives to ribbons was just that: something he must have done all his life to get and keep approval from those above him.

When the straw from half of the bale had covered the two bodies, I stepped across to James. He looked at me with the face of a questioning child, as he fell; the knife stuck firmly in his chest. I covered him with the unused straw remaining from the bale. I would like to be able to say that it was the sight of the hanging body, which stirred a rage inside me and making me do it. But I can't. I think if I looked inside myself at that moment, I would have found nothing.

Having taken a life in cold blood and feeling nothing, my only thought was: 'So this is how it is. You fight. You kill. You keep moving. Just like they taught me.'

I went outside and saw that Ellen and Lucy had pumped water into buckets and cleaned the yard of blood. If someone came by they would not see anything amiss. It would be a while before anyone thought to look into the empty stall and then they would see straw. They'd only discover the bodies if they put a horse in there. Neither Ellen nor Lucy asked me about James, who they had seen go into the stable with me, and not come out.

I requisitioned a wagon from the carriage yard next door to the stables to act as an ambulance to take Brushes with us to the Rawlins House in Ripley, which was the safest of houses in the freest county in Ohio.

I reckoned we could get there by sundown.

Forty-one

Brushes had woken occasionally on the journey to Ripley but relapsed almost as soon as he had done so. His breathing was shallow and his pulse light. I had gradually eased the ligature as the journey progressed. He had lost so much blood, but the bleeding had stopped.

The Rawlins House was high on a bluff overlooking the Ohio River. We were not challenged at any stage of the journey.

No soon as we arrived that Ellen said she had to go to Boston. I told her that I needed to take Lucy to Canada and would stay until Brushes was ready to travel. She looked troubled at that but said nothing.

Lucy and I sat with Brushes after Ellen left. His breathing was still shallow. I was exhausted but what was keeping me going and stopping me from sleeping was realizing that I could sit with Lucy without thinking about the next step of our escape, the next map to recall and the hazards which were ahead of us and the dogs and Patrol which were following behind us. We could be together with no urgency of the chase or worry of what the next day would bring.

Occasionally I would sense that Lucy was looking at me as I watched over Brushes or looked out of the bedroom window. When I looked up at her, she would smile at me. This was the first time I felt relaxed and unworried since Dr. Holmes's fateful conversation.

After an hour Mrs. Rawlins put her head round the bedroom door.

"I'll stay with him," Mrs. Rawlins said. "You two get some rest."

We went downstairs into the parlor. Lucy looked out over the Ohio River with her back to me. I sat on the sofa and rubbed my temples. Fatigue was washing over me now. Then Lucy spoke, quietly but distinctly.

"Neil came to me in my bed on the top floor of the plantation house. He put his hand over my mouth so I couldn't scream. I wouldn't have tried to scream even if I could. Martha slept nearby. I didn't want her to hear me or what he was doing to me. He usually finished quickly and with a grunt. When he left I saw that my sheets were red with blood."

Her voice was even, without emotion.

"It was regular. Every night he was home. I would be in my bed, the door would open. I would smell the whiskey and hear the breathing. I shut my eyes so I couldn't see him. But I felt his presence, standing over me. It was no different each time. The next and the next and the next. After a week I stopped bleeding and Martha no longer changed the bed-sheets."

Lucy paused. I felt that she was going to say more. I dug my fingernails into the palm of my hand hard trying to create enough pain to smother what I was hearing. I looked down at my hands. My right palm was bleeding. Lucy turned around and came to the sofa.

"Just as I started to show I was pregnant, Brushes took an interest in me," she said. As she did so, she took out a handkerchief and wrapped it round my hand.

"It was when Victoria was in town with Neil. The children were out. I had finished for the morning. He was getting some horses ready to go to the blacksmiths, rubbing one of them down. I liked to watch him work and had spied on him quietly for a long time. Just watching him with the horses. Do you know I spied on you and him when you came in the summers?"

I shook my head.

"You both concentrated on the horses so I figured you'd never see me." She paused. "Where was I?"

"Brushes was getting the horses ready"

"He had his back to me. He couldn't have seen me but he knew I was there.

" 'You have a little one coming,' he said to me. It wasn't a question but I took it as one. I shook my head. He carried on grooming.

"Then the tears came to my eyes and I started to nod. I had been sold for learning to read. Maybe I would be again for having Neil's baby. More than anything, I was so ashamed."

Lucy paused, looked at me and then continued.

"I was crying and Brushes picked up the horse's front foot and said, 'The Mistress knows he comes to you.' It was like he was saying it to the hoof. I nodded, though he could not have seen me."

" 'Will she sell me away?' I asked him. I had reckoned that she might know of the visits, but could deny them to herself. Now, I thought, the baby would change things. As I talked, Brushes groomed the horse. I told him my story. How I was sold naked in the market place. How they touched me as I stood on the block. How they talked and sneered. He could see my tears and feel my fears, but he didn't look at me directly as he carried on grooming. I could feel him accept me and care for me. I would do anything for him then.

"I knew what the horses felt like when they came to him. Whatever he did, he would not look directly at them, but they would become interested in him. Something draws them to him and the same thing drew me to him. It draws me to him now as I watch him breathe and wonder if he'll get better. Then, all those years ago, through my tears I could see that Brushes had not stopped the grooming. He said to me, 'You better sleep with me. You wear your nightgown, but you sleep with me.'

" 'Master Neil?' I said. I was afraid of what Neil would do to him for trying to protect me. Defiance could mean the whip or the branding iron and this was defiance.

"He stopped working on the horse and, for the first time, he looked directly at me. He dropped the hoof pick and started laughing and said, 'I guess Master Neil won't want to come to me as well.'

"The colt started to rear. He was one of Brushes' conquests and had been given to Neil because only Brushes could control him. 'Hey Fragment,' he said to the colt. 'Easy. I guess you've never heard me laugh before.'

"All the people I had seen would jerk on the lead or reins and shout at the horse. Brushes just talked quietly as it listened. Fragment reared up one more time to make a point and then stood still as if nothing had happened.

" 'If he wants to come to me, he'll sell you.' I said to him. I didn't want to mention the whip or anything else that might happen to him for protecting me. I was frightened to even say the words.

" Then he said, 'I reckon he needs a good story to explain your child when it comes.'

"Neil didn't come to me any more. I was safe with Brushes in the quarters. Nobody said anything. It wasn't as if these things hadn't happened to me, but it did feel like he protected me. It was when I started to show a lot that Victoria looked at me strangely. She didn't say anything. Her voice got higher in pitch when she talked to me. She would look away sometimes as if she did not know where to put herself.

"Then we went to Boston and you came. You know I was ready to hate you when you did. If William or Dr. Holmes had told me I could have given you away, I would have said to them that was what I wanted. But when you came, I wanted you to be mine and always have. I gave you away so you'd be free, not because of where you came from."

I felt that I had been hit on the head with a hammer and punched in the stomach all at once.

"Why are you saying all this?" I asked. My voice was high pitched as if I was being strangled.

"So you know why I had to go to Woodburn and why Brushes takes me to Canada now. He only stayed for me. He'd have been long gone but for me. I stayed to see you and to watch my own son grow up free and then know me as his mother. Brushes must take me to Canada. You must go and be a soldier."

"I'm tired Mama," I said. It was all I could think to say to her. The shock of what she said about Neil was still hurting and I could take no more. I thought back to the dream of me taking her to freedom whilst I was in uniform. It had come true in its way. She was right. Brushes had to be the one take her to Canada.

I felt a rising rage at Neil but I did not have the means to express it - least of all to her. Lucy's words, "the next and the next and the next," reverberated in my ears as I blacked out, exhausted.

Forty-two

When I woke I rubbed my eyes. It was midday and I had been carried to a bed.

As I looked over the river to the Kentucky side, the thought of what to do next came to me. Crazy or self destructive it might be but I knew what I had to do.

Lucy was with Brushes. She was wiping his brow. He was propped up in bed, sweating with fever but somehow he looked stronger. Sleep was reviving him and the fever was somehow helping.

"I don't know how to thank you," I said to him. "If you hadn't taken his hands off my throat, I wouldn't be here."

He smiled and Lucy put her finger to her mouth to gesture him not to speak.

"It's okay," I thought I heard him say.

"How long until you're ready to go?" I asked.

"One week, maybe two," Lucy said. "At least that's what Mrs. Rawlins says."

"Looks more like two to me," I said. "I could send Pierce here and he could take you both to Canada."

"You're going to be a soldier?" Lucy asked.

"I need to see Grace first. I want to help with the Railroad."

"She wants you to be a soldier."

"I'll meet her in Philadelphia like she asked me to. I've got to find out about Tracker. I'll stop off in Baltimore and pick up Pierce. I'll have

233

him sent here after I've got to New York. He can take you to Canada."

Brushes spoke in a whisper and with a twinkle in his eye.

"Tracker told me about Pierce. Told me he lets no one else ride him."

"I'll tell Pierce about you," I said. "He'll take you both on his back. I'll have something to eat and then leave. I've got a lot to do before West Point's term starts."

Forty-three

The train and horseback got me to Baltimore in two days. As I approached the Circus, I saw someone hailing me from the other side of the street. It was Horton Field. He was waving frantically, but in a friendly manner.

I waved back, revulsion welling inside me. The man, who set the trap for Tracker and me to walk into and had sent the Stimsons to capture Brushes, was hailing me as if I were a long lost friend.

"Hullo, Mr. Field." I said. I was about to gesture to Campbell's front door as an excuse not to meet, but I saw Field start to cross the street. I went towards him.

"You remember my name," he said as we met in the road. "How kind. How are you and where have you been?"

"Oh out and about," I said.

There was an amused look in his eye. It was the one of the chess master who has been bested and knows why.

"Anyway," he said. "I was just hailing you to say that I'm dining at your uncle's tonight. Will I meet you there?"

I was being drawn into a conversation and felt revulsion as it was happening, but I saw no way of avoiding being civil and pretending that we weren't enemies.

"Oh yes, I've got to pick up my horse," I said.

"Back to West Point soon?"

"Yes, just a few days now."

"Do you need a horse there?" Field asked.

"No, I just want it for the trip north. I'll see you at the house. What time are you expected?"

"Seven. I'll see you there."

At the Ruffin Plantation, Pierce pretended not to recognize me as I tacked him up for the journey to Philadelphia. As I tried to rub his muzzle, he looked away. He was making clear his resentment at being left behind. I reckoned that he would be sulking for another week. This mood would be a matter of pride for him which he could sustain for as long as he could.

It was six-o-clock. I had to get moving before Horton Field arrived. Victoria was in Boston and my cousins were away so the only person in the house would be Neil. Perhaps the empty house had caused Neil to change the venue of the drinking sessions, I wondered. Whatever the reason, its emptiness suited my purpose.

Better to do it early, I thought. There was no time to lose.

I led Pierce to the front of the house and asked him to wait. I thought of tying him up, but if he panicked he would pull at the rein tying him and either run away or hurt himself in the process of trying to get free. If he had freedom to move, he would not stray far.

I walked in the front door as I had many times as a child and adult. It felt strange that this would be the last time I did so. I went into the kitchen, lit a lamp and took it back to the parlor.

"Uncle Neil!" I shouted.

A quiet voice came from a wing-backed chair. Neil had been sitting in it all the time and in my haste and concentration I had not seen him.

"I'm here. Welcome."

I set the lamp down on a side table. The sun was streaming in. In an instant I could see fear and the recognition of my intentions in Neil's eyes.

"Horton Field will be here soon," he said. I could sense the bravado in his voice and could feel that was the only pretense he had left.

"Not for an hour," I said.

The look of fear in his eyes turned to panic and then suddenly a sly relief.

"He's often early. We often talk about you. He knows."

Neil then gave me an account of their drinking sessions. I felt that it was not just to buy time but a confession.

"Are you going to shoot me now?" he asked. The fear had gone. The time he had taken in talking gave him some relief. I looked out of the window.

"He's not here, there's no-one approaching," I said. "He's late sometimes isn't he?"

The fear returned to his eyes and he nodded in assent. "What do you want?" he said.

"I want you to come with me."

I had my gun, but there was no need to use it. Neil got out of the chair.

"Where to?"

"Upstairs. Lead on."

I followed, carrying the lamp.

"Which room?" he asked as we got to the second floor landing.

"Up one more flight," I said.

"You've never been up there before."

"You have. Go on."

There were three rooms off the third floor landing, which was dark with neglect. All the rooms faced the back of the house, the corridor was off the stairs with no windows so that the house looked like a two-storey building from the front. I did not know which was Lucy's room. He must have felt my uncertainty and pointed to the middle door.

"That's Martha's old room," I said.

"No, it's this one. No one's been in here since...since. Victoria wouldn't have it used again after you were born."

"Open the door," I said.

The room was small and narrow with a view of the quarters and the corn fields beyond. We stood inside looking at an empty bed with no mattress, just the bedsprings covering a dusty floor which had not been swept for years. Paint was peeling on the wall, brown curtains hung at the window covered in cobwebs and dead flies lay on the window sill.

Neil was swaying and sweating. The climb up the stairs had made him breathless, but the sight of the room seemed to change him.

"You raped her and then you sold her," I said.

He stood silent. He wiped the sweat from his brow with his sleeve and staggered to the window where he propped himself, panting with exertion. Victoria had said many times that he was proud of me. There was no pride in his face, but rather a recognition of something understood.

I had arrived in a state of cold rage. Lucy's telling of her rapes at his hands had led me, the one who had emerged from the darkness of those awful nights, to this moment of revenge. I had wondered on the journey from Ohio what he would say when we got here. Then he spoke.

"Horton'll be here soon."

I was, just then, unsure whether he said that to deter me or simply warn me. Downstairs when he said the same thing there was fear and bargaining in his voice. Now there seemed to be acceptance.

I'd shown no mercy to the Stimson boy and had determined to show none to him. His look of defeat and acceptance gave me pause as we stared at one another. My feeling of hatred dissolved with my resolution. The man was pathetic. There was enough of me in him that made me hate him and be sick with myself for doing so at the same time.

We looked at one another for a full minute. I was the first to speak.

"I have to destroy this place." I said.

"And you want to destroy me?"

I was about to reply when a familiar voice carried up the stairs from the downstairs hall.

"Neil!"

Horton Field had arrived.

"Neil, where are you?"

I nodded at Neil. "Tell him," I said.

"Up here. In the maid's room."

The shouting increased his breathlessness and he staggered, catching himself on the bedpost.

"I'm coming up. Tell him not to do anything stupid."

I did not think what I was about to do was stupid. Fitting certainly. Reckless perhaps. It was the obliteration of the scene of a crime. It was something which I had to do. It meant the likely destruction of my army career. This place, part of which I had inherited, had to be destroyed. It was not only the scene of a crime but was also the place of the continuance of many crimes, the victims being housed in the quarters I could see through the window behind Neil.

I threw the lamp at the window. It fell to the floor and flames engulfed the curtain making a whumping sound. Neil moved forward away from the flames. I took the gun out of my belt and pointed it at Neil, who shut his eyes in acceptance. I did not shoot but threw the gun at the window. I had wanted him to suffer and atone but the urge to kill had gone.

He opened his eyes. There was nothing that he could say. For the first time, I saw shame in his face as he looked at me. It was at that moment that Horton Field appeared in the doorway. He had a gun.

"Don't shoot him," Neil shouted to Field. The room had quickly filled with smoke.

"Then let's leave now," Field said and went towards the stairway. Neil did not move. He stood paralyzed. I pulled him out of the burning room. He resisted my grip and said, "I'm coming." I let go my grip and saw that Field had already run down to the second floor landing. I started down the stars. I looked back and saw that Neil was not following. I went back up and smoke stopped going me further. The fire had taken so much hold in the bedroom that I saw the bed tilt through the smoke as the floor started to give.

Field came back and stood beside me. He choked and backed away.

"It's no use," I heard him say and then he ran. If I had my gun with me I would have shot him then.

Through the flames, I could see nothing in the bedroom and the heat coming from it made it impossible to enter. Neil had to be somewhere else if he was alive, however the smoke was overwhelming. I looked around and saw a figure lying prone on the floor down the hallway outside Martha's bedroom door. It was hard to make out because the smoke was so intense. I was choking and my eyes were burning. I had to take a breath.

I ran down to the second floor bedroom and heaved some fresh air into my lungs, soaked a hand towel in water from the bedside bowl and put it round my face. I ran back upstairs through the smoke, which had thickened. I could no longer see the end of the hallway. The figure, if it was there, was invisible through the smoke. My eyes were smarting and my face was feeling the heat from the flames, which had taken over the bedroom. They were now licking out onto the landing starting to cut off the route to the prone figure.

Neil had passed out, flames were starting to approach his prone body from under the bedroom door. I picked him up. He was surprisingly light. His clothes were baggy. His frame had wasted as drink had replaced food and appetite.

As I carried him down the stairs to the ground floor, I heard the sound of the top floor starting to fall into the one below and I felt the heat of flames. I ran out the front door which I had entered just half an hour before.

Neil's face was black, his breathing shallow and quick. The house was a tinder-box. Flames were coming out of the windows of the second floor that were exploding one-by-one. The roof was close to collapse. I was awestruck at the speed of the destruction. In just five minutes the house had become beyond saving.

"Was anyone else in there?" Field asked. His presence surprised me. I had dismissed him from my mind after he had run away.

I shook my head and then received a blow from the butt of Field's gun.

Forty-four

I had not been unconscious for long. Field had hog tied me and put me in his wagon, leaving Neil to be tended by a field hand.

He stopped the wagon first at the Sheriff's office in Pratt Street. He was told by the Deputy Sheriff to take me to the County Jail and then have a charge sworn out against me by Neil on the following day. In the meantime I could be held under arrest in the County Jail at Towson.

It was on the journey from the sheriff's to the jail that he told me the story I already heard of my 'twin', his grave in the churchyard in Boston and of Neil's suspicions about me as related to Field in that drinking session ten years previously.

He was almost friendly as he spoke and was matter of fact as he said that a conviction for arson would get me out of the Academy. I did not belong there, he said. Once out of the Academy, and after a decent interval of jail time, I could be exposed. That's what had to happen and that's what would happen, he said.

The County Jail near Baltimore had a wing for serious offenders on the third floor behind the tower. I was in a cell by myself and with a blinding headache. Through the prison bars, I could see that the sun was rising.

I had not slept that night and had paced up and down in my cell. My rescue of Neil seemed to be a heat of battle instinct as was my near reflex to shoot Field. I was annoyed at myself for throwing my gun away.

I did not regret that the house had been destroyed. However I had many other regrets. The biggest was the loss of Tracker. Impetuousness had made me walk towards the Patrol when good sense would have made me abort the mission and try another time. Impetuousness made me stick to the mission of torching the house at the time Horton Field was visiting.

Now the time available before I was due back at the Academy was fast diminishing. My life had changed so much in a few short weeks. It was to change again. Horton Field would have his wish. I would be thrown out of West Point.

Unlike when I approached the Patrol on the night of Lucy's escape, there was no Tracker to guide me, no Grace to give me the use of her Railroad and inspire me and no Lucy to rescue.

I was alone.

Part of me felt pleased that I had done what I had to do. The rest of me felt regret at its timing, inspired only by rage. The loss of Tracker gnawed at me, his loss being caused by the same fault that had brought me to the jail.

That night I appreciated the irony. My experience made me a better soldier, just as it was about to disqualify me from being one.

Then there was the knowledge that Horton Field knew my secret. Whatever had prevented him acting on it must have gone with the fire. I could see myself being transported from the County Jail in Towson to the slave jail in Pratt Street. Perhaps to Campbell's, where Ellen had worked.

As the sun rose high in the sky my satisfaction at having done what I felt to be the right thing, gave way to despair.

Forty-five

I had heard the other prisoners being let out for exercise and meals. My door remained shut. I had spoken quietly and distinctly to the guard as he passed my cell.

"Do I get breakfast?" I called out.

He broke stride slightly indicating that he had heard me, but walked on pretending he had not. I repeated the question at lunchtime and the same thing happened.

There was a jug of water in the corner of the cell and I drank sparingly during the day. When water on a marsh is low and you do not know how long you have before the next well, you should make sure your men only sip sparingly, the better to preserve what they have.

I did not touch the water until mid-day and then only a mouthful. From where the sun had descended, it was four o' clock when the guard, who made me miss breakfast and lunch, came to my cell and unlocked it.

"You have an appointment with the Warden."

The Warden's study was on the third floor of his house, which was a three-storey structure with a tower in the middle which went up to a fourth level. The cell block was behind the house.

I followed the guard across and up the stairs.

"Shouldn't you be shackling me?" I asked.

"Not unless you want me to."

The warden looked about fifty years old with black hair brushed back and a fleshy lined face, which spoke of weariness and boredom as well as the relishing of responsibility.

"Thank you. You can leave him here."

The guard left.

"What do you have to say for yourself?"

"Nothing, sir."

"You were brought here by a man who said you were an arsonist and attempted to murder your uncle."

I stayed silent. I had been taught, if captured stay silent.

"Do you not want to rebut the charges?"

I stared straight ahead.

"Well, you don't need to. Your uncle, who it is said you tried to murder, says you saved his life and the fire was an accident which only destroyed joint property."

"I'm free to go, sir?"

"He says you've been like a son to him."

I said nothing.

"Why didn't you tell the Sheriff this before you were brought here?"

"Am I free to go, sir?"

"You can see yourself out. Down the stairs and out the front door. Your uncle says you'll be in a hurry to get back to the Academy. He sent a man here with your horse. It's outside. Good luck trying to get on him."

"Thank you, Warden."

"I'm West Point 1845. I have one bit of advice for you. Before you leave the army, make quite sure you will not end up at a place like this."

"In jail?"

"No. As a warden. Good luck."

Forty-six

We made quick time to Philadelphia. Pierce was fresh. Nevertheless Ellen was right, there was no time to lose before I had to get back to the Academy. I would miss seeing the Holmeses. I reckoned I had only a few hours in Philadelphia before I had to leave for New York.

I came to the house where, it seemed a lifetime ago, Grace had sent me to Lynchburg and I started my time with the Railroad. I gave three sharp knocks and then a cough. There was silence. I could hear no footfall. I waited a minute and knocked again. Again there was no reply.

Grace was not there. Suddenly I realized that her promise to meet me, made in the woods where she met Lucy and talked of her sister and where she re-assured me of Tracker's indestructability, meant more than I had realized at the time. I had felt, as I rode from Baltimore, both dread and expectation.

I had to make myself conspicuous to the Railroad and I went to the coffee house where I had gone with Wilson Calhoun as he tested me out. I sat down at the table where I had sat before.

The same man took my order. It was just coffee. I had to buy something. My stomach could take no food. I doubted that I could hold down any coffee, but I had to force myself.

"Do you mind if I join you?" a familiar voice said. Then it spoke again.

"Excuse me young man, do you mind if I join you?"

245

I looked up. Wilson Calhoun had a lot of samples in one hand together with a briefcase and he was trying to hold a cup of coffee at the same time. If someone did not take the coffee from him, either the paper or the coffee would spill over the floor.

I stood up quickly and took his coffee.

"Mr Calhoun," I said. "Of course."

I helped him with his paper samples. He placed the briefcase beside him.

"Nice to see you again, young man. Now I am sure you can order a second cup of coffee and keep a tired salesman company a while."

"Of course, sir. Excuse me."

"Not eating?" asked Calhoun.

"No sir."

"I don't blame you," he said.

He lowered his voice.

"I followed you here from the house. You were not paying attention"

I grunted. I could not even smile at my inability to feel or spot him.

"Where are you staying?" he asked.

"I'm on my way home."

"Not staying at the Giraud?"

This was a hint, I felt. I had planned to make a start that day, but I could stay overnight if I left early the following morning.

"Yes, I'll stay overnight there and leave first thing. I was supposed to meet someone..." My voice tailed off.

"The Giraud's a bit grand for a salesman, but it's amazing the people you meet there."

He had said that in almost a whisper before continuing a long, loud and complicated explanation of all the different types of paper he was trying to sell.

His message was clear. Grace was at the Giraud.

I took that news with relief and dread. But Pierce would be glad of the overnight rest.

It was a five minute ride to the Giraud. I quickly dropped Pierce off at the stable. They had a room ready in my name. I declined the services of a porter, ran up the stairs to the room and opened the door. Grace was not there.

I felt disoriented. Calhoun had as good as told me that Grace would be waiting for me there. The room was empty. I must have misunderstood the message.

It was early evening. I had left Pierce without thanking him and so I went down to the stables. There were four horses in our set of boxes and only one groom, who was rubbing Pierce down.

"It's okay," I said. "I'll do this."

"You like giving orders don't you?" the groom replied. He was facing away from me, but I recognised the voice as I would do for the rest of my life.

It was Tracker.

It was as well that there was no one else in that set of boxes. I let out a scream. Emotion flowed over me. Relief was the least of it. The heaviness of guilt lifted. The image of Norbert washed over me as I saw that Tracker had not, after all, suffered his fate. I looked at his legs as he turned to face me. He was not lame. I started to cry. I wanted to speak but could scarcely draw breath.

It was a long time before I was in any condition to hear what had happened.

Horton Field had arranged for three farms to be patrolled and on that Saturday night. The Smith family, Dick, Tim and Jake, were to watch the area around the Robinson's farm. Field was to ride and check out all three patrols to see how they were doing. The Smiths tied up their horses at the rear of the property about one hundred yards from the slave quarters and walked quietly around the farm. After checking the front on foot, their orders were to walk back to the rear, mount their horses and then ride separately, first around the perimeter and then one of them was to go north, another east and the other west. To the south was a cornfield and then some woods. Those woods were nearly impassable on horseback but the Smiths could ride through the cornfield.

Jake heard the sound of our horses from the back of the house. They were at the front having just walked around the farm.

Jake did not want to wake the household and look foolish if he had made a mistake. So he signaled to his father and brother and whispered to them, "To the back." They started to walk back to their horses. Dick saw a heap in a ridge. It was Lucy and me laying prone. But he was too far away to be sure that someone was there and sufficiently far away for me not to realize that we were in sight. By the time we had got up to run to the cornfield, Dick had concluded that the heap was a natural ridge and was scanning the horizon. He then looked back to where the heap was and saw that it was no longer there. It was night and he thought his eyes could be deceiving him. To make sure, he mounted his horse and trotted to where Lucy and I had lain.

By the time he got there, Tracker had already met us in the cornfield and had sent us running to the back way of escape. Tracker did not follow us. Jake and Tim had mounted their horses and caught up with their father at the spot where he thought he saw the heap. Dick told them what he had seen and said, "They must have gone into the cornfield." They looked through the field and, even from the vantage point their horses' backs gave them, could see nothing

Tim dismounted. "I'm going into the corn. Y'all look out and tell me where they are if you see them." Tim took out his iron bar that he had used to cripple Norbert.

"Where are you, Boy?" he shouted.

Tracker was crouched, still and silent in the cornfield having seen and heard everything. He pulled on a corn stalk and broke it. It snapped with a loud crack. Tim reckoned that whoever made the noise was about fifty yards from where he stood. He ran towards where he thought he heard the noise.

It was the signal Ada and Nathan Fleming had been waiting for. On the horses they had taken from Butler's farm, they charged towards Dick and Jake hollering loudly. Dick and Jake's horses shied in shock.

The piece of paper, which Nathan had been given by Tracker at the Butler plantation, contained a map to the Robinsons. Tracker had whispered that they were to help disable the Patrol on his signal, which was to be the crack of a broken corn husk. If there was no Patrol, they were to go their own way north.

Under cover of the noise made by Nathan and Ada, Tracker moved silently and swiftly. He was quick and methodical. Tim had no chance. The piercing scream belonged to him as his iron bar came crashing down on his own kneecap.

As Tim writhed in pain, Ada and Nathan had taken down Dick and Jake Smith. Nathan had his horse kick Jake as he tried to stand up. Dick was too old for combat. Jake was so distracted by his brother's screams and winded by the kick that he offered no effective resistance and did not even reach for his gun. Dick's rifle was kept on his horse's saddle and that horse had bolted. Tracker stayed out of sight of the Smiths, he did not want to be recognized. He would return to the area. The others would not.

Dr. Robinson had woken with the commotion caused by Tim's screaming. When Robinson came out of the house, Dick and Jake were tied up. Tim was so badly injured he could not move. Nathan held Jake's gun and pointed it at Dr. Robinson.

"I'm going to have to tie you up, sir," he said.

"I see," said the Doctor. "And my wife?"

"I'm afraid so sir."

"Let me look after his leg first," the doctor said pointing towards Tim.

"Yes, sir, but you must be quick."

There was not much Robinson could do to Tim's smashed leg. He soaked a cloth in Epsom salts and lay it on top of the knee cap and handed Tim a bottle of one of his better whiskeys.

Louise Robinson spent the next two hours on her bed, tied up with her husband. Dick and Jake lay in the parlor downstairs also bound with rope. All that could be done with Tim was sit him against a tree trunk with whiskey.

When Horton Field came to check on his Patrol, he didn't see them and he thought they were patrolling away from the house. He dismounted and walked round the front of the farm. It was Tim's moaning which alerted him to the fact that something was wrong. Field ran to Tim, who was incoherent, but he did point to the Robinson's house and it was not long before Field had untied Dick and Jake and Dr. and Mrs. Robinson.

"Who tied you up?" Field asked.

"Some niggers," Dick replied. Field looked at Dan Robinson, who nodded in agreement. Everyone was in the parlor except Louise Robinson, who was sitting on her bed, holding her arms across her chest and rocking herself, and Tim, who was outside under the tree.

"Were they your niggers?" Field asked.

Robinson shook his head and went upstairs to see Louise. She was still rocking and looking straight ahead. Robinson asked her if she was alright. She did not reply but shut her eyes and continued to rock back and forth.

Field went to the slave quarters and knocked on the door. In spite of all the noise that night, none of the slaves in the quarters had stirred themselves and all of them said that they had not heard a thing. He went back to the house. "You'd better check on your niggers," he said to Robinson.

Dan Robinson, who had now left his wife's bedside, went to the quarters and saw that Lucy had gone. Everyone else was present.

To any on-looker Louise Robinson's distress was enormous and life changing. Field was instrumental in Robinson paying most of his savings to buy Lucy to nurse his wife. The sight of her staring ahead and rocking herself made him angry and determined.

He alerted the other patrols to find us. Their dogs lost the scent in the swamps. Frustrated, Field then went to Captain Fleming. Tracker did not know what was said between them except that immediately afterwards he went to the telegraph office to send the Stimsons back through Maryland to Kentucky.

"Where are the Stimsons now?" Tracker asked.

I told him of the man lynched by them hanging in the woods with his bloody shirt cut to ribbons by James and his legs in irons, of the train ride to Cincinnati, of my overnight rush to Woodburn and how Brushes used the leg irons to fight the Stimsons and how he pulled James Stimson's hands from my throat just as I thought I was about to die. I recounted how I killed James Stimson in cold blood leaving the bodies of the three dead brothers in the stable.

"That thing with the knife and leg irons. That thing..." Tracker's voice tailed off. As he said it, the sight of the hanging corpse came back to me and hit me like a train. I had squashed the full horror in our flight as if my mind had turned off enough senses to allow me to function. Now it came back to me. It was almost as if I was standing in front of the tree.

Tracker carried on rubbing down Pierce. He was staring at me out of the corner of his eye as he did so. I started to breathe deeply to stop my head spinning. I was not holding it together.

"You know, that thing...the sight of that lynching will never leave you," Tracker said. "Those things never do. That's why they do it."

"Do you ever think..." I said.

Tracker cut me off.

"All the time. They'll get me one day."

"I didn't mean that. Do you ever think about the people you kill? That hanging body haunts me, but not the Stimsons, not even the boy James who looked so helpless as I killed him."

"You know the thing that haunts me most?"

"No."

"What they did to my mama's back. Nothing's worse than that to me. That's what I think of when I kill."

"Do you always think of something when you kill?" I asked.

"Only that."

"What would you say if I told you that I don't think of anything then?"

He looked at me quickly.

"Nothing?"

I let his question hang in silence.

"Where's Grace?" I asked eventually.

"I don't know where she's gone."

I explained about Sally and the map which Lucy gave her when we met in the woods.

"Well, I guess we know where she's gone to but not where she is."

251

Forty-seven

I expected to find West Point hard when I got back for the final year. I expected having been in the field to make me impatient with the theories from my studies and my detachment from my comrades to continue as the gulf between us became deeper from my experience with the Railroad.

The detachment did continue, but was hidden behind a veil of goodwill. I knew how to be a false friend now in the sense that I was not and would never be as they thought I was. In the previous term I cut myself off from my friends, but this term I made a conscious effort to be sociable.

I expected it to be hard to talk about what I did in the holidays and discussed this with Dr. Holmes on the journey back to the Academy.

"You know what my best friend once said to me?" Dr. Holmes asked.

I wasn't sure if he was speaking of Father, the judge, or Dr. Emerson. "No." I said.

"John Ruffin told me what he had been taught him in an ethics class by way of a joke. It was in the form of a question: 'Why lie when the truth can be so misleading?' the teacher said."

I decided to speak about my times with Brushes in previous holidays; times with Brushes which I had never shared with them before. All I had to do was change the time-frame. I rarely had to do so, however, because I became a very good listener. My friends wanted to talk about their holidays and did not especially want to listen to what happened in mine. I was happy and relieved it was that way.

Occasionally I got nightmares of the lynching, but they did not affect my studies, rather they told me why I was there. Grace and Lucy wanted me to be a soldier and that is what I would be. Mathematics now came easy to me and no longer held me back. The big change was my appreciation of life in the field. What was theory to my classmates was real to me and almost a recitation of practical exercises with the added appreciation of the value of knowing terrain, which we cadets had always underestimated and our instructors tried to get us to appreciate. My understanding of it stood out and within six weeks I was rising to the top of my class.

The Superintendent calls in the top cadet and it was with a combination of ease and pride that I answered the summons to see him. There was no greeting of congratulation, however, and Delafield gestured me to sit. He had a letter in front of him in writing I recognized.

"I've been asked by Dr. Holmes to give you some leave."

My heart jumped. Perhaps Grace had returned and he was giving Delafield an excuse for me to go see her.

"He says there's a medical emergency and you should go to the Emersons."

"Emergency? Is it Mr. Emerson."

"No; his daughter Ellen has been taken ill. I can give you a week."

It's a nearly three-hundred-mile ride to Concord. I was able to do it in just over a day. I rode as if possessed, each horse doing its best for me for five hours and then slowing down to an exhausted walk as I looked to find an inn where I could change horses.

I'd not seen Ellen since we parted in Ripley. I hoped for visits to the West Point Inn, but they never came. Neither did any letters. I looked out for them daily on the letters table. There were letters from Aunt Victoria about how Maud was recovering; from Dr. Holmes about how he was looking forward to my passing out and with news from Harvard; from Wendy Holmes about how he wanted to be a soldier but his father, Dr. Holmes, wanted him to be a lawyer and not follow him into the medical profession and even letters from Mr. Emerson who sent one of his lectures for me to critique and share with my fellow cadets. But nothing from Ellen.

I didn't write her either. That time, when I pulled away from making love to her and feeling her tears as she turned away from me as the gulf between us opened, returned to me as I rode to Concord. We had been driven apart and I was at a loss to know why it was. As the West Point term progressed, I had hoped that time would heal and we could get back to how we were – to how we had always been, from those first moments of friendship as children, to that first time we made love, to the shared times together as she visited me and sent notes via Lester, the cellarman's reliable postal service. What had caused her to turn away from me in tears, what had caused her to steel herself against me was something I could not fathom and dared not ask her. I wondered if I would ever get the chance and whether she would live to see me or whether she would be taken from me.

I was tired on arrival at Concord, but with plenty of energy in reserve. I'd had longer marches and longer rides before. Dr. Holmes opened the door to me.

"Waldo is sitting with her now," he said. "She's sleeping. We've been expecting you about now and he'll come down when she wakes. Come through here."

He gestured to Emerson's study where all those weeks ago I heard the stories of the Underground Railroad from the mad and wild John Brown.

"She was pregnant," Holmes said as we sat down. "She's lost the baby."

"Oh God, so that was it."

"That was what?"

"Why she was so distant from me."

"Can you tell me this; did you love her?"

"Yes. I do love her. I always have, you know that."

"Waldo and I thought that. Did she love you?"

"Yes of course. I'd have never been with her if I hadn't."

"Can you say therefore, why she'd want to make herself lose the baby?"

"What?"

"You heard. If she loved you and you loved her, why would she want to make herself lose the baby?"

"What do you mean make herself lose the baby? How could she do that?"

"That's what I want to know. Waldo found her bleeding to death in her bedroom with a piece of wire inside her and a dead foetus beside her. I ask again, sir, why would she want to make herself lose the baby."

My nameless dread found its answer.

"How far gone was she?"

"Three months."

"Could it be any older?"

"No. If anything it'd be younger."

"Oh God," I said. "Oh God. God help her and God help us."

"What do you mean? Why would she want to lose your baby?"

"Because it wasn't mine," I said. "It wasn't mine."

I had never burst into uncontrollable sobbing before. Never. Not even after learning of Lucy's life, loves and loss. But now that nameless dread which had seeped inside me and I had pushed away, hoping that all would be well, had found expression.

Dr. Holmes hit me across the face. I'd never seen him so angry and contemptuous. He was red in the face and shaking with rage.

"That's enough self-pity for one day. Answer my question now."

The slap restored me almost immediately.

"She slept with a man named Horton Field to find out where Lucy was," I said. "We didn't know where she was. She's been sold by Fleming. Field bid for her as an agent, bought her and then she disappeared. It must be Ellen who found out from him that Lucy had gone to Dr. Robinson."

The color drained from Dr. Holmes's face.

"That can't be true," he said. "It must have been yours. We'd have never let her go join the Railroad if that was going to happen."

"I haven't been with her for four months. The baby can't be mine. When I went into the trader's office they were gossiping about her and Field. Tracker told me about where Lucy was; he said it came from their best spy and Grace told me who their best spy was. That's how it must have been."

We sat in silence.

"Best wait for Waldo. He's angry with you."

"Don't tell him. I'd rather he stayed angry with me than...than..."

From behind me in the soft but penetrating voice he had came the words, "Don't tell him what?"

"Mr. Emerson," I said. "You have every right to be angry with me. Please sir, how is she?"

"She's waiting for you, she says she heard you come in, though Lord knows how, I didn't hear you. Go now, she's very weak and is asking for you." Emerson's voice was mild, then it hardened.

"Wendell here will tell me what you both want to keep from me about my own daughter," he said. "She's my daughter you know. I have a right to know what happened to her."

"I'll go to her now, sir," I said and left them to talk. As I mounted the stairs I heard Emerson's muffled cry of heartbreak.

Ellen was asleep, her breathing was regular. I sat beside her and took her hand. She squeezed my hand back and then pulled me towards her.

"Don't speak," I said.

She let go of my hand and beckoned me to her.

"I love you," she whispered. "You're the only man I've ever loved. The only one I'll ever love. You know that."

"I know," I said. "And I love you. You know that too."

"Stay with me."

And I did. Her breathing was regular but shallow to start with but, over time, got deeper. Dr. Holmes looked in occasionally, as did Mr. Emerson.

When Dr. Holmes first came in to see us I asked him what could be done. As I did so I was holding her hand.

"The only medicine she can have right now is rest and being with the one she really loves." As Holmes said this Ellen squeezed my hand and smiled.

The sun streamed into the room when Ellen awoke.

"How long have you been here?" she said.

"Three days."

"Have you slept?"

"No. I've been with you."

"And I with you. I with you. Go get Papa and have some sleep yourself."

I slept for a full day and Dr. Holmes woke me.

"Ellen's out of danger now."

"Where is she?"

"Sitting in her chair in her bedroom."

Ellen was pale but alert and reading a galley proof.

"One of Holmes's new books he wants me to edit," she said. "He says I mustn't travel for a while."

"Ellen," I said.

"Can we talk another time please? Just stay with me a little and help me with this work. You being with me is all I want today. You must go soon and I don't want us to talk for a while. I just want us to be. For a little while anyway. Can you do that Jack? Just be and not do?"

"I'll try," I said.

I stayed the rest of the day and we didn't talk about anything except West Point and editing Dr. Holmes's new book. We didn't talk about Lucy, Brushes and, Grace. Not about Tracker, the Birdwatcher and the Railroad. Not about the Dick Smith or the Stimson boys. And not about Horton Field.

"Can I come to your passing out?" she asked as I was about to leave.

"You can visit before then," I said.

"I'm not travelling for a while Jack. I will write you though. There's lots going on in Concord and Dr. Holmes has a book out."

"Please write me," I said.

"I said I would."

"Yes you did, but please write me."

"I said I would. Now go."

The rest of the term passed quicker than I expected. I allowed myself time to read the regular letters, which came from Ellen and Dr. Holmes, at my spot overlooking the Hudson. In each letter I searched for news in code of Grace and Sally and in each letter I found none. The only hope I had was Tracker's words to me that Grace would never be caught, but that I knew to be as false as the certainty that one day she and Tracker would be caught. I tried to see them in visions, but that gift had left me.

Victoria wrote that Neil kept up the pretense that she was away, temporarily, looking after her sister. Dr. Holmes wrote that Horton Field reckoned that by trying to expose 'reality' he would ruin himself and so would remain without it. I understood from one letter that his drinking sessions with Neil had stopped. The sentence read: "Mr. Field has one less drinking companion." Given that Ellen's weekly letters were all postmarked from Concord, the source had to be Tracker.

I did receive letters from attorneys acting for Neil asking for money to replace the house. The 'accident', as they termed it was, in law they said, my fault. I instructed attorneys to prevaricate and then after a decent interval of quibbling to say that I would pay for the building of a two-storey house to my own architect's design, but not on the exact site of the old one. The quibbling lasted for most of the year.

The letters I treasured most came from Lucy in Canada. She wrote in the persona of an aunt called 'Lady'. There was nothing in them about their escape. But she wrote that 'Buddy's' work as a groom in Hamilton, Ontario integrated them into the community quicker than anyone could have imagined. His salary was good and they were building a house, which, they hoped, would be ready by the time I had my first leave, if I had the time. I tried also to see Lucy and Brushes in visions, but that too was not to be.

Ellen had told me to 'be' and not 'do'. But at West Point I did. I studied and drilled; studied and drilled, determined to be at the top of the class.

Then, a month before, passing out I had a dream. It was as if I was placed in the skins of two women. One was standing at the top of a barn looking out over a plantation and the other woman had come to meet her. My consciousness was moved between them as if switched at will by an unseen hand.

Forty-eight

The Dream

The sketch of the property and surroundings showed that nothing had changed in twenty years. All was as remembered, written down and passed on for this moment.

She saw a short black female figure come into view and walk towards the barn. As she watched the figure approach, her relief was overwhelming. She stood back thirty feet inside the barn's attic looking at the approaching figure. The sun was behind the barn and she could see out into the light, but she would not be seen in the darkness of the attic.

The figure walked alone, looking around her as she did. As she approached the barn she became more and more tentative. Her stride shortened and, about fifty yards from the entrance, she stopped.

The message had been perfectly given. She was to stand fifty yards from the barn door and wait for someone to come. She would be met when the church service finished. That would be after the last psalm. She had been told to wait no more than five minutes and then, if no one met her, to go back to the quarters. The sound of singing floated across the field to where they stood. One waiting for the other's arrival. The other looking to see if she was the one.

There had been hope before. There had been false sightings and reports of her sister over the many years since she started her branches of the Railroad.

Now this.

Her anticipation was dampened by her previous disappointments.

The figure looked right. The right size. The right age. The right everything. The key question was whether it would move in the right way. Now was the time to be patient. She had to wait.

The singing tapered off. Then it started again. The words were distinct: "If it had not been the Lord who was on our side..." It was the last psalm of the service and a short one.

The figure stood still, but from the attic she could see the signs of anxiety in it. First there was the clasping and unclasping of the hands and the thumping of the thighs. Was that enough? she asked herself. No, she had to wait for the movement which she remembered the five-year-old-girl would make when anxious and waiting. Maybe she had grown out of it, she thought. What if it was just the hands that was all that was left to recognize?

She watched as the figure bent its knees and then raised itself. Up and down, up and down, anxious, excited and near heartbreak.

The last psalm had finished five minutes ago. The figure had counted every second since the singing stopped.

The excitement which had caused the figure to move up and down gave way to grief. Her dreams had told her this was the time. Now it was happening, she had thought. The world was moving for her, she had thought, and she would see her girl again just as she had been promised in her dreams.

It was not to be. The five minutes she was to wait had passed, each heartbreaking second of it. She had to go back.

She allowed herself thirty more seconds. Maybe she had counted too quickly in her anxiousness, she thought. This time she started to count the seconds out loud.

"One stop. Two stop. Three stop," she said. Slowly. Each count took two seconds. That way the thirty more seconds would be a whole minute. She knew this, but had started to persuade herself that it would be only thirty seconds when counted that way. Enough to correct any error in counting the five minutes, but no more.

She was fooling herself and she knew it. Her voice broke. "Four stop" came out as a cry. She bent her knees again, but this time her

260

legs gave way and she fell forward. Her sight blinded by tears.

Then she felt a presence. She had heard no approach. She had felt no footsteps. Yet now she knew someone was with her. Alarmed at this, she wiped her tears, her eyes still cast to the ground as fear and self-reproach seeped into her heart.

"Remember me, Vallie?" a voice above her said. Sally looked up and saw black homespun covering a slight figure, five feet four in height, with a face carrying a broad smile and tears.

"Aysie?" Sally said, her voice breaking.

"We have to go."

In a single movement, Grace took Sally's hand, pulled her up and ran with her to the woods.

Forty-nine

June 1860

It was Passing Out. I was awestruck by the numbers of guests my fellow cadets had invited for the day. They seemed to be far greater than mine. Their guests could not all watch the Ceremony as there was a limit of ten. But the Parade, where there was no limit on guest numbers, was the real spectacle. Some of my southern friends even invited a few of their 'People'.

Their 'People' were their slave domestics and stable hands (inside and outside men as both sexes were called collectively), chaperoned by overseers and supervisors of both colors.

The 'People' could not sit or stand with the white relatives and friends at the Parade. A separate area was roped off for them. They could wait and watch there, whereas everyone else could move around and watch where they wished. After the War, the need for a separate roped off section disappeared and special temporary stands were built on the Plain for all the audience to watch the Parade.

Dr. Holmes had been to Canada for me to see if it was possible for Lucy to come. The message she came back with was that Tracker had deemed the enterprise too risky. Black faces with no white supervisors would be an object of suspicion. They could get to the Academy, but there was no telling what sideline in kidnapping some of the chaperones or their hangers-on would have.

There was still no word from Tracker about Grace. The dream, which had been so vivid, had gone like a sunset. All it told me was that

Grace had found Sally, not that they had escaped the Patrol.

My ten guests were Maud and Victoria and the Holmes and Emerson families: Dr. and Mrs. Holmes, Dr. Holmes's brother John, Mellie, Wendy, Ned, Mr. Emerson and Ellen.

I realized on that morning that the feeling that my supporters were small in number stemmed from the fact that the one person I wanted to be there would not be. I had wanted to talk about this with Ellen as we met at sunrise at my special place overlooking the Hudson. Somehow she did not give me the chance and changed the subject when I tried to raise it. Finally, as our time was up and I had to go to my quarters, I tried one more time.

"Lucy won't be there." I said.

She changed the subject again.

"Who is your Cadet Captain? I need to see him."

"Why?"

As I asked the question, her eyes recessed slightly and she got that hunted look I knew so well. I backed off from habit.

"Never mind," I said, deflated and hurt. "It's Jeremy Ralston, he's my Cadet Captain."

The preparation for the Parade was long and painstaking. Creases knife sharp; brasses and swords gleaming; boots shining. Eventually, we moved off. Each group, headed by their Cadet Captain, marching to the sound of the band. We were all as one, looking straight ahead.

There was a thirty-second interval between each group. I was in the third group and was relieved that I could see the first two and watch what they were doing. They marched in perfect time, all to the command of their Cadet Captain.

We moved off and our marching took us to the Plain. Once on it, we were to go past the domestic and ground staff first, then past the separate roped off crowd and finally to the main central of the Plain where the principal guests and the academic staff stood.

The command from Cadet Captain Ralston came over a minute before it was due.

"Eyes Right."

We were all good enough soldiers to obey immediately as we marched past the roped off section notwithstanding that Ralston had got his timing wrong. A lesson in obeying orders regardless, I thought.

I looked deep into the crowd in that section as I marched because I saw immediately that Ellen stood within it. She took my eye and then she took my eye to them.

They were unmistakable. Looking at me as my eyes met theirs, wanting to wave but restraining themselves for the occasion.

Lucy and Sally.

Next to them was what appeared to be an old man leaning on a stick. I'd have bet anything that the 'man' was exactly five feet four inches in height.

I was about to break down, but the discipline of the marching routine made me continue. Marching had its uses. I would have never held it together that morning had I known they would be there waiting to watch my march past. I thanked Ellen inwardly. Then the second order from Ralston came as I stared back at Grace, Sally and Lucy.

"Salute."